I0614810

THE
ZALEM
CRISIS

THE ARMOURED BUTTERFLY SERIES

The A'zyon Warrior
The Zalem Crisis
The Crowned Guardians

THE ZALEM CRISIS

THE ARMOURED BUTTERFLY BOOK TWO

TRUDY ADAMS

AMBASSADOR INTERNATIONAL
GREENVILLE, SOUTH CAROLINA & BELFAST, NORTHERN IRELAND

www.ambassador-international.com

The Zalem Crisis

The Armoured Butterfly, Book Two

©2021 by Trudy Adams
All rights reserved

ISBN: 978-1-64960-104-9
eISBN: 978-1-64960-154-4
Library of Congress Control Number: 2021941372

No part of this publication may be reproduced, distributed, or transmitted in any form or by any means, including photocopying, recording, or other electronic or mechanical methods, without the prior written permission of the publisher, except in the case of brief quotations embodied in critical reviews and certain other noncommercial uses permitted by copyright law. For permission requests, contact the publisher using the information below.

This is a work of fiction. Names, characters, and incidents are all products of the author's imagination or are used for fictional purposes. Any resemblance to actual events or persons, living or dead, is entirely coincidental. Any mentioned brand names, places, and trademarks remain the property of their respective owners, bear no association with the author or the publisher, and are used for fictional purposes only.

Scripture taken from the New King James Version®. Copyright © 1982 by Thomas Nelson. Used by permission. All rights reserved.

Cover Design by Megan McCullough
Interior Typesetting by Dentelle Design
Ebook Conversion by Anna Riebe Raats

AMBASSADOR INTERNATIONAL
Emerald House
411 University Ridge, Suite B14
Greenville, SC 29601, USA
www.ambassador-international.com

AMBASSADOR BOOKS
The Mount
2 Woodstock Link
Belfast, BT6 8DD, Northern Ireland, UK
www.ambassadormedia.co.uk

The colophon is a trademark of Ambassador, a Christian publishing company.

To Maria and Rowie

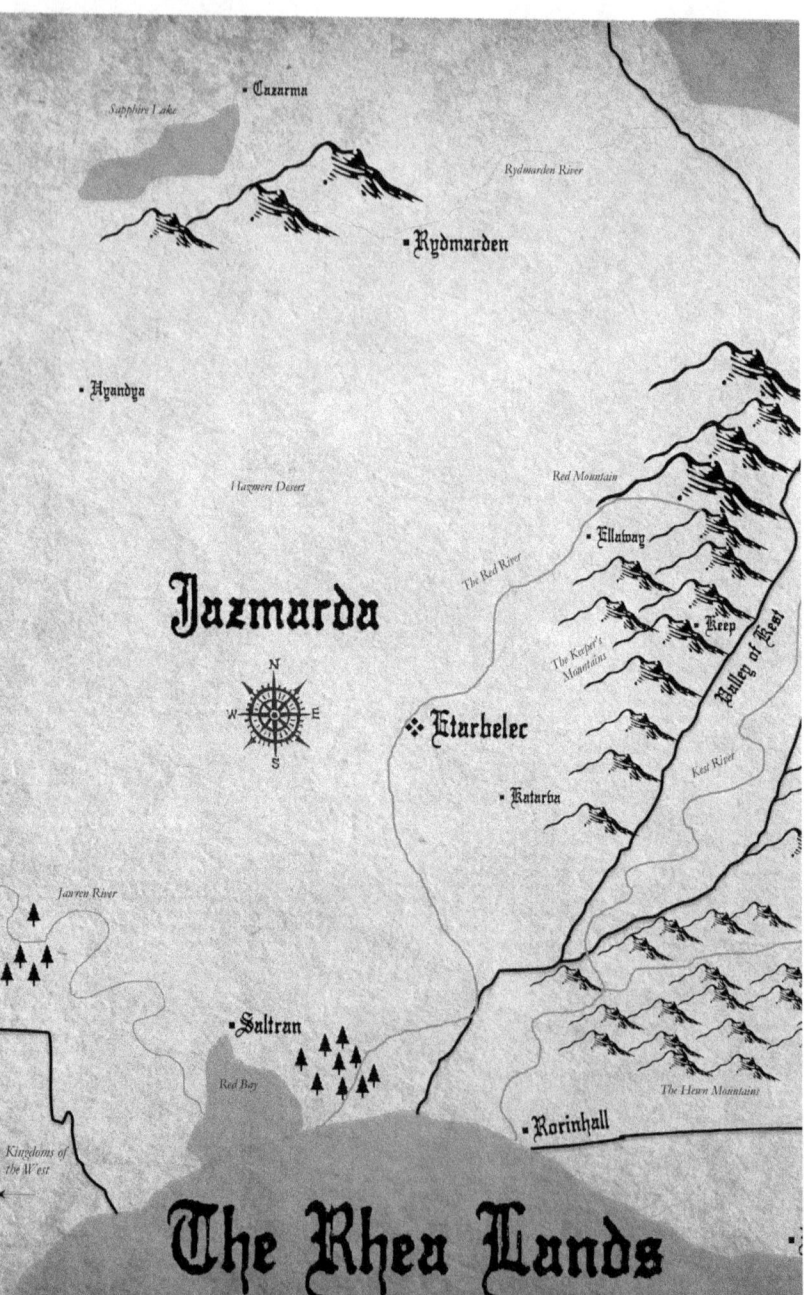

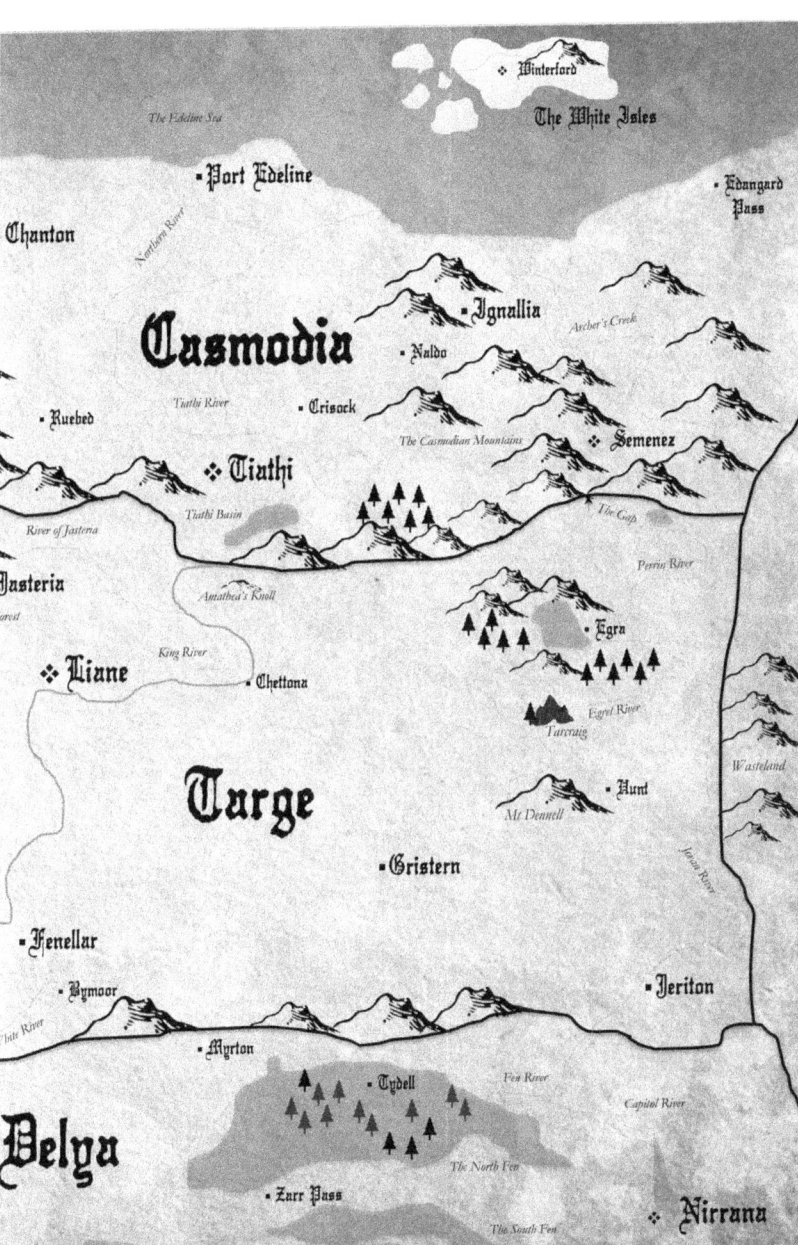

CHARACTER PRONUNCIATIONS

Adaliah—Ah-*dar*-le-ah

Alel—Ah-*lel*

Amaz—Ah-*marz*

Anash—Ah-*nash*

A'zyon—Ah-*zigh*-on

Bagred—*Ba*-gred

Benne—Ben

Bylon—*Bye*-lon

Cades—*Kay*-dees

Cazine—Ca-zeen

Darj—Darge

Dayle—Dale

Edangard—Ed-an-*guard*

Elhian—El-*high*-an

Elryane—El-*rye*-an

Erran—Eh-ren

Hazaka—Har-*zack*-a

Jenethea—Jen-*ee*-thee-a

Kadram—*Kad*-drem

Lowelan—Low-*ell*-an

Samela—Sa-*mell*-a

Sirvan—Sir-*varn*

Zalem—*Zay*-lem

Zavad—Za-*vard*

LOCATION PRONUNCIATIONS

Rhea—*Ree*-ah

Liane—Lie-*anne*

Semanez—*Sem*-a-nez

Fenellar—Fe-*nel*-lah

Sharlard—Shar-*lard*

Etarbelec—Eh-*tar*-be-lec

Katarva—Ka-*tar*-va

Myrton—*Mer*-ton

Tydell—*Tie*-del

Levanna—Leh-*van*-ah

Rorinhall—*Roar*-in-hall

Egra—*Eh*-gra

For a full list of terms used in the *Armoured Butterfly* series, please visit www.trudyadams.squarespace.com.

You shall not be afraid . . . of the pestilence that walks in darkness.

Psalm 91:5-6

PROLOGUE

Dead will the boy be if the lady does not abstain.
Dead will the lady be if her dear king does not pay.
Dead will the Ghosts be if the general does not recall.
Dead will one and all be if Queen Targe does not obey.

The paper in my hands was old, and the words were fading. The edges had crumbled over time, and it smelt like leather. That was all I noticed at first when I found the note lying on the King of Casmodia's throne in Tiathi. It had been tied with a black ribbon, and someone must have delivered it in the night.

I read the words again.

Dead . . . Dead . . . Dead . . . Dead . . .

'Elhian? Elhian!'

1
RETURN TO LIANE

If you reach the small hill to the north of Liane before midday, before the shadows are stretched by a falling sun, you can see the city glistening ahead of you like a pearl. In the spring, the first things you notice are the sweeping meadows, farms, and King River, all teeming with life and rejoicing at the end of winter. The meadows dress themselves in tiny flowers that afford a purple lustre known as the Royal Carpet, which invites you to the Targian capital like you're a long-lost friend.

Liane itself spreads out in an easy manner. It rests below its hilltop palace in the same way a youngster burrows into its mother. There's something about it that invites you closer, that offers you peace and safety within its walls.

'Adaliah?'

I turned at the sound of my name and watched as the King of Casmodia rode towards me on his white horse, Leuk.

'I thought you said you could keep up!'

Elhian Edangard smiled. 'The carriage is ahead of us. That last diversion cost us more time than you said it would.'

'Well, it's been a while since I've travelled through this countryside.' I leant down to stroke my horse's neck. Bagred was turning his ears, listening to the woods. 'I want to see as much of it as I can.'

Elhian peered at Liane. It compared to our home, Tiathi, like gold to copper. 'Do you miss it?'

'A little, but my real home was Kest, not Liane. Even though I lived there, it's not the city I miss so much as my cousin. The cousin I had before Ethaniel's and Jeri's deaths, that is.'

'You don't think she's still grieving, do you?'

'No, it's just that her letters to me are always void of emotion, like she's forgotten how to feel. Now we need her counsel, and I'm worried.'

'Worried about her—or the note?' Elhian asked.

I didn't answer. Leaves were moving on the trees, but there was no wind.

A man jumped out of one and pushed Elhian from his saddle. He tried to pin Elhian to the ground, but Elhian reached for a rock, struck it against the side of the man's head, and pulled out a dagger from his boot. I dismounted Bagred, sword in hand, but Elhian thrust his dagger into the man's stomach first. He shoved the man off him. Bleeding, the man pulled himself to his knees and screeched at Elhian like a wild animal. I cringed and stepped back, taking in his black armour and the patch of blood on the side of his head. He looked hungry and thin, but it was something in his eyes that convinced me he was mad.

'The traitor must die!' he yelled. His voice was husky and tense, like his throat was half the size it needed to be. 'The High Zalem will prevail!' He pulled Elhian's dagger out of his stomach and attempted to stand. He shrieked again, so piercingly I felt compelled to cover my ears. I kicked him backward. He collapsed into the dirt, turned to Elhian with a snarl, and died with it set on his face.

Elhian looked at me. I opened my mouth but didn't know what to say. Elhian poked the man, testing for a response. Assured that he was definitely lifeless, Elhian proceeded to search the man's pockets.

'Do you think it was one of his kind that left the note?' I asked.

'Perhaps.' He pulled out some coins from the man's front pocket and turned them over between his fingers. 'I don't recognise these . . . but they look ancient.' He held one up. There was a symbol pressed into the gold—a crescent moon overlaid with an eye. I wasn't sure about the eye, but the crescent moon was the symbol of Anash, the great dark spirit that was said to linger in the night and bring torment to mankind. He was known as the invisible Prince of Death; those who worshipped him were usually in pursuit of great power. Elhian kept the coin and left the others scattered over the man's chest.

I looked out at Liane again. The view no longer seemed as beautiful, nor the sun as warm.

We arrived at Liane Palace a few hours later. The Casmodian carriage brought us into the courtyard while a servant took our horses to the queen's stables by a less public route. People had gathered to welcome us. They cheered when Elhian stepped out of the carriage door. I mused with a smile that although he was the King of Casmodia, he was more appreciated in Targe than at home. In Targe, he was the slayer of Cades, the kingdom's foremost enemy. To many in Casmodia, he was still just the murderer of their former king.

I heard the people's cheers rise as Elhian reached back towards me with an open hand. Taking it, I stepped out to a warm reception and waved to the sea of smiles as the Queen of Casmodia for the first time.

Casmodia was an uneasy kingdom for some time after Cades' death. Elhian had to deal with several men in high positions who openly disputed his right to the throne. I supported him as much as I could, but my time was stretched amongst him in Casmodia, Alexia in Targe, and the Keep in Kest.

Still officially the Keeper of Kest, I had to play my part in maintaining peace between Jazmarda, Casmodia, and Targe. I was no longer able to reside at the Keep, though, so Alexia and I installed a contingent of men and a trusted captain there to act as steward—Darack Symes. Without the Armoured Butterfly, messages were sent to Liane Palace the traditional way—on horseback. I committed to travelling to the Keep every three months to keep a check on things. The commitment continued after I married Elhian and made my home in Tiathi, and would last until Alexia had a second child and they were of age.

In the meantime, Elhian persevered in his reign with a few supporters and managed to reform his court, but even now held little trust for the people around him. We had, of course, planned to delay our wedding after the Northern Invasion but not for the entire year and a half it took. When it did finally occur, Casmodia secured stronger relations with its Targian neighbour, but I knew some in Targe judged Queen Alexia Elryane for her quick forgiveness of a kingdom that had brought Targe to its knees and murdered her husband and child. They did not know what was going on inside, though, for she was, as her General Darj Ryder described to me in a letter, 'a master of hiding her heart behind her duty'.

Still, having not spent time with her since our wedding six months earlier, I longed to see her now and was disappointed when Lord Fenton of Egra, one of the men of her court, came down the palace stairs to greet us in her place.

'Her Majesty sends her deepest apologies,' he said, bowing to us. 'She is still holding court.'

'Of course,' Elhian said. 'We are two days earlier than we said we would be.'

'Yes, but come—I will take you to her.'

The criminal who knelt before the throne with a royal guard on either side of him was more afraid of Her Majesty's presence than his punishment, I think. Lord Fenton told me the man had never seen her before, and even now, he was only staring at the ground. The tall, warm throne room was filled with priests, nobles, councillors, and courtiers, all judging him. A breeze shifted the long, green banners that hung from the ceiling with nobility, reminding us all that we were in the presence of royalty.

The criminal shook as a chancellor introduced his matter to the queen in a loud voice that echoed around the room. He bit his lip and lifted his gaze to the steps that were just ahead of him.

I saw the queen through his eyes. There was the long, burgundy gown, lavishly embroidered with gold thread, that draped over the stairs. Resting on her knee was the jewelled sceptre she held as a symbol of her authority. The diamond necklace on her chest sparkled in the light with every breath. Long earrings embraced her beautiful but serious face, and her ebony hair fell over her shoulders, curling at the ends. The famous Targian crown with its twelve points was set on her head, heavy but grand. Finally, her startling blue eyes, full of calm confidence, were focused on him.

As he began to plead his case, speaking too fast to be coherent, Her Most Glorious Majesty Queen Alexia the First, my cousin, leaned to her right with an inherent coolness. She stared at the man with boredom and, with her spare hand, tapped her jewelled fingers over the armrest. I could see the criminal watching her nails arch and fall on the gold surface.

Elhian and I listened to the proceedings until we were distracted by something to our left. Two maids had appeared and seemed to be chasing something. That something was forcing the councillors to move out of the way, some of them uttering protests as they did so.

'I have heard it all before,' the queen said, interrupting the criminal's plea. 'The point is you have been found engaging in treasonous acts yet again, for which I can no longer show mercy. You will contemplate your actions in prison, so you may have some explanation to offer Ru'ach when you meet him.' She indicated with a wave for the guards to take him away.

It was only then that she, too, heard the commotion to her right. She turned to see some of the men near her in a fluster, stepping back. A small child ran between them.

'Mother!' the little girl called when she saw Alexia. 'Mother!'

I had to put a hand over my mouth to stop myself from laughing as the princess stumbled up the steps towards the queen. If Alexia was embarrassed, she was hiding it well, but I knew the maids responsible for the girl would be spoken to later. Princess Eva tripped on the stairs, but the queen gathered her up into her arms before she fell.

Eva snuggled into her neck. 'I found you, Mother.'

Alexia suppressed a smile, as I'm sure many others did. Before she could decide what to do with her daughter, the main door to the throne room opened, and we all turned.

General Darj stood in the doorway, clutching his arm. His shirt was covered in blood, and a group of men were behind him, looking back over their shoulders.

2
THE ARROWHEAD

Alexia's mouth dropped when she saw the general, but she quickly recovered and sent for the physician. 'Help him to his bed,' she said to the soldiers that accompanied him. They nodded and left.

Darj was not easy to injure, and I couldn't imagine what enemy might have caught him so off guard.

'What does he think he's doing, interrupting court like that?' I heard one lord say to another as the doors closed again. 'He's not in the War Room now!'

'Injured or not, he presumes too much!' the other said.

I turned to Fenton, who was still standing with Elhian and me. 'Don't worry about them,' he said, reading the distaste in my face. 'There are just some who think military affairs and politics should be kept separate.'

'How so, when politics defines the need for an army?' Elhian asked. 'One would not exist without the other.'

Lord Fenton hesitated, and I knew he didn't have an answer. However, he smiled as if he simply didn't want to bore us with an explanation. He was a plain-looking man with a thick, black moustache that he kept flattening down with his fingers.

He escorted us out of the now-chaotic room and into the hallway. We stood with him until the queen arrived through another door, at which point he bowed and returned to the throne room.

'Adaliah,' the queen said to me with affection. She had taken off the Targian crown and was now wearing a smaller, gold circlet. She gave me a warm hug. 'I'm so pleased to see you.'

'And I you!' I held her tight, the long six months of separation over at last.

She reached out her hand to Elhian, who took and kissed it. 'You are most welcome, Your Majesty,' she said.

'Thank you,' Elhian said. 'Can we go to Darj?'

'Yes, we will,' the queen said. 'I am just waiting for the physician.'

'Do you have any idea who might have done it?' I picked Eva up and kissed her cheek.

Alexia shook her head. 'He's been away for a fortnight, visiting the barracks in Levanna and Gristern. He is late to return. It was raining last night, so I assumed that was the cause of his delay. It never even occurred to me he might have been hurt.'

I set Eva on her feet. The little girl clung to her mother's skirt and refused to let go. She looked up at Alexia with blue eyes and dark eyelashes that reminded me—and most likely Alexia—of Ethaniel and Jeri. Out of the nearby window, I could see the statue a mason had carved as a monument to the ones Alexia had lost. Set in stone stood her Ethaniel, who held the reins of a horse, upon which their son Jeri was seated. Jeri was smiling. Ethaniel's youthful, strong figure was seriously set, and he was gazing up at Alexia's chambers, ever watchful.

She saw me looking at them. 'Yes, they are frozen in time now,' she said. 'Forever young.' I could see it passing over her face: the inescapable sense that her loss had been so unjust and, worse, a waste. She would have to grow old without them.

The physician came rushing down the hallway with the three maids Alexia had sent to find him. Alexia picked Eva up again, and Elhian and I went with them all to Darj's apartments.

The general's rooms were at the back of the palace with easy access to the barracks further down the property. We walked through the empty War Room, where conferences were sometimes held around a large table, and into Darj's private apartments.

He was sitting on the edge of his bed, holding his arm and grimacing. An arrowhead was firmly planted in his flesh. The physician began wiping the blood away, but Darj tried to get up and greet us.

'Please, don't trouble yourself.' I put a hand on his shoulder to encourage him to stay seated. I flinched as the physician removed the arrowhead from Darj's arm. Blood gushed down his sleeve.

'Da!' Eva called with concern from her mother's hip. She wriggled her way down and climbed up onto the bed for a closer look. 'Sore?'

'I'm all right, Evie,' Darj said behind clenched teeth.

'What happened?' Alexia asked.

'Men in black clothes,' Darj said. The physician put the bloodied arrowhead on a table. 'A hundred of them, maybe more. They killed some of my men.'

'A hundred of them?' Elhian asked, glancing at me.

Alexia picked up her daughter and sat with her next to Darj. 'Did they say what they wanted?'

Darj shook his head. 'They just . . . raised themselves out of the grass on our way home. I didn't even know they were there until it was too late. There were too many . . . We just had to get away. But I know who they were. The arrow . . .'

The physician proceeded to stitch the wound, and Darj couldn't speak until he was done. Beads of sweat formed on his forehead, and he only took a breath once the needle was taken away. 'It was a Zalem arrow.'

'Zalem,' I said. The mad warrior had used that word.

Alexia turned to address the physician and maids. 'Thank you for your assistance. Please, take the princess and leave us.'

They turned to go, but Eva wouldn't leave until she was allowed to kiss Darj's cheek. I saw some of the pain fade from his face as she did so, and he smiled at her as a maid took her from the room.

'How do you know it was them?' Elhian asked.

'See the arrowhead.'

Elhian picked up the black arrowhead and wiped the blood away. I moved next to him and saw what he was now pointing to. A tiny crescent moon with an eye was engraved into the iron.

'I think we met one of them earlier today,' I said, and Elhian and I told them what had happened on the hill. Elhian showed them the coin he'd kept.

Alexia took the physician's cloth and rinsed it in a basin. She wiped the remaining blood off Darj's arm. 'The Zalems haven't been spoken of in years,' she said. 'Many doubt they even exist.'

'I wish I was wrong, truly.' Darj watched as Alexia wrapped a bandage around his wound. 'But if they attacked Elhian, too, then I know I'm not. They were too close to Liane, Alexia. I'm not sure the city is safe.'

3
THE SECRET ROOM

Her Majesty's Secret Room could only be found through a passage in the palace library. The following day, Alexia, Darj, Elhian, and I walked across the library's marble floor and climbed the stairs to the second of three levels. King Jepath, our paternal grandfather, had built the library for his wife, Queen Clair, from whom I took my middle name. Her large portrait still hung in a predominant position over the main hearth. In between the aisles of books and scrolls were one or two scholars and priests, but it was mostly a grand, quiet section of the palace that Alexia loved.

We followed her along the second-level balcony and through a confusing array of passages until we came to a wall of ancient scrolls.

'These are the original Cazinian Papers,' Alexia said, pointing them out. She carried a candle.

'How did you come to have Jazmarda's key artifact?' Elhian asked.

Alexia shrugged enigmatically and dragged a shelf away from the stonewall. 'Kadram felt they were safer in my care,' she said. 'Don't mention it to King Hazaka if you see him though, or you will be forced to endure a long and mournful speech.'

Elhian laughed while Alexia leant on the wall with her spare hand. It turned as if on a vertical swivel. Through the gap was a passageway. Alexia lit an oil wall lamp so we could see the other, normal door at the far end. We stepped inside and shut the stonewall behind us before going through the second door.

Behind that was a small room I hadn't visited since I was a little girl. In the time that had passed since then, Alexia had made it more comfortable than the cold storeroom it used to be. The walls were draped in red silk, and when Alexia lit some more candles, their light gave the small space a warm, orange glow. Beneath our feet was a rug weaved with every shade of green. The furniture—four chairs, a table, a cupboard and a bookshelf—were some of the most exquisite woodwork pieces in the palace. On the wall was a beautiful painting of the Targian plains.

I walked to the window and opened its stained glass panes to the night breeze. Alexia settled in what she named her favourite chair while Darj uncapped a jug of honeycomb he'd requested from the kitchen. It was a traditional Targian bedtime drink made from milk, honey, vanilla, nutmeg, and a bit of brandy. Darj poured us all a cup with his good arm.

'Alexia,' I said, taking a seat, 'I'm sure you've gathered we didn't just come to celebrate Eva's birthday.'

Darj handed her a drink, and she took a sip. 'Yes. What do you need to tell me?'

Elhian pulled the note out of his pocket. 'Someone gained unlawful entry to our castle in Tiathi,' he said. 'No one saw or reported them. We wouldn't have known they had come at all, but they left this on my throne.'

He handed the note to Alexia, who read it to herself. 'I see.' She passed the piece of paper to Darj. 'It's a threat against all four of us.' She spoke as if such a thing were commonplace, like someone expecting a storm on a summer's eve.

'Yes,' Elhian said. 'I can only assume it is these *Zalems* who left it for us.'

Darj moved to a candle and held the piece of paper in front of it.

'Don't burn it,' I said.

'I don't need to.' Darj studied the paper. 'The light is enough to answer your question.' He pointed out a watermark behind the words, a faint but clear crescent moon with an eye over the top. 'We all know the crescent moon is a symbol of Anash. The eye is a symbol of his followers, that they are always watching us. Together, they form the mark of the Zalems.' He read the note again. 'If nothing else, this tells us they believe you have a debt to pay, Elhian, presumably because you killed Cades.'

'Do you think Cades was a Zalem?' Alexia asked Darj.

'I think he must have been connected with them, yes.'

'I remember him mentioning them once or twice,' Elhian said, 'but I never knew who or what they were.'

Darj took a seat beside Alexia. 'They are a sect,' he said. 'They lash out whenever they believe there is a "wrong" in the world or whenever they feel a need to exercise their power. It's just like them to give vague instructions as a threat. They're good at riddles.'

'What do you mean by "lash out"?' I asked. I knew less about them than Elhian.

'A house set on fire, important people abducted, graves desecrated . . . Their methods are based on fear, just like Anash. They have never been identified. They have never declared war or unified against a kingdom. Well, not yet. No one knows how many there really are, but they always leave a trace of their existence, such as this.' Darj paused and read the note once more. 'With this, they are becoming more active, more present. If Cades was an ally of theirs, I'm sure they feel his slayer is not welcome to the crown of Casmodia. But what I'd also like to know is what obedience they expect from you, Alexia, and what I need to remember.'

The four of us fell silent. 'Well, if it is fear they want,' I said, 'then we cannot show it. Neither the Zalems nor Anash will have power here.' I could remember the constant anxiety I'd felt throughout the Northern Invasion all too well and wasn't prepared to endure that again. I took a sip of honeycomb. 'Are you still having the dinner for Eva's birthday tomorrow night?'

'Of course,' Alexia said.

'You should leave the city,' Darj said. 'Adaliah and Elhian as well.'

Alexia scoffed. 'I am not going to just flee and hide. I will not abandon my people, nor will I cause them panic by running away.'

Darj leant forward in his chair. 'Alexia, the Zalems may well be planning to tempt us to war—'

'Yes,' Alexia interrupted, 'but Adaliah is right. Whatever their plan is, we cannot show them fear.'

It wasn't until the next morning that I got some time alone with my cousin. I was grateful when she suggested we go for a walk as I longed to speak to her, but I hardly knew what to say as we passed through the palace gardens together. My mind kept thinking of the madman's piercing scream.

We reached a stone seat by a lily-covered pond and sat down. 'What?' Alexia asked with a soft smile when she caught me trying to read her expression. She was wearing diamond and sapphire earrings and a matching necklace that made her eyes seem particularly deep and blue.

'Nothing.' I linked my arm through hers. 'I've just missed you, that's all. I've been worrying about you actually.'

'Oh, Adaliah, I'm fine, really.'

'Yes, but . . .' I searched her eyes for the high-spirited woman she once was. 'Are you happy?'

She withdrew her arm from me and wrapped it around her waist. 'Now is probably not the best time to ask me that, with all this talk about the Zalems.'

'Yes . . . Do you think they will pose a significant threat?' I was finding it hard to comprehend that we could be facing another enemy within two years of the last.

'If what Darj is saying is true—that they were working through Cades and failed and are now intending to do it themselves—yes, I do. I haven't studied the Zalems, but I know enough to say that we could be threatened with an enemy more complicated than Cades. Do you remember him saying he needed all four swords to fulfill his plan? I thought he meant his plan to take over Targe, but now I wonder if that's all he had in mind.' Alexia stood and stepped towards the pond before turning back to me. 'I can't think of being happy when my kingdom and my people may yet again be in danger.'

I stood as well and put my hands on her upper arms so she couldn't turn away from me. 'I know you love your kingdom and take much pride in your duty, but you are also human. You are a woman, entitled to know love—'

'I do know love.' Alexia fiddled with her necklace. 'I have you, I have a daughter—'

'I know,' I said, though I knew she was avoiding my point on purpose. 'But I want you to promise you will let yourself be happy again.

Not for Targe, for me, or for your people—not even for Eva. I want you to be happy for your sake.'

Alexia met my eyes. 'Even after regaining your memory and knowing the full extent of the evil that killed the ones we loved, your hope and passion is inexhaustible, isn't it? Your spirit shines through your eyes as if it has never known disappointment or fear.' She looked away. 'I feel withered and tired next to you.'

I was surprised she was willing to admit as much. 'I have known disappointment, but I will not let Cades continue to ruin my life now that he is gone. Nor should you. You deserve a happier life than this.'

She gave me what I think was a humouring smile. 'If you say so.'

I drew her into another hug. 'I do because I love you. It's what Ethaniel would have wanted, too—and Jeri.'

Alexia was saved from saying any more when she saw someone running up the path towards us. 'Here's someone who will be excited to see you,' she said.

I turned and smiled when I saw the young boy coming our way. 'Zavad Erowen!'

'Adaliah!' he called, running straight into my arms. 'I mean, "Your Majesty". How long have you been here? How come I haven't seen you? It's been so long!'

'I know.' I laughed. 'You've grown so tall since I last saw you. How old are you now? Eight? Nine?'

'Nearly ten!'

'Practically a man,' I said, ruffling his hair. 'Where are you going?'

'Darj is training Zavad to be the next general.' Alexia winked at the boy. 'They've been spending a lot of time together, and he has a lesson this morning.'

'Yes, archery,' Zavad said, 'so I can learn to shoot like the queen!'

Alexia returned to the palace, but I accompanied Zavad to the training yard outside the barracks, happy to see his development. There, the general was waiting for him with a freshly bandaged arm. Darj assured me the pain had reduced to almost nothing, but then scowled when he picked up a bow for Zavad.

'You must take care of yourself,' I said to him while Zavad collected arrows. 'The queen relies on you, you know.'

'The queen is a very capable and independent woman.'

'Yes, but . . . '

'It's good to see you, Adaliah,' he said, giving me a pleasant but firm smile. 'How is married life suiting you?'

I grinned. 'Rather well.' He laughed in his quiet way and handed Zavad the bow. 'When shall we see you married, Darj?'

'Me?'

There was more shock in his voice than I'd expected. 'Yes . . . I'm sure you've thought about having a family of your own, of finding a wife . . . ' I studied him for anything that might give him away, but he continued to look at me like I'd suggested he take up embroidery. Then, when he could think of nothing to say, he turned to Zavad instead and helped him place an arrow on the bow.

'The arrow is the most accurate and careful way to kill,' he said while I watched on, apparently dismissed from the conversation. Zavad listened to every word, placing full confidence in his tutor. 'All you need is a steady hand.' Zavad pulled the bow string back, his thin arm shaking slightly from the pressure. 'Try not to think about anything. All that matters is your arrow and your target.' Zavad aimed at the target on which they were practising. 'Now,' Darj said, leaning close to see where Zavad was directing the arrow. 'When you're ready, shoot.'

Zavad took a deep breath, squinted, and released the arrow. It flew through the air and hit the target. The shot was too low and weak, and the arrow bounced off.

'Why do I find this so difficult?' Zavad asked. He turned to me. 'This is my third archery lesson, and I still haven't come close to hitting the target.'

'It's often a matter of perseverance,' I said.

'What sort of soldier will I make if I can't shoot?'

'I'm not a skilled archer either,' I said. 'Nor is Darj, if he's honest. We can make use of it when we have to, but we prefer the sword. Alexia has had training with sword fighting, but she prefers the bow. You just need to find out what you're good at.'

'Perhaps the queen should teach me.'

Darj's smile faltered. 'Why?' he asked.

'Well, everyone knows she's the best archer in the Rhea Lands.' Zavad's eyes brightened with excitement. 'Everyone knows her perfect shot saved Adaliah on the Tiathi Basin.' He raised his bow again and pretended to shoot something in the distance. I couldn't help but smile. 'And I was there, remember?'

'Yes,' Darj said, 'and so you will also remember that she got herself shot only a few seconds later and could have been killed.'

'Yes, but—'

'Zavad . . . ' Darj sighed. 'It's not important how good you are at archery, or sword fighting, or whatever it is you learn. What's important is what kind of person you choose to become. I know plenty of men who have trained hard, but a great fighter is nothing if they don't believe in what they're fighting for. Being a soldier is about risking your life for a cause, believing in it so much that you're prepared to die for it. It is the willingness to take that risk that makes life so much more precious.'

I watched as Zavad thought about this eloquent speech with all the seriousness of an almost-ten-year-old. 'Well, when I can fight, I'll be able to protect the palace from those cloaked men.' He ran across the grass to pick up his arrow.

Darj glanced at me with a frown. 'What do you mean?' he asked when Zavad returned. 'What did you see?'

'Cloaked men, two of them, near the palace chapel.'

'Perhaps they were churchmen,' I said.

Darj seemed appeased by the thought. 'Yes, that would make sense.'

'No, they weren't churchmen,' Zavad said.

'How could you tell?' I asked.

'Because they were wearing black cloaks, and both of them had daggers.'

4
A COLD KNIFE

'I would like to propose a toast,' Elhian said, sitting next to me at the long dining table that night. He rose his hand to hush the small party of forty people. They lined the table in a room filled with exciting smells of freshly cooked meat, rare fruits, and other culinary delights.

Elhian topped up his glass with wine. 'To the loveliest Crown Princess of Targe on her second birthday and her mother the queen.' He raised his glass to them, and those in the room lifted their glasses in turn. 'May blessings be upon them in every way.' He drank from his cup and smiled at Alexia.

The four of us had spent much time that afternoon discussing the potential threat to Liane and Targe. I was glad to have some time away from it all; I found no joy in entertaining the idea that the enemy may be lurking outside. Darj had found no evidence of the Zalems in the palace, despite Zavad's observation and a thorough search, but he still felt it was unsafe. Zavad was rarely wrong, and he never lied. Darj had tried to talk Alexia into evacuating again, without success.

'Darj, you above all know my duty as queen,' she'd said, 'and how I must weigh risk against my reign. If I were a common woman in a common house and you were asking me to leave, then of course, I would agree with you. But whether or not we like it, I am the monarch of this kingdom. I must stay until the very last.'

After dinner, it was time for the princess to go to bed, but the rest of us began to dance. Elhian smiled warmly at me as he bowed ahead of the first dance. I curtsied in response, wearing a long, blue gown in honour of Casmodia. He slipped his hand around my waist and drew me close, touching his cheek against mine.

I felt myself glow as I leant into him. Something in me settled in being back in Targe. I loved Elhian and had come to think of Tiathi as my home, but I was more content in Liane. If Elhian knew this, he didn't mention it. He just twirled me and made me laugh until the Zalems were all but gone from my mind. Then, he kissed me as the music ended. The people clapped and cheered around us, and I couldn't help but smile.

After the second dance, we left the floor for a short break. Elhian took the opportunity to speak to Darj, and I crossed the room to join Alexia. I realised when I drew near to her elevated seat that she was in conversation with a man crouching beside her. He was an older man, and I could tell by his velvet green robes that he was an important member of the church. Alexia wasn't facing him, but I knew by the look in her eye she was not impressed with whatever it was he was saying. His face also spoke of frustration. I moved behind them under the guise of getting a drink from one of the servants who stood nearby.

'But that's just it, isn't it,' the man said. 'It's been two years and nine months since your husband passed away. That means there has been nine months in which it has been perfectly acceptable for you to take a second husband. And yet, I hear you will not even consider the suitors who have asked for your hand.' He spoke harshly, more so than I felt he had a right. I half-expected Alexia to banish him from the room for his impertinence. 'You know your throne would be safer with a husband.'

'Archbishop Dennear, what is it that bothers you?' Alexia asked dryly.

I recognised the name. Alexia had once written to me about him. She'd described him as an 'unintelligent, forcefully arrogant man, who tries my patience more than King Hazaka ever did'. At the time, I'd smiled at the scorn in her words. Now I knew she'd meant every one of them.

'We have an heir and are quickly regaining wealth after the Northern Invasion. How is my throne unsafe?'

'With all due respect, Your Majesty, we all thought your throne was safe when you had Ethaniel and Jeri.'

'Exactly!' Alexia said. 'Being married then did not increase the security of the throne—it only broke my heart. I have no intention of going through that again.'

This saddened me, and I had to stop myself from interrupting.

'That's what this is about? Your heart? Love? Your Majesty, there is no room for love! You have your duty. You owe it to your kingdom, to Ru'ach. What if something happened to Princess Eva?'

Alexia gave him a sharp look. 'Nothing is going to happen to my Eva. I would die first.'

'Then your line would be gone forever.'

'Adaliah would become the monarch, and then her future child. It would still be in the family.'

I ran my hand over my stomach and hoped she wasn't relying on me having a child soon. None grew there yet, and a part of me hoped it wouldn't until the threat of war was gone. Besides, the Targian crown had to stay with Alexia's line. Targe would be changed forever if it didn't.

'And Targe would be lost as part of Casmodia. You need more sons!'

'Are you so ignorant of Targian law? As the only surviving child of my first husband, Eva will retain her right to the crown even if I have ten sons.'

Dennear groaned. 'I know you are only a woman, but—'

Alexia stood and glared down at him. 'Archbishop Dennear, I am told you respected my father. It was because of that I authorised your promotion. But now you must also respect me and the decisions I make. Press me any further and I will not hesitate to demote you. I am not ready to consider marriage again, and I will not be rushed into it at your request or anyone else's. If the Great Spirit wishes me to remarry, he can tell me himself.'

Archbishop Dennear stormed away from her as I took a long sip of my drink. He glared at me as he passed. I smiled politely at him and, seeing that Darj and Elhian had been watching as well, crossed the room again to speak to them.

'I assume the archbishop was testing Her Majesty's forbearance for the third time this week,' Darj said.

'How did you know?' I asked with a smile as Elhian put an arm around me.

'Well, she didn't seem to be enjoying his company,' Darj said, smiling as well. 'But then, the happy, ever-laughing Alexia was lost in the Northern Invasion, and she has not danced since Ethaniel died.'

'There is hope for her, though,' Elhian said. 'She will find herself again.'

Alexia was smiling at her guests now. She was an attractive woman, a regal pillar of strength. But also like a pillar, she had become stoical and silent. I put my hand on Darj's arm. 'Darj . . . I had hoped—'

A distant rumbling interrupted me. It sounded like thunder at first, and I wondered if there was a storm. But then, a clearer thud sounded, and I knew it wasn't forthcoming rain. There were shouts of distress somewhere in the palace. One or two guests rushed to the main door to see what was happening. Another crash made the floors vibrate.

Darj left me and ran towards Alexia. 'Get down!' he yelled, and then he pushed her to the floor himself. There was another crash, close by and loud. A few screamed. As the palace vibrated again, Darj covered Alexia, shielding her from falling debris. Elhian and I ducked behind a table.

'The palace is under attack,' Darj said to the room full of startled people. He pulled Alexia to her feet. 'Get to safety, all of you!'

The people began to run out of the nearest door. Elhian directed them, but neither Alexia nor I moved.

Another loud crash crumbled part of the wall. 'Your Majesty,' Darj said, tugging at Alexia's arm. 'Come, you have to get out of here.'

'Eva.' Alexia pulled away from Darj and ran to get her daughter.

I moved to go after her, but Elhian grabbed my hand. I grew impatient when he hesitated. 'What?'

'If it comes to it,' he said as the ground trembled again, 'we'll meet you in the Yellow Forest.'

As I ran into the hallway, a gust of cold wind blew the candles out, and I was surrounded by blackness. With one hand on the wall, I felt my way alongside it to Eva's room and only stopped when I thought I glimpsed a figure up ahead. 'Alexia?' I called. The figure seemed to flinch and disappear. I convinced myself I had imagined it.

I took a few more steps, then held my breath and listened, keeping still. I heard something brushing against the wall and felt the hairs on my arms prickle. My heart started thumping. I saw a dark, cloaked figure standing at the door of Eva's chambers, just up ahead. I couldn't move. I knew by then I wasn't imagining it.

'Darj?' I heard Alexia say somewhere ahead of me. 'Darj!' she called louder and a little shrilly.

I looked over my shoulder, but no one was coming. I knew I had to find the courage to get to her. I felt the wall for guidance again and pushed ahead as quietly and as quickly as I could.

Once at the door of Eva's room, I saw Alexia moving towards the hearth with a candle. 'It's all right, Evie,' she called out to her crying child. 'I'm here.'

I opened my mouth to let her know I was there, too, but she dropped her candle. My eyes adjusted to the dull light, and I saw the cold hand that had clasped over her mouth and the arm that wrapped around her waist like a leathery vine.

The darkness suddenly seemed impenetrable. Panicking, Alexia elbowed her attacker, and he loosened his grip. She struggled again to get free, but his hand slipped from her mouth to her throat. She tried to call out but couldn't speak. I could hear her fighting to breathe.

All this happened in the few moments it took for me to cross the room and push her attacker to the ground. Alexia scrambled away while I fought the man on the floor. With a sudden rush of adrenaline, I wrenched the knife out of his hand and stabbed him with it. He called out but died quickly. It was the first kill I'd made since the war. I felt cold.

I pushed the feeling to the back of my mind. 'Are you all right?' I asked Alexia, standing.

'I . . . ' She rubbed her throat. 'Yes.'

I pulled Eva out of her crib. 'Come on,' I said, passing the princess to Alexia. 'We must get out of the city now, while we can. Darj and Elhian will meet us in the Yellow Forest.'

'But I can't abandon the palace. I'm not supposed to leave my people.'

'How can you say that even now? Can't you see that Darj was right? That Zavad had seen someone coming in?'

'I must stand my ground.'

My adrenaline turned to anger. 'Alexia, these men aren't here for your people—they're here for us. You must leave—for your daughter, if for nothing else!'

The palace shook again as it took another hit, and it was only then that Alexia gave me a reluctant nod. She followed me out of the room, and I noticed the Zalem symbol tattooed on the man's ankle as we passed.

We rode out of the city under the cover of darkness, Eva secured to Alexia's front. I glanced over my shoulder and saw something out of the corner of my eye. A flash of movement. 'Alexia!' I called, unsheathing my sword.

She reached for the bow on her back.

Two horsemen came upon us on our right. The second one rode straight into me, into Bagred. He crashed to the ground, taking me with him.

I landed awkwardly. A sharp, unnatural pain filled my shoulder, and my foot was trapped under Bagred.

While I struggled to get free, Alexia struck the first horseman across the face with her bow. The man recovered and pulled my cousin and her daughter off their horse. Eva was crying.

I tugged harder at my foot. The pain in my shoulder filled my entire being. I wanted to vomit.

The first man kicked Alexia's head. Her body went limp. Eva started screaming.

More men arrived. They kneeled around Alexia's body. I couldn't see what they were doing to her, but one of them picked up Eva.

Bagred managed to get back to his feet, but my foot was still stuck in the stirrup. I tried to reach out to free myself, but my shoulder seized up. Before I could stop myself, I cried out. This drew the second man's attention back to me. He leant down with his sword handle and delivered a blow that left me senseless.

5
ODAVAN

When I awoke, the first thing I heard was the river. I opened my eyes with a throbbing headache that made living unbearable. I groaned and tried to move, but everything hurt. I managed to roll onto my side. Realising where I was, I sat up despite the pain.

'Kest,' I said out loud, an intoxicating sense of familiarity passing through me. I had woken by this river before. 'Adaliah,' I said quickly. 'My name is Adaliah.'

At least I had not lost my memory.

I staggered to my feet, groaning out loud again at the pain in my shoulder. The moon was still high.

Where is Alexia?

I looked about, trying to orientate myself. I found my sword lying in the dirt. It was the tree-blade, the one Elhian and I had pulled out of the tree in the Northern Invasion, probably not far from where I was now. I had brought the Life Sword with me to Targe as well but, in our hurry to leave, had left it back at the palace.

I picked up the tree-blade and, hearing a noise behind me, turned on my heel and pointed my sword into the darkness. 'Who's there?' I heard something take a step towards me. A tall, dark man appeared, only just visible by the moonlight. 'Who are you?'

He peered at me as if fascinated. 'I am Odavan, a Jazmardian fisherman,' he said, speaking with a thick accent. 'I am not a soldier and do

not wish to attack you, A'zyon Warrior, or I would not have saved you.'
He studied me with brown, almost black, eyes. 'I brought you here. Your
shoulder was dislocated, but I put it back in place while you were asleep.'

'How do you know who I am?' I asked, lowering my sword and
rubbing my shoulder.

'I fought with King Hazaka Cazren in the Northern Invasion. I
saw you in battle.'

'But you just said you're not a soldier.'

'I was not before the war, and I am not now.'

I looked around again at the silvery river, the silent trees. 'Have
you seen anyone else tonight?'

'Not here, no, but there is something I found that belongs to you.'
He disappeared in the darkness again and returned with my black horse.

'Bagred.' I reached up to stroke his face. He snorted gently, as if
disturbed from a pleasant sleep. I ran my hands over his right side and
felt the swelling where he'd been hit. 'Where am I?'

'You are standing where you killed Jag at the end of the Northern
Invasion.'

I reviewed my surroundings again. Yes, there was the dagger I
had thrust into the tree, the one I had killed Jag with. There was the
riverbank where Kadram had revived me after death. This was the last
place I had seen the purple wisp of the Armoured Butterfly. And now
I was here again, in pain again, alone again.

I considered the fish Odavan cooked me but couldn't bring myself to
eat it. I had the strange sensation that the ground was moving. My
shoulder was throbbing, and my head felt like someone had filled it
with water.

I dropped my food altogether and grabbed my sword when I heard another set of footsteps approaching. Odavan raised a hand to silence me and motioned for me to lower my weapon. I did, but only a little. He turned and beckoned someone forward.

A young and beautiful Jazmardian woman stepped out of the darkness. Her body was toned like someone who lived off the land, and her face held a sense of wisdom and understanding. She met my eyes, and her gaze gave me a sense of peace. I lowered my sword completely and watched as she spoke to Odavan in their tongue. The woman kept looking at me with concern as she talked, and the expression on Odavan's face became more and more serious, but I had no idea what they were saying. Odavan whispered something next to her ear and gave her a lingering kiss that made me think they wouldn't see each other for some time.

The woman shrank back into the darkness.

'Who was that?' I asked, sitting down again.

'My woman. She was tracing the men who attacked you but says they have disappeared.'

'You saw the men?'

'It was I who chased them away from you.'

'Then you saw Her Majesty? Queen Alexia?'

Odavan drank from a goatskin water bottle. 'I saw her.'

'What? Was she all right?'

'She will be fine. It was fortuitous that we met. You must come with me.'

'What?' My head was pulsating now. None of it made any sense. 'Why should I go with you?'

Odavan smiled, a little smugly I thought. 'Because dead will the boy be if you do not abstain.'

The poem. 'How do you know about that? Who is this boy?'

'All you need to know is that the wheel has begun to turn and you must play your part. The Zalems tried to work through Cades, but now they are doing their work for themselves. The High Zalem himself must die for this to be stopped. No one knows how to defeat him, except for one man, and it is that one man who sent me to find you.'

'But why me?'

Odavan shrugged. 'Only Ru'ach can answer that. All I can say is this: you have been chosen, and you alone can do it.'

I wished I were still unconscious. 'I have to find my cousin and Elhian and Darj.' I stood and moved towards Bagred. 'Now.'

Odavan watched me. 'I will camp here for two more weeks. Come back when you have changed your mind.'

The night felt eerie as I made my way back to the path in the Yellow Forest, trying to find the spot where I'd been knocked down. I flinched when I heard a horse neigh ahead of me but realised it was Darj and his horse Guntar. Darj was kneeling on the ground next to Alexia's horse. It had a black arrow protruding from its neck.

'Darj?'

He looked up. 'Adaliah! Where is the queen? Where is she? Where is the princess?'

I'd forgotten how formidable Darj could be. 'I . . . I don't know . . .' Tears formed in my eyes. It occurred to me that just a few hours ago, I'd been dancing in Elhian's arms. 'We were attacked . . .'

'Yes. One of them stayed behind, saw Elhian and me, and did this.' He gestured towards Alexia's dead horse. 'Elhian ran after him with two of his royal guards.' He stood and cupped his mouth with his hands. 'Alexia! Eva!'

Silence.

I rubbed my arms and hugged myself.

'Alexia! Eva!' Darj called again.

A child's cry sounded somewhere to our left.

'Princess!' Darj yelled.

'I think it came from over there.' I pointed to a spot where the ground fell away to a stream.

Darj ran to the edge of the small dip, and I followed. 'Eva?' he called again. We saw her standing in the middle of some scrub. 'Eva!'

She saw us and burst into tears. We hurried down to her, and Darj knelt so she could run straight into his arms. He held her closely and rubbed her back.

'Where's Mother?' he asked once she settled a little. He passed her to me, and I kissed her cheek. She was still crying. 'Where is she?'

Eva looked somewhere behind us. 'There,' she said. I followed her gaze and saw a piece of torn cloth in a tree.

Darj rushed through the scrub, and I carried Eva behind him.

'Where is she?' Darj asked again.

Eva pointed to the ground this time, just a few steps away from us. We found the queen lying amongst the foliage, her skin so dirty, we could only just make out her figure in the moonlight.

We hurried to her, and Darj knelt by her side. Her dress was ripped, and she had blood all through her hair and down one side of her face. Her skin looked cold from the night air, but when Darj placed a hand over her heart, he said he felt a beat.

I closed my eyes in relief.

'If they weren't going to take her with them, why did they drag her out here?' I asked.

'My guess is she crawled here herself, trying to get away or possibly looking for help.'

Darj lifted her torso up and used his free hand to hold the torn cloth to her head wound. As he touched her face, she threw her head back and cried out as if she'd been stabbed. The muscles in her throat became unnaturally taut, and the colour drained from her face.

'Alexia!' Darj tried to hold her still. She thrust back again, her eyes unopened. 'What's happening?'

'I . . . I don't know. It's like she's having a fit!'

She continued to toss and recoil from Darj's touch. It lasted for another minute or so and then stopped. Her body relaxed again.

I checked the pulse in her wrist; it was steady, if a little fast. 'Perhaps . . . perhaps it was just a nightmare,' I said, but I could see the same fear I felt etched on Darj's face.

He held the cloth to her wound again, and this time she didn't move.

6
MISSING

Darj settled Eva next to her mother on a bed of furs Elhian and Darj had brought with them from Liane. With no tents or anything else to use as shelter, we would all be sleeping under the sky. Morning was soon to dawn, but the prospect of at least a few hours rest was still desirable.

I examined the forest that encircled us, searching for any sign of Elhian. He had not returned after chasing the last soldier, and I was beginning to worry. *He is a capable warrior,* I kept telling myself. *He can handle one man.*

I woke after about two hours, disappointed at how tired my body still felt but feeling unsettled, as if darkness was lingering nearby. The forest was eerily still. I turned over and realised that while Eva and Darj were still sleeping, Alexia was gone from her bed.

I circled the camp in search of her and was about to call Darj to help me when I saw a ghostly white figure ahead. It was standing in the morning mist, further off and near a small brook. I walked towards it as if stalking prey, but then realised it was Alexia in her pale shift. She was standing wholly still.

'Alexia?' I called, softly at first, but louder when she didn't respond. 'Alexia!' I called for a third time, now standing right by her.

She flinched and turned. I realised too late she had her bow in hand. She struck me across the face. I fell, reaching for my nose.

'Adaliah!' She gasped. 'I'm so sorry; I was startled. I didn't know it was you.'

Blood ran into my mouth. 'I think you broke my nose . . . '

She leant forward to check the damage but stopped, picked up her quiver, and loaded her bow. She loosed an arrow just past me. A body fell to the ground. Alexia shot another arrow; another body fell. Then another, and another—one perfect, deadly shot after another as men in black armour fell around us. The Zalems were ambushing us. The gold-tipped, green feathers, unique to the queen, cut sharply through the air. Alexia turned behind her, and the last man, realising that his comrades had been killed, dropped his sword and slid to his knees. Alexia bent her bow back.

He raised his palms. 'Please, stop!'

A snarl crossed Alexia's face. It reminded me of the madman who'd attacked Elhian. She walked behind him and pulled up his pant leg, revealing the Zalem symbol on his ankle.

She shot the arrow. The man elicited a whimper as he fell forward into the dirt, dead.

The look on Alexia's face was made all the more frightening by the cold sunrise.

I found myself backing away. 'Alexia . . . '

She rubbed her neck like it was irritating her. I pinched my nose, trying to stop the bleeding. My head was throbbing.

'They attacked my home,' she said flatly, like someone other than herself was speaking. 'They tried to hurt Eva, and I will not lose another child.'

Darj was awake by the time we got back.

'What happened?' he asked, jumping to his feet when he saw my face.

'It was an accident,' I said. Alexia told him about the ambush. I wanted to tell him about the surrendering man, but not with Alexia nearby.

It took an hour before my nose stopped bleeding. By then, I felt like I had a cold. The loss of blood made me exhausted, as if my head weighed twice as much as usual, but with Elhian still missing, I couldn't close my eyes for a second.

It had been hours since Darj had seen him. There was no sign of him returning. It wasn't until midday, after the three of us had spent the morning searching the forest for him, that one of his Casmodian royal guards came stumbling towards us.

I hadn't allowed myself to fear the worst up until that point. I'd wondered whether Elhian had just chased the man further than he intended to, as I did when pursuing the Life Sword in the Northern Invasion. But what could he have that Elhian would want so much?

Perhaps he's lost.

As with most men, I knew he'd rather continue wandering aimlessly than admit he didn't know where he was.

Or perhaps he'd been injured.

That was the furthest I'd let my thoughts go. But when I saw the soldier covered in dirt and, worst of all, leading a riderless Leuk along the path, my heartbeat thinned.

'I'm so sorry, Your Majesty,' the guard said. He attempted to bow to me, even though he was obviously in pain.

The fear began to creep over me until I could barely breathe. 'Please . . . don't . . . '

Don't tell me he's dead.

I involuntarily pictured his broken and bloodied body lying in the dirt. Had he been felled with arrows? Impaled? Had he been beaten and stoned? Was he dying right now, alone and cold, unable to call for help?

'I lost him.'

Alexia reached for my hand and squeezed it.

'Elhian or the Zalem?' Darj asked.

'Both. I lost sight of His Majesty and Peyton, the other guard. I traced them to a cave, but I was too late. Peyton I found dead, and the king was gone.'

'Gone?' Alexia asked. I couldn't speak at all.

'They must have taken him,' Darj said. 'It's just what they would do—abduct an important person—and they see Elhian as the slayer of one of their own. I . . . I shouldn't have left him.'

All I could think was that abduction was better than death.

'Where would they take him?' Alexia asked.

'I don't know,' Darj said.

I rubbed my forehead, tears pricking at my eyes.

Elhian is missing.

'What is your name, soldier?' Darj asked.

'Karlen.'

'Thank you for coming back to find us, Karlen.' Darj moved towards Guntar. 'Alexia, do I have your permission to call your councillors to Chettona for a meeting?'

'Yes. We cannot go back to Liane yet.'

'Ride with us, Karlen,' Darj said. 'We may yet need more of your help.'

7
THE CAPTAINS

Chettona was home to just a few hundred people and built intimately against the ever-flowing King River, Targe's central life source. A few locals once found gold dust in the water, which had inspired many to try and find the source of gold further upstream, but no one had succeeded. Instead, most of them found work on the farms. Riding towards the town four days later, we passed healthy fields of corn and wheat.

The tranquil setting brought me no comfort. By then, my mind was wild with fear. *Elhian, Elhian, Elhian* . . . I kept saying his name over and over in my mind, like that would somehow conjure him back.

Ru'ach, please protect him. Please keep him alive!

We passed through street markets, where people were selling meat, vegetables, herbs, and spices, and rode to the small barracks that housed the local soldiers and Captain Ival Fort, who, since the war, had been promoted to head of the town's military contingent.

'Do you think Ival Fort can help?' Alexia asked Darj as we dismounted outside the barracks and tethered our horses, including Leuk.

'If nothing else, he can give us men for the search,' Darj said.

I walked inside ahead of the others and found Ival sitting at a desk, talking to two men we had not expected to see. One was a tall man with shoulder-length, black hair that looked stiff from lack of washing. A lock near his temple was plaited with a green bead at the end. The other man was shorter, rounder, and balder, with a missing tooth and wide lips that made his smile look like a child's.

'Xander? Raggin?' I said as the others came in behind me. 'What are you doing here?'

The three men looked up with surprise.

'Queen Alexia!' Ival bowed to her before taking Darj's forearm in a friendly greeting. Xander and Raggin did the same, though they seemed quieter. 'I'm glad you're all safe,' Ival said. 'We just heard news of the attack on Liane Palace.'

'That's not all of it,' Darj said. 'Elhian is missing.'

'What?' Raggin asked with a scoff. 'The King of Casmodia? Missing?' The three men glanced at each other with disbelief and turned to me. I knew my expression was pained, and not just because of the bruise Alexia's blow had left. It was taking all my strength to not panic.

'Yes,' Darj said. 'These attacks . . . I believe they have been instigated by a cult called the Zalems. Have you heard of them?'

Raggin slapped Xander's back with a sudden realisation, causing his tall friend to lose his balance and utter a profanity at him. 'I bet that's who the men were at Hunt,' Raggin said.

Xander began to nod. 'It's rare for you to make sense, but I think you could be right.'

'What happened at Hunt?' Darj asked.

'Wait,' Ival said, raising a hand. 'One thing at a time. What are we going to do about King Elhian?'

Raggin jumped in before Darj could answer. 'Xander and I travelled with Elhian Edangard for weeks during the Northern Invasion,' he said. 'He may be young, but I find it hard to believe he's in more trouble than he can handle.'

He gave me a weak smile, but I remained silent. Even if I wanted to speak, I didn't have the words.

'But we need to do what we can to find him,' Darj said. 'Ival, please arrange for the queen's council to meet here and send word to the captains of each town, asking them to be on their guard. In the meantime, Xander, Raggin, if you have news for us about Hunt, we'd better hear it.'

It wasn't until after we ate that night that Xander began to tell us their story. Like Ival, Xander had been promoted to captain after the Northern Invasion, and Hunt was his post. He lived there with Jacinth, a young and pretty woman he'd married within six weeks of meeting her. The last I'd heard, they were expecting a child.

'Our daughter was born eleven nights ago, the same night as the attack,' Xander told us as we sat around a table. A servant cleared our plates. 'I was just holding her for the first time when I heard a ruckus outside our window. Someone was yelling at people to move aside.'

'That was me,' Raggin said, chuckling. 'I had to meet my ward, didn't I?'

'I never agreed to you being the guardian.' Xander gave him a bored look.

'I have to be; you don't have any other friends!'

Xander couldn't help but laugh, but he stopped when he realised we weren't in the mood for a joke.

He cleared his throat. 'I introduced Serene to him. Raggin was romanticising about how he'd like to have one—even though he'll never find a woman who'll have him—when my front door burst open. A soldier stood there with a sword in his hand, yelling at me to come.'

'I handed Serene to Jacinth, and Raggin and I ran outside. There was a tower of flames down the street. Two buildings—you know the blacksmith and small chapel? They were on fire, but my men were already throwing buckets of water over them and working the well as fast as possible.

'There were seven or eight bodies nearby, all of them my soldiers, and behind them was . . . well . . . ' He stopped and moved his eyes towards Alexia.

Her daughter had fallen asleep in her arms. Up until then, she'd just been gazing at Eva's peaceful face. I'm sure she'd been listening, but it had yet to move her to any illustration of emotion. I wondered if I would become like that too, if Elhian . . .

'What?' she asked, looking up when she realised Xander was waiting for her.

Xander clasped his hands together and rested them on the table. 'The headstone they made for Prince Jeri . . . It was broken and desecrated with the Zalem symbol.'

Alexia's mouth dropped. 'So, my son is still not allowed to rest in peace?'

None of us could think of anything to say, and silence endured for a minute or so.

'I took a sword off a nearby man,' Xander said in the end, 'but I couldn't see an enemy. I asked my soldiers where they were, but they hadn't even seen them.'

'I couldn't believe it either,' Raggin said. 'I mean, how could they just walk in, do that to Jeri's headstone, and leave unseen? Why would they want to?'

'It was beyond repair,' Xander said. 'We knew it must mean something, though. That's why we rode to Chettona with the intention of continuing on to Liane tomorrow. We wanted to tell you face-to-face. But now, of course, we discover that Liane Palace has been attacked as well.'

We talked late into the night, and then Ival led Alexia and Eva to the first of two small rooms while I followed. 'This is the best we have.' He opened the first door.

Alexia stepped inside, recoiling a bit from the potent smell of straw and sweat. A doll was sitting on a simple bed.

'One of the men who cleaned the rooms left that for Princess Eva as a present,' Ival said.

'That is very kind,' Alexia said. 'Please thank him for me.'

We left them there, and Ival took me to my room further up the hall. 'I know you must be going mad with fear,' he said, opening the door, 'but everything will be all right. I can't help but think they're using King Elhian as a pawn in their game and that he is not the main objective. He is known to be an intelligent and valiant warrior. I feel certain he will outsmart them at their own game.'

Ival Fort had been a prisoner of Cades for six months before we freed him from an underground dungeon in Semanez. When we'd first found him, he'd looked underfed and wild. He still looked somewhat wild. His hair was matted and pushed back, as if blown by the wind and frozen in place, and he looked older than when I'd last seen him, but there was a kindness in his eyes that made him seem so sure about what he said.

'Thank you,' I said, meaning it. I wanted to have the same faith he did, but the fear of the unknown was still too strong.

What if he's killed? Ru'ach, you are the King of Life. Please be with him!

I had been desperate to get to my own room, thinking that some silence would help appease the noise in my mind. It didn't. I lay in bed thinking about Elhian, the Zalems, and Odavan. Had the Jazmardian fisherman known this was going to happen? Could I have prevented it by going with him as he'd asked? I had no reason to trust him, but still, I wondered.

I gave up trying to sleep an hour later. Seeing that candlelight was still shining from Alexia's room, I visited her and began pacing her floor. She sat on the end of her bed and watched on as I became more and more anxious.

'I can't stand this,' I said quietly, not wanting to wake Eva. 'Doing nothing.'

'We are doing everything we can,' Alexia said. 'Darj will organise a methodical search in the morning. We will not stop until he is found.'

'He's been gone for days. Something has to be wrong. Why won't anyone admit that out loud?'

'Adaliah, Elhian is a good warrior and an even better man. If he is in trouble, you can trust him to handle it. He has faith; Ru'ach will protect him. Perhaps you should go to Jazmarda to find out what you can, like that man—Odavan, was it?—said. Our people are in danger, and we need to do what we can.'

'Would you have abandoned Ethaniel for your people?'

She straightened. 'To wear the crown is to make hard decisions.'

'That is just an excuse you use so you don't have to feel anything again.' I spoke far more harshly than I intended, but the shame didn't register until later. 'No pain, but no love or happiness either.' Alexia flinched at my words, but I went on before I could stop myself. 'You talk about Ru'ach, but even now, you are not truly connected to him.'

'I made my peace after Jeri and Ethaniel—'

'You sought his help, and he gave it—that is all. You are cold, but I am not. I love Elhian!'

'And what would he have you do?' Alexia asked, raising her voice a little. 'Leave your home, your kingdom, and your people to be destroyed on account of him?'

'He is the king!'

'He is also but one man!'

'Did Cades cut out your heart?' I yelled. Eva woke up and started to cry. 'Because that "one man" is everything to me!'

'You pushed us to leave Liane,' Alexia said, picking up Eva. 'At least you would not have been separated had you stayed.'

'Ethaniel was killed because he stayed.'

'Why do you keep bringing him into this? He's dead, Adaliah. And yes, he died defending me, something I will have to bear for the rest of my life.'

'So you're blaming me for leaving Liane?'

Alexia groaned. 'Adaliah, go and see what Jazmarda might be able to do for us. You cannot be a wife when you must be a queen. Your husband's search will be safe with us.'

'What, just as Jeri was?'

The words hung in the air like a slow arrow. Despite everything else I'd said, it was only then that she paled with anger.

I felt sick.

What have I done?

My fear was attacking one of the most important people in my life.

How could I touch on such a wound?

Tears filled my eyes. 'Wait,' I said, raising my palms. 'I'm so sorry. I didn't mean . . .'

But I could see the repulsion in her face.

'Get out of my sight,' she said, her piercing blue eyes burning through me. I now understood how criminals felt before her. 'Leave!'

I turned and hurried out of the room, passing Darj in the hallway.

8
IVAL

Alexia didn't speak to me the following day, and I knew she wanted me leagues away. I intended to satisfy her and had my opportunity when I found Raggin and Xander in the stables, saddling their horses with Ival and six other men. 'Where are you going?' I asked.

'Darj thinks the Zalems have come from the eastern wastelands,' Raggin said. 'He's asked us to see if we can find one between here and Mount Dennell and force some information from them.'

'I'm coming.'

'We'll be gone for days,' Xander said.

'I don't care.' Without giving them a chance to protest any further, I ran to get Bagred.

'What was that?' Ival asked as we walked by a small stream two days later. We'd decided to give the horses a rest and were leading them along the path. The road was mostly made for easy travelling but was now going up a slight hill. So far, we hadn't seen anyone but a few journeymen and a family travelling to Gristern.

'I thought I heard something,' Ival said. 'It sounded like a dying animal.'

We stopped and listened. Xander turned to Raggin with a grin. 'It's him,' he said.

Raggin was gripping his stomach and trying to catch his breath. 'All right, so I'm not as fit as I used to be,' he said. 'I need another war, just for exercise.'

The men laughed as we walked on.

'You'd need more than that to lose all that weight,' Xander said with a nod towards Raggin's middle.

'The women say it makes me cuddly.' Raggin patted his belly with affection.

'Which is why you're still single.'

I smiled to myself as they continued to banter but stopped in my step when two strangers appeared ahead of us. They were dressed in black armour. Zalems. I was surprised to see them out in daylight, as if they were not just some dark creatures that nurtured evil in the night. It seemed they were becoming more confident in whatever it was they were planning. I reached for my sword, insulted that they felt they could walk around Targe in such a way.

'Did you get Jacinth drunk before you proposed to her?' Raggin asked.

'Why is it so hard for you to believe she fell for me sober?'

'Well, have you looked in the mirror lately?'

'Shut up!' I said to them, pointing to the men ahead of us. I crouched low to the ground.

Xander and Raggin quickly realised what was happening and crouched low, too, as did the others.

Ival moved closer to me. 'Let's take them hostage.'

'They're coming this way,' I said. 'Wait until they're close.'

I'd noted by then that they had bows and arrows on their backs and swords sheathed by their sides. I could also tell by the dust on their pant legs that they had covered a lot of ground on foot, but they didn't seem tired.

Once they were closer, Ival stepped up and pointed his sword at them. The soldiers stopped and glanced over their shoulder. Our men surrounded them.

'Don't move,' Ival said. 'You're outnumbered, so I suggest you surrender.'

The soldiers put their hands in the air. 'Who are you?' one of them asked. I didn't recognise the accent, but it clipped the ends of the words in a severe way.

'I am Captain Ival Fort of Chettona, and you are now captives of Queen Alexia of Targe.'

The first one gave a shrill whistle. Ival struck him across the face and pushed him to his knees, but it was too late. More Zalems appeared further up the path—ten by my count. They took out their weapons and sprinted down the hill. One of them shot the man beside me.

I raised my swords and let them come. One ran at me; I impaled him and then another, fueled by days of pent-up anger and frustration. The sword moved easily in my hands, and I didn't have to think about what I was doing. My father had trained me well. I deflected a strike and slashed a third Zalem across his back.

To my right, two of our men fell at the hand of one Zalem, whom Xander then impaled from behind. Raggin threw a dagger into the chest of another.

It wasn't long before there was only one left. Ival brought his sword upon him until he had the Zalem on his knees. 'Cooperate, and we may spare your life,' Ival said.

But the Zalem pulled a dagger out of his shirt and thrust it into Ival's stomach.

'No!' The word charged out of my mouth.

The Zalem spat in Ival's face and withdrew the dagger with an angry scream.

Ival fell to his knees, blood discharging down his front.

Raggin pushed the Zalem into the dirt and started kicking into his body. Xander grabbed his friend's arm and pulled him away. 'Stop, Raggin. We need to talk to him.'

Scowling, Raggin turned the Zalem onto his front and roughly bound his hands behind his back.

Xander and I helped Ival move onto his side to stop him from choking. Xander pulled Ival's shirt up. He tried to stop the flow of blood with his hands, but we both knew there was nothing he could do to heal such a deep wound.

Ival gripped my hand. 'Tell D-Darj . . . Tell Darj I'm sorry.' Blood bubbled out of his mouth, and before I could say a word, he passed away.

I held Ival's hand for a bit longer, too numb to react. It wasn't until Xander reached over to close his eyes that I was able to place his hand over his heart and let go.

'Xander,' I said, 'this isn't fair.'

'Of course not,' he said softly. 'This is war.'

Raggin kicked the Zalem again. 'You have just killed a good man!'

'So have you!' the Zalem yelled.

Raggin dragged the man to his feet by his hair. I winced to see the pain in the soldier's face. 'Tell me where King Elhian is!'

'Why would—'

Raggin gripped the man's throat. I thought he was going to crush him. A bit tighter, and the man's neck would snap like a rabbit's. 'Tell me!'

'Sharlard,' the Zalem said with a gasp. He kicked hard at Raggin's knee, forcing him to let go.

The Zalem scrambled away but came straight into Xander's path. Xander's sword fell, and Ival's death was avenged.

Xander and Raggin barely said a word on the trip back. When we arrived at the barracks in Chettona, they went straight upstairs to wash.

Outside, members of the queen's council were arriving in answer to Darj's call—some on horseback and some by carriage. Men, women, and children lined the streets as members of the council tethered their horses, spoke to each other, and walked into the barracks to meet with Darj and Alexia.

Despite my fatigue, I trailed them inside and hid in the shadows by the doorway of the meeting room. Once the men had settled, Darj leant over a map he'd pinned to the table with two knives.

'We have sent men to search here, here, but not here,' he said, waving his hand across the colours and lines on the old parchment.

More than twenty men sat along the two sides of the table in the stronghold, glancing at each other and mumbling between themselves. Some of them were old. Some were dressed grandly. Some remained silent, and others were leaning forward like they were brimming with suggestions.

'We expect Captain Ival and the others back at any time,' Darj said.

Alexia was sitting at the head of the long, chipped table with a far-off look in her eyes.

'Your Majesty?' Darj asked. 'What do you think?'

She blinked, returning to the present. 'Well, we know Elhian has been taken by these Zalems,' she said, 'but what do you suppose they want with him?'

'How are any of us supposed to know that?' one of the councillors asked. 'They are a secret society.'

'Lord Bannard,' Alexia said, addressing the man, 'if we have any information about how they think, how they operate, whether they would have imprisoned Elhian or killed him straightaway, whether they are making some statement or if they are just acting to promote terror ahead of a bigger, more forceful attack, surely you can see how understanding these things would help us.'

I recoiled when she spoke about Elhian's potential death so calmly. I wanted to reveal myself and say something but knew that whatever came out of my mouth would be tainted by anger and exhaustion.

The council fell silent, and Darj fiddled with one of the knives that was pinning the map down. He pulled it out of the table, and one half of the map furled across the other.

'They won't have killed him,' he said, so firmly I was relieved. 'But I fear you are right, that they are promoting terror. They didn't attack Liane, just the palace. It wasn't about conquering the city, not then. They wanted to flush us out and to signal their return. I think they have decided to no longer remain secret.'

One of the other councillors leant forward. It was Lord Fenton of Egra. 'I think if we are to learn more about the Zalems—which I believe is where we should start—travelling to Delya would be the most helpful course of action.'

'What makes you say that?' Alexia asked.

'As I mentioned before, legend has it that's where the Zalems originated. To solve a problem, one must go to the source. Right now, you need information, and fast. That is the place you are most likely to find it, and the Delyan Rivermen may even be willing to provide help, now that they have a new king. Providing, of course, visiting him would not prove too uncomfortable for Your Majesty.' He added this with shy haste.

'If Her Majesty had accepted King Thane's offer, perhaps we would not now be in this predicament!' This was Lord Bannard again.

'Let me remind you that King Thane and I mutually agreed after a prolonged discussion that such a thing would not be in the best interest of our kingdoms.'

Thane Markus was one of many who had sought the widowed queen's hand, but to his credit, he was considered one of the better suitors. Some members of the court had criticised Alexia for rejecting his offer instead of seizing the opportunity to bring the two kingdoms together. Members like Lord Bannard and Archbishop Dennear.

'But,' Alexia said, 'I would not hesitate to visit him and his brother Ren in Nirrana if it would help us find King Elhian and uncover more about the Zalems' plan. What do you think, Darj?'

Darj was still staring down at the table with pressed lips and folded arms.

'Of course, if I didn't know you better, Your Majesty,' Lord Fenton said, 'I would respectfully suggest you stay in safety and let someone travel in your place.'

Darj scoffed. He knew as well as me that Alexia would never do such a thing. Alexia raised an eyebrow at Darj with a small, amused smile. 'Yes, well,' she said to Lord Fenton, 'you and General Darj both know I am not one to shy from my duties, and I don't intend to start now.'

'Well, at least the princess—'

'I will not be separated from the princess,' Alexia said. 'Now, if what you say is true, then I think Darj and I should travel there, as you suggest. We will leave you all to ensure Targe is ready for battle and to continue the search for King Elhian. Have riders arrived in Casmodia yet? The sooner they are able to bring men down to join the search for their king, the better.'

'We had word this morning that they have arrived in Tiathi,' Darj said.

'Very good. You and I shall leave tomorrow.'

'Your Majesty, a word of warning,' Lord Fenton said, running a finger over his moustache. 'If you really must go, I think it would be best if you don't cross the border as the queen. From what we've seen, the Zalems are cunning. They seem to be tracking you already. While you are in Delyan territory, I think you would be safer if you posed as a commoner.'

'That would mean no guard for an escort,' Darj said, frowning.

'I'm afraid it would.'

Alexia thought about this for a long time before she nodded. 'Thank you, Lord Fenton. Your advice will be taken into account.'

About an hour later, Darj and Alexia called a recess and found me sitting at the dining table in the next room with Xander and Raggin.

'You're back,' Alexia said, now raising her eyebrow at me.

'You might have told us you were going with them,' Darj said to me aside. 'Alexia did not appreciate finding you missing, too.'

I pressed my lips together.

I am the last thing Alexia cares about right now.

'Where is Captain Ival?' Darj asked. 'We require his report.'

I glanced at Xander and Raggin, who were staring into their drinks.

'What happened?' Alexia asked.

'Your Majesty,' Raggin said, clearing his throat. 'I regret to report that Ival . . . Captain Ival has been killed.'

'What?' Darj leant on the table.

The men explained all that had happened and how the Zalem had said Elhian was in Sharlard.

Darj thought about this as he sat down. 'Sharlard . . . That's the name of the rumored Zalem city, but I don't think anyone knows where it is.'

So it was pointless.

We fell into silence for some time, all of us thinking about Ival's sacrifice. What if it was only the beginning? Perhaps that was what Alexia had meant when she said Elhian was but one man. Was his life more important than Ival's?

'Raggin,' Alexia said, disrupting my thoughts, 'I want you to become captain of Chettona in Ival's place.'

Raggin nearly choked on his drink. 'I can't do that! Replace a man of Ival's character?'

'Raggin!' Darj said, frowning at him.

Raggin took his meaning, and his cheeks flushed. 'I'm sorry, Your Majesty,' he said. 'Of course, I will do what I can to serve you. I only regret that it is under these circumstances . . . and that we have lost one of the best captains I've known.'

'I understand,' Alexia said, 'so please protect Chettona in his honour. You must keep your men vigilant. Xander, you must return to Hunt and do the same. The Zalems could attack at any time, and I would feel better knowing you are both at your posts and ready to defend my people.'

'Then that is what we will do, Your Majesty,' Xander said, 'and only hope it doesn't come to that.'

9
THE PROPOSAL

I woke just after midnight feeling cold and disturbed. I'd dreamt of Ival but couldn't remember much about it. I was just left with renewed feelings of dread and sadness. I didn't dwell on them long, though. I heard footsteps outside my door, and thinking it was Alexia, I went to see if she were all right or even willing to talk to me.

I was desperate to heal the rift between us. Hurting her was the last thing I wanted. How could I say such things? The thought that she despised me made me feel sick. I couldn't help but think she blamed me for Ival's death as well . . . or maybe I was blaming myself.

When I opened the door of her room, I could hear whispering. I saw Eva asleep, but Alexia wasn't in her bed.

'I will let you go,' a man said softly, 'if you promise not to scream.'

My eyes widened. I stepped further around the door and found Alexia once more in the grip of a black-clothed man.

'Let her go!'

He looked up and threw a dagger at me. It landed in the door just near my face. 'Move and I will kill you.' His voice was distinctively raspy.

Even from where I was standing, I could see his small, shining eyes.

He waited until I raised my palms before uncovering Alexia's mouth. She turned to him. Her hands were shaking, but no fear was visible in her face. 'Who are you?' she asked, stepping back.

He took hold of her wrist to stop her retreating any further. Alexia winced. 'I am a messenger of the High Zalem. He offers you his hand in marriage. You must obey if you want to save your people. If you do not accept within a month, the Casmodian king and Targian boy will die.'

'Where is the king?' Alexia asked. 'And who is this boy you speak of?'

He hesitated. 'The one the general was training.'

'Zavad?' I asked. 'You have Zavad? He's just a child!'

'Just like Jeri,' the man said. Alexia took in a sharp breath. 'The stupid boy—what happened to his grave is nothing less than his memory deserves.'

I'm sure she knew he was trying to bait her, but I felt renewed guilt in that her son's name was being used against her yet again.

'What happened in Hunt is just a message, a hint of what is to come,' he said. 'Consider your answer carefully.'

'I would never consent to such a thing,' Alexia said. 'Marriage is an alliance, and I will not align with evil and darkness.'

'We all have darkness inside us.'

'But we also have the power to choose whether or not we will feed it,' Alexia said.

The Zalem smiled. 'Sometimes, that choice is made for us.' He pulled Alexia in until her face was almost touching his. Her upper lip curled as she smelt his breath. 'Tell anyone that we have spoken and I will kill them. I will visit you soon for your answer.'

He placed a long kiss on Alexia's hand and exited out the window.

I pulled the dagger out of the door and hurried after him, but by the time I reached the windowsill, he was already out of sight.

Alexia scrubbed her hand with a cloth until it was red. 'We can't tell Darj.'

As I was lying in bed the next morning, I heard Darj in the street, saying goodbye to the members of the council as they prepared for their journeys home.

'Make sure the palace repairs continue,' he said not too far from my window. 'And under no circumstances stand the army down until you hear from me.'

'Try to keep Queen Alexia's identity a secret as long as you can,' Lord Fenton said to him. I got up and looked out the window. Fenton had stopped by Darj on his horse. 'I know you are not keen to go to Delya, but I promise I would not recommend it if I didn't think it would help.'

'Fenton, I wouldn't act on your suggestion if I didn't believe it was worthwhile.'

'Good luck then,' Fenton said as he rode away.

I went downstairs to join Darj and Alexia for breakfast. Alexia slouched uncharacteristically over the table while Darj cut some fruit for us in his usual silent service. His dark hair hung over his forehead a little, and he seemed deep in thought.

I knew how much Alexia had come to depend on him since her husband died. I longed to tell him what had occurred the night before but knew Alexia had forbidden it because of the Zalem's threat. What if we told him, and the Zalem was faithful? What if Darj was killed? Alexia rubbed her neck again like there was too much weight sitting on it.

She reached out to take some fruit. Seeing the bruises on her wrist where the Zalem had gripped her, Darj took her hand in his for a closer look. Alexia jumped at the unexpected movement. I saw genuine fear in her eyes.

Darj saw it, too. 'What is it?' he asked. He looked at the bruises more closely. 'Who hurt you?'

Alexia withdrew her arm. 'It's nothing,' she said. 'It's just an injury I incurred at Liane.'

Darj frowned at her. 'No, it's not.'

'Yes, it is,' she said, meeting his eyes.

Darj thought about this, and I knew he was already beginning to understand.

I saddled Bagred in the stables later, forcing back tears. Elhian's disappearance, the conflict between Alexia and I, the ultimatum she'd been given, knowing now Zavad was somehow caught up in everything, and Ival's death—it all weighed on my mind.

While I still felt uncertain about it, I was prepared to take the journey Odavan had called me to. It had to be better than doing nothing. Karlen, the Casmodian royal guard, had volunteered to travel with me as an extra sword. Darj encouraged it, for while he agreed I was doing the right thing in pursuing this lead, he was reluctant to trust Odavan when we knew so little about him.

I didn't complain; I was glad to have the company, even though I hardly knew Karlen either. He was younger than me, which meant he was very young, and he had eyes that were a darker brown than most Casmodians. He had to have come from a noble family to be a member of the Casmodian Royal Guard, and yet he rarely lifted his eyes to look at me—a rare display of genuine humility. He had said little since returning to us but was saddled and set to ride out, his thick, brown hair tied back from his face. We left Leuk stabled at Chettona's barracks, ready for his master's eventual return.

Darj came to see me off and handed me some bread to take. 'Will you make it in time?' he asked.

'Odavan said he would wait a fortnight, which gives me the four days I need to travel back and a spare day.' I stored the food in my saddlebags.

Darj put a hand on my shoulder. 'When you cross those mountains into Jazmarda, don't forget who you are,' he said. 'Yes, you are Elhian's wife, the Casmodian queen, and Alexia's cousin. But right now, you need to be the A'zyon Warrior. It is she who does what she must, despite her fears.'

I nodded with a faint smile. 'Darj, about Alexia . . . I know you heard what I said that night. I don't know what came over me. I know she only wants what's best and right, and so do I. I just need a better reason to fight for it than duty.'

'Love, you mean?' Darj held Bagred's reins while I climbed up into the saddle.

The cynicism in his tone didn't elude me. 'If Alexia were ever to suddenly go missing, what would you do?'

'You know I would ensure her safety at all costs, just as I have always done.'

'Why?'

He didn't hesitate. 'Because she is the queen and I took an oath to protect her.'

I smiled, shaking my head. 'You may have fooled everyone else, Darj, but I think you and I both know your devotion to Alexia goes far beyond duty. The only reason I can even consider going to Jazmarda when Elhian is in danger is not only because I feel I must, but also because I love him and need to do something, just as you would for Alexia.'

'Adaliah,' Darj said hotly, 'I don't know what you're accusing me—'

'I am not accusing you of anything!' I sighed. 'I think I'd better leave before I offend anyone else. I will find you all soon.'

'The queen and I will travel through Levanna, Fenellar, and other southern towns to put them on guard before we reach Delya. I think we should reach Bymoor in two weeks. We will wait for you near the White River.'

'I will see you there.' I couldn't imagine that Elhian wouldn't be found by the time we met again. Perhaps we wouldn't even need to go into Delya.

It'll all be over soon.

I glanced back at the barracks, feeling a mixture of guilt and frustration. I'd wanted to talk to Alexia numerous times, but she refused to even look at me. Her pain ran deep, and I had brought it back to the surface.

How could I hurt her like that?

'Tell Alexia how sorry I am,' I said. 'Tell her I love her always and protect her and Eva for me, whether it be for duty, or for love, or both.'

10
THE DART

The sky clouded over with rain as Karlen and I rode through the Yellow Forest. We travelled along a damp path through the ancient trees until we came to the east bank of Kest River.

I watched the powerful, constant flow of the river. It seemed louder than usual, almost overwhelmingly so. I closed my eyes and thought back to the evening when I had almost been beaten to death in the water. I remembered Cades' panic when he'd realised how I was going to cleanse the swords. Thinking about how it had ended with him and Jag and how we were still struggling now, I no longer felt that justice had been done.

'You came back,' Odavan said, appearing out of the woods. 'You are a wise woman.'

'I'm not sure about that,' I said, 'but I don't know what else to do.'

'You will not regret it. Hazaka himself encouraged me to come for you.'

I hadn't seen the King of Jazmarda since the end of the last war, and my main memory of him was of a boy king who wanted glory without having to earn it. I wasn't sure what to think of the fact he had something to do with my call to Jazmarda, but while he was an immature monarch, I didn't believe he was treacherous.

'This is Karlen,' I said. 'He will be coming with us.'

Odavan eyed him. 'If that is what you want. We will leave in the morning.'

It took most of the following day to get to the hut nestled up on the Kestian hill, where Elhian and I had found the tunnel-way during the Northern Invasion. Without a word to either of the men I was travelling with, I went inside to shelter from the rain.

I'd heard Elhian recount more than once how the ride up the Kestian mountainside had been tedious and tiresome when he'd first travelled it with Xander and Raggin. Now, I remembered it for myself. The road was mildly better since we'd last passed through. Alexia had paid to have it improved so the Kestian passage to Jazmarda was quicker and easier, but even now it was overgrown with tangled vines and branches in places I found dark and forbidding.

Inside the hut, I was greeted by a Targian solider named Sam, who worked for Captain Darack Symes and, by extension, me. The hut was now Sam's outpost, one of many that fed information back to the Keep. Sam was a man in his thirties and of few words. He had been shelling nuts before our intrusion and now moved aside so I could warm myself by the fire, but I barely had time to feel its heat in my fingertips.

'We should keep going,' Odavan said, coming in.

I wanted to argue that I was tired but knew Elhian wouldn't be helped while I rested.

Two days later, I rode down a hill on the other side of the mountains and saw Etarbelec in the distance. There, the Jazmardian king lived in his oversized palace. Not that I had been there before or could see it closely now, but Odavan had spent a good part of the trip telling me about it. From what I'd heard, Hazaka Cazren had enough grand rooms to house most of the city's poor, and after his second son was born in the autumn, he'd even had his own lake built at the rear of the palace so he 'could have somewhere quiet to think'.

I thought of Alexia's secret room in her palace. She now seemed utterly conservative.

'Could we make it to the city today?' The sooner we arrived and found what we needed to know, the sooner I could begin the ride back to Alexia and Darj and find Elhian. I wanted nothing more than to be lying in his arms again.

'We are not going to the city,' Odavan said, pulling his horse up next to mine.

'What?'

'The man I am taking you to see does not live in Etarbelec.'

'But . . . but you said that King Hazaka himself . . . '

'Encouraged me to come and find you, yes, but I never said we were going to Etarbelec.'

I looked back towards the great red city and frowned. 'The one thing I was looking forward to despite everything was being able to visit it.'

'Another time,' Odavan said. 'We are travelling to a small village called Katarva. It is closer to us than Etarbelec. We should reach it by sundown.'

Odavan rode on, and I was about to follow when Karlen came up beside me. 'Your Majesty,' he said. 'Please, make sure you drink plenty of water.' He handed me a goatskin bottle.

'Thank you.' I took it from him and gulped down the water, especially grateful as I could feel my skin burning under the sun. 'Thank you for coming with me so far.'

'I have let the king down. It's because of me that all this has happened.'

I hadn't realised Karlen had taken so much upon himself, but he had barely spoken until then.

'No, it's not,' I said. 'King Elhian would not blame you for what the Zalems have done, and you shouldn't either. Your help is appreciated.'

He nodded to show he accepted what I said, but I knew he didn't feel the truth of it. A young boy, Karlen reminded me of the soldier Naclen, who had died in the last battle of the last war. I didn't sense the constant anger at the world in him I'd felt in Naclen, though. Karlen was just sad.

The ground beneath us began to turn dusty red. The grass, which in Kest had been thick and lush, was now tall, spindly, and a dark olive green.

'When you rub it between your hands, it smells sharp, like citrus,' Odavan said, 'but it is useless for both eating and medicine. Any good Jazmardian healer will tell you that.'

Odavan said Etarbelec had only a few trees for shade—and those had been planted specifically—but a thick type of tree I'd never seen before grew confidently and in large clusters along the road to Katarva.

'They're beautiful in their own way,' I said as we passed under the low branches. Some of the leaves brushed against me. They were prickly. 'A bit defensive, though.'

'So would anyone be if they lived in this climate, I think,' Karlen said as he loosened his collar. 'We are far from the snow-topped Casmodian Mountains here.'

I felt a sharp jab on my neck. I reached up to rub the spot, thinking I had just brushed against more leaves, but something was sticking in my neck. I pulled it out.

It wasn't one of the trees' leaves. It was a tiny dart, and on my fingers were traces of my own blood.

Before I could think of what that meant, my vision began to blur. My body slouched over, so far that my face almost touched Bagred's neck.

'Your Majesty?' Karlen asked. I slipped to the ground. 'Adaliah!'

11

THE JAZMARDIAN BLESSING

I woke when men in dark hoods attacked me. I'd been lying flat on the red ground but stood, unsheathed my sword, and killed the man closest to me, and then another. I moved to attack the third, but it was as if my sword was melting in my hands. It was too hot to touch. My hands were blistering, and I shrieked as my flesh began to fall away. I fell to the ground and came face to face with the first man I'd killed. Except it wasn't a man. It was Alexia. Blood was pouring down her face thick and fast. I let out a shrill scream, and then everything went black.

'Adaliah, can you hear me?'

I jolted upright.

'Are you all right?' Karlen was squatting in front of me.

My eyes widened. 'It was a dream,' I said. 'It was a dream . . . I didn't kill Alexia . . . '

Karlen's expression of concern deepened. 'You must have been hallucinating again.'

'It seemed so real . . . ' I put a hand on my stomach and tried to calm the dread I'd felt at seeing Alexia's dead face.

'It's the poison in the dart,' Karlen said. 'You've been other-worldly for the last three days.'

'I have? Where am I?'

Karlen explained that after the dart hit me, Zalem soldiers attacked. 'They are hunting you. If it wasn't for Odavan, we'd be dead. Only a few escaped his sword. He picked you up, and we rode without stopping to Katarva. You've scarcely slept since we arrived. The poison seemed to be driving you insane.'

'Yes, that's what it felt like.' I rubbed my hands together to reassure myself they were intact.

'Try and get some rest, now that you've come back to us. It's night time outside, and there is nothing for you to do now.'

I was covered in a cool layer of sweat, but I didn't even have the strength to get up and wash, so I took his advice and lowered myself back onto the thin bed. Karlen, satisfied that I would be all right, left to get rest as well. But I lay awake for at least an hour, thinking about how Alexia had shaken so violently when we found her in the Yellow Forest. I wondered if she had been hit with a dart then, too.

Karlen brought me a small plate of bread and cooked eggs for breakfast. After I'd eaten, he invited me to follow him out of the hut, where I was confronted with a blinding sun and shielded my eyes. My vision slowly adjusted, and soon, I could see the dark-skinned women sitting around a communal fire, cooking, cleaning clothes, and talking in their native tongue. Most of them wore bright-coloured clothing and had a child or two playing at their feet.

One of them stood and walked in my direction. She was dressed in a red and purple dress and carrying a basket of exotic fruits, most of which I didn't recognise. She gave a gentle nod and lifted her basket as if offering the fruit to me.

'Thank you,' I said and reached out to take one. Just as I touched the leathery skin of a green berry, a look of horror passed over her face. I thought I must have misunderstood her offer and retracted my hand. She dropped her basket altogether and pushed me sideways with a garbled yell. I stumbled and was inclined to be irritated, but she fell to the ground with a whimper. At first, I didn't understand and thought she had fainted in the heat, but then I saw the arrow protruding from her chest.

There was a slow moment as the other women turned and called her name as if expecting her to get up like nothing had happened. One of them ran over and shook her shoulders. The friend pulled her hands back; they were covered in blood. She screamed, and it was only then that we all came out of our stupor.

The women grabbed their children and ran from the street. I scoured the trees and saw the legs of a lone archer standing on a thick branch.

Karlen handed me his sword, and I threw it with all the force I had.

It hurtled through the air and hit the archer in the chest. He fell from the tree and crashed through the roof of one of the huts.

'Well done,' Odavan said, running over.

'Another Zalem,' I said.

'Who is this that brings bloodshed to Katarva?'

Odavan, Karlen, and I turned to see a large man with a tall staff—a Jazmardian elder. He wore a hard expression, the sort that comes from having seen too many painful things.

'This is Lady Adaliah Elryane,' Odavan said.

I smiled a little at the old title and surname. I hadn't been called that since my marriage to Elhian.

It impressed the man with the staff, however. His mouth turned in a small smile, too, and he no longer looked as severe. 'Then you had better come inside.'

The air was thick and sweet-scented inside the elder's hut. I couldn't decide whether the smell was of lilies or something else, but I closed my eyes and breathed it in. It filled me, calmed me.

Outside, the villagers were burying the archer and singing. It was a lamenting sound, and that surprised me. I hadn't expected them to care about the soul of someone who had killed one of their own. I hadn't thought the Jazmardians would be that generous and forgiving, but perhaps I was judging them by their past mistakes, or their king.

The woman who had saved my life would soon be buried, too, and mourned by those who loved her. I wondered if she had a husband or children. Why had she pushed me out of the way? I saw them gathering flowers for her and knew I would never forget the woman with the fruit basket.

'Adaliah,' the elder said. He heightened the sounds in my name and made it sound magical. 'It is good that you have come.' He reclined on a cushioned chair, while I sat on a mat before him, the two of us alone. 'I am Erran. Ru'ach told me I needed to meet with you.'

'Why?'

Erran leant forward. 'A great evil awoke on the second anniversary of Cades' death, on the Targian princess' birthday. Now, your husband's life is in the palm of the High Zalem's hand.'

I remembered how the messenger who had threatened Alexia in Chettona had said she would have to marry the High Zalem, but I didn't understand what the title meant and hadn't been allowed to ask Darj.

Erran saw my confusion. 'He is the captain of the Zalem cult. He must die if this evil is to be quelled.'

'Then tell me where he is, so I can ensure he does,' I said.

Erran calmly placed a finger over his mouth, indicating for me to be silent. 'It is not up to me to tell you where he dwells but to tell you how to defeat him, for a sword alone will not be sufficient.'

'But the sword is what I know,' I said, unsure what he was getting at. 'It's what makes me the A'zyon Warrior.'

'Yes, but for this mission, you need more than that. The High Zalem is more powerful than you can imagine. He has a way to steal identities, Adaliah. He makes people forget who they are.'

'I've already survived that,' I said, thinking of those longs months I'd endured without my memory.

'No, he takes much more than memory. He has the power to make your will, your values, your personality, and your dreams all diminish. If you're not already a Zalem, you'll become a Ghost enslaved to his will.'

I thought back to the insane man who had attacked us outside of Liane. I could still see his wraithlike eyes when I closed mine. Had he been a slave to the High Zalem's will?

'What is a Ghost?'

'The High Zalem has two levels of followers. The Zalems are soldiers who have joined the cause willingly, worshippers of Anash. The Ghosts are those he exercises his power over, forcing them to be on his side. They follow him out of blind obedience. I believe it is his mission to turn the whole population of the world into Ghosts. That day is fast coming, but you must stop him. Now, I can give you a blessing to help you overcome his power with the sword, but it must be done with the Kestian sword, the Life Sword. Where is it?'

'I left it in Alexia's palace.'

'Adaliah, you may not have known it, but you cleansed the sword of its darkness for this purpose.'

'I did it to stop Cades.'

'That was only the first step in cleansing the world of Anash's evil. Now, you must collect the Life Sword before you face the High Zalem. I can give you a blessing that will protect you from his evil, but there is a condition.'

'What?' I expected him to tell me Alexia would have to marry the High Zalem after all and was already trying to think of a counterplan.

Erran asked for the tree-blade, and when I gave it to him, he held it up near a window. The sun glinted on the clean metal. 'You must make a commitment.'

'A commitment to do what?'

'You must promise that even if every Zalem comes against you, even if they make war against Targe and Casmodia, against your beloved husband and cousin . . . If you want the power to destroy the High Zalem, to stop a war . . . Adaliah, you must not spill one drop of any human blood but his from this day to that, or all will be lost.'

12
COMMITMENT

'I can't do it,' I said, hugging my knees as I sat with Karlen outside Erran's hut. 'If someone moves to attack my family, I have to protect them. Even if I never wanted to spill blood again, I wouldn't be able to stop myself if someone I loved was under threat. It's what my father trained me to do—to defend my family, my kingdom, and myself. The Zalems are trying to kill me, Karlen. Erran said it's because they know I have been chosen to kill their leader, because of what I did at Kest River last time. They will do anything to stop me, and I have to protect myself. I wouldn't even make it back to Kest without breaking the deal.'

'I can protect you, and if it can help the king . . . '

'I don't know how to do it this way.'

'Like anything: one step at a time. If Ru'ach has asked you to do this, he will provide a way.'

I looked up at the sky—the sun was setting for the day, and I could see a star already. Had Ru'ach asked me to do it, or Erran?

I could hear the villagers singing again, but the song was joyful this time. There was an innocence about it that I found encouraging, as if not all the world was wrestling with darkness yet.

'What if Elhian is already dead?' I asked softly. 'What if the High Zalem is already warring against us? What if it's too late?'

'You don't know that,' Karlen said. 'I would not dream of advising Your Majesty, but I do believe there is still hope.'

I remembered the poem Elhian and I had found in our home. The words played through my head as I thought about how our lives were tangled up in each other's. I meditated on the poem's lines in reverse, trying to make sense of it.

Dead will one and all be if Queen Targe does not obey.

That one made sense: we would all die if Alexia didn't agree to marry the High Zalem. She would be forced to choose between her life and ours. I knew if it came to it, she would make the honourable decision. That's what worried me.

Dead will the Ghosts be if the general does not recall.

Erran had said the Ghosts were slaves, a step lower than the Zalem soldiers. But I still didn't understand this one, except that Darj had some important information or access to knowledge he'd forgotten about.

Dead will the lady be if her dear king does not pay.

This one was easier: they wanted Elhian to pay for his 'debt'—the killing of his father to save his kingdom and mine. If he didn't, my life would be the price. I knew he would never accept that but still felt sick when I tried to imagine what was involved in his repayment.

Dead will the boy be if the lady does not abstain.

Obviously, I was the lady, but it only occurred to me then that the thing I was to abstain from was spilling blood. The Zalems must have known Erran would give me the blessing, but it was like they wanted me to have it. They wanted me to abstain . . . and were threating to kill a boy if I didn't.

They want me helpless in battle, unable to fight.

They were taunting me, threatening me to make sure I adhered to the blessing and couldn't fight against them. They obviously didn't think I could actually defeat the High Zalem, and this way they got me off the battlefield. I'd also be easier to kill if I couldn't fight back, and killing me seemed to be their primary goal.

But what boy's life was in my hands?

'Zavad,' I said out loud, my heart sinking. 'They will kill Zavad if I don't adhere to the blessing and abstain from spilling blood.'

'What?' Karlen asked.

'Never mind.' I knew what I had to do. In fact, I didn't really have a choice. 'I will let Erran give me the blessing. Let's pray I don't lose it before meeting the High Zalem.'

Erran led Odavan, Karlen, and me to a clearing in the trees just outside Katarva. He piled some leaves and set them on fire, filling the air with the citrus smell Odavan had told me about. He added several sprigs of sage and asked me to kneel. He began to speak in his own tongue. I wondered what he was saying and if I were right to go through with it.

He could be cursing me for all I know.

But somehow I knew he wasn't. It was the way a breeze swathed around me, like I was being dressed in invisible silk ribbons. As he went on, the smoke from the leaves began to turn white, and I felt a surreal calmness.

'To defeat the High Zalem and receive the blessing,' Erran said, speaking in the common tongue for the first time, 'you must promise to not spill any human blood but his from this moment to that. Will you make this promise?'

I took out my sword and gave it to Odavan, as well as the dagger I kept in my boot. 'I will.'

'Then you must hold fast to your promise or lose the blessing needed to defeat him. May Ru'ach preserve your life.' The smoke twirled upwards, and embers fell from the sky. They floated onto my cloak, and I breathed in the scent of sage. I felt something different stir in me, a new strength that I knew wasn't my own. It didn't feel unnatural. Rather, I felt protected. Empowered, like a flame had been lit inside me.

Erran nodded his head to me. 'May the Jazmardian blessing serve you well.'

13
SACRIFICE

Karlen, Odavan, and I arrived back at Sam's hut in Kest just at nightfall a couple of days later. It was raining again, and we were all soaked. Sam invited us in and offered us some dry nuts to eat while we waited for him to cook some vegetables.

It took me some time by the fire to feel dry and warm. I sat staring into its flames, thinking of Elhian and how he'd looked when I'd walked up the church aisle towards him: handsome, composed, regal, but a hint of emotion in the smile he gave me when he saw me approaching. I'd realised then, deep down somewhere, that we'd be a part of each other forever.

'I will travel with you to Kest River,' Odavan said, standing behind me and bringing me back from my thoughts, 'but then I must leave to be with my woman.'

'Fine.' I had too many things on my mind to care much about what Odavan wanted to do. Part of me blamed him for the predicament I now found myself in, and I kept wondering how I would be able to protect my loved ones without spilling blood. My weapons were sheathed on Bagred, and there they would have to remain.

Odavan lay down to sleep, but Karlen put more wood on the fire. 'You're still waterlogged,' he said.

'It doesn't matter,' I said. 'I don't think I will be able to sle—'

My gaze fell on the sealed letter Sam was now holding out to me. 'A runner brought this to me yesterday,' he said. 'He asked me to give it to you on your way back to Targe.'

Adaliah C. Edangard was written on the front. Taking it from Sam, I broke the golden seal.

'What does it say?' Karlen asked.

I read it aloud. '"The blessing Erran gave you did not stop the threat against the boy. The poem was written in Dragon's Breath ink. The moment you draw any blood other than the High Zalem's is the moment the boy will die. If Alexia is not soon crowned the High Zalem's queen, you will all die in the same way. She is on her way to Delya, but the only answer she needs is in her father's pact".'

The signature was illegible, but familiar somehow. I studied it for some time, trying to think where I had seen that scribble before.

'Dragon's Breath ink?' I wondered. I knew Dragon's Breath was a rare and deadly poison, but I wasn't sure what Dragon's Breath ink was.

'Did King Amaz have a pact with the Zalems?' Sam asked.

I read the letter again, remembering how Cades had said something once about the 'promise' King Amaz supposedly made to him regarding Alexia.

I folded the letter. 'I . . . I don't know. I have to get to Alexia. We'll ride for Delya first thing in the morning.'

I spent that night hoping that when I rode into western Targe, some of the angst I felt would ease a little in the familiar lands. It didn't. I was tense with apprehension and determination as we crossed the border, the two making uneasy friends within my heart. 'I'm sorry,' I said when Karlen heard me sigh. 'I'm just tired.' I didn't add that my sleep was full of terrors about what they might be doing to Elhian. Visions of his flesh being ripped apart, of him being branded with hot irons, had haunted me for most of the night.

'I understand,' Karlen said, and we rode on in silence.

The two of us had woken before sunrise and found Odavan already gone. There was no note, no mention of goodbye—only a horse gone and some tracks left in the wet ground. From those, we deduced he had ridden north, presumably to reunite with his woman. I could only assume he'd heard what I'd said about leaving and made his own plans.

Having said goodbye to Sam again, we now continued to travel towards the southwest of Targe, intending to cut across the bottom corner of the kingdom in hope of reaching Delya faster. It was an area less populated than the rest of Targe and the only Targian land totally covered in mountains. The Hewn Mountains weren't tall and grand like the mountains in Casmodia, however. They were rugged, forbidding, as if the rest of Targe had soaked up the kingdom's beauty and shunned its ugliness to one corner. Dark grey rocks covered the ground in sharp ridges, and the only animal that welcomed it as home was a type of black bird that nested in the uncomely crevices.

'I haven't been near these mountains since I was a little girl,' I said. A wispy fog hung on the rocks as if Ru'ach had breathed warm air over them. 'I'm not even sure where the path is, or if there is one.'

'You made it through Kest once with little more than an animal's track. We will find something here.'

I smiled at Karlen, wondering where he drew so much certainty.

It started to rain, and Karlen and I heard thunder somewhere in the distance. We found shelter in a small cavern that was wedged in between two tall rocks. We had to climb up to it on foot. Poor Bagred was forced to weather the rain outside with Karlen's horse.

The water drizzled down every crack, shimmering on the rocks. Karlen stood near the opening with his face turned towards the sky. I found some dead sticks inside the cave and used them to get a small fire going. I cooked the fowl I had hunted earlier, but it was a tedious process.

'Do you think Casmodia will fight to find Elhian?' I asked.

Karlen took the piece of meat I was offering him. 'I think the people would rally, yes. We can be a headstrong nation and not as loyal as the Targians are. But whatever the people think of his actions, Elhian is still the rightful king, and there is not yet another legal heir to replace him should he . . . be unable to reign.'

I rested a hand on my stomach. 'No . . .'

'So, they would not risk a stranger ascending the throne.'

I thought about this. 'It's not quite the same as being loyal to him, though, is it?'

'No,' Karlen said, 'but it's a start. I believe in Elhian. I always have. You see, he knew my father. He was a nobleman up by the Edeline Sea. When my father died, men started to treat my mother with disrespect. They started harassing her, threating to make her unvirtuous. Elhian heard of it and sent two royal guards to protect our home until those men realised she was not to be mistreated. I admired those guards so much, I made up my mind to become one. I wanted to protect others as they had protected my mother.'

'You're a good man, Karlen,' I said. 'A gift to your kingdom.'

He took another bite of meat and chewed slowly, then stopped. His brown eyes were alert. I heard what had attracted his attention: footsteps, voices, and both drawing near to us.

Karlen unsheathed his sword and peered out into the rain. Someone pushed him backwards; he tripped and fell.

Four men climbed in. One lunged at Karlen with a black sword. Karlen rolled out of the way and got to his feet. He impaled the first one—the one who had pushed him—and kicked him down. The soldier landed in the dirt near me, his sword within reach. I moved to pick it up, but Karlen saw me and kicked it away.

Having left my blades sheathed on Bagred, I had no choice but to watch helplessly as Karlen fought the remaining three men. He managed to wound one's arm, but the soldier lunged back and stabbed his sword into Karlen's leg.

Karlen cried out as blood ran down his thigh. He pushed through the pain to land a heavy blow on the soldier's shoulder, crushing him to the ground. He ran his sword through the third soldier's middle, pushed the fourth to the ground, and impaled him, too.

Karlen wiped the sweat off his brow and tried to catch his breath, but something pinched his stomach. A sword point appeared. Blood leaked out around it.

The first soldier hadn't died after all. In fact, he'd crawled over to his sword. Karlen stabbed him again, this time right through the heart. The man dropped to the ground, now undoubtedly dead.

But Karlen fell to his side.

'No!' I moved next to him and put my hands over his wound, trying to stop the blood pouring out of his stomach, but nothing I did helped. I was reminded of Ival and knew it was hopeless.

Karlen began to convulse. 'I'm sorry . . . '

The colour was draining from his face, and I was getting blood everywhere. 'No, I'm sorry. This is my fault.' I put a hand on his forehead, trying to settle him. 'I should never have brought you with me.'

'If you had drawn blood,' he said, 'we'd all be condemned.' He met my eyes. 'For the king.'

His body shook for another minute, and then there was nothing.

14
INTO DELYA

After that, I rode hard for eight days: first to Fenellar, where the resident lord told me the queen and general had passed through just two days before, and then further south until I came to the foot of the mountain range between Targe and Delya. There, I found the small Targian village of Bymoor, and the local innkeeper told me that a man and woman had passed through with a small child that afternoon and that they had said something about camping by the White River.

They must already be posing as commoners.

The moon was rising, but I mounted Bagred again and rode on, quickly coming to the White River and following it until I had to rest. I drank some water but was rationing what was left of my food. Hungry and sore from riding and sleeping on hard grounds, I lay down on the grass and drifted into a tormented sleep.

A cold hand fastened over my mouth. Jerking, I opened my eyes and realised with a mixture of surprise and relief that it was Alexia. She was crouching beside me and wearing only her thin shift. It was cold, and I was about to chide her for not dressing warmly, but she lifted her finger to her lips. She pointed to something across the river.

Turning my head and squinting in the dark, I saw five men dressed in black cloaks. I thought I must have been dreaming, but I could see them even after blinking several times. They were walking along the eastern side of the bank in a single line, and after a minute, they were out of sight.

'Come on,' Alexia said, getting up.

I took Bagred's reins and followed her back to Darj and Eva. The two of them were sitting next to a small fire further up the river. 'Alexia,' Darj said, 'where did you . . . ' He saw me and stood. 'You're back!'

'Yes.'

'Was the trip worth it?' he asked.

Alexia sat beside her daughter. She'd barely even looked at me. Eva was playing with her doll. 'I guess so.'

'Where is Karlen?' Alexia asked.

Karlen. I hadn't even been able to bury him. *How many others will perish while I stand by?*

'Dead?' Darj asked.

I nodded.

'That's the second time you've come back without one of the men who went with you,' Alexia said under her breath.

I looked at her, hurt. 'You weren't there.' I was racked with exhaustion and not up for arguing with her. I already felt like the bringer of death. More than anything, I was disappointed that she was still harbouring anger against me. Maybe I didn't deserve her forgiveness, but the lack of it made me feel even more fragile.

'Have you heard anything about Elhian?' I feared the answer to my own question.

Darj shook his head. 'I'm sorry.'

I turned my face away to hide the tears that had formed in my eyes. I longed for him with all my being, but somehow, it wasn't enough to draw him back to me like I wanted.

'Are you hungry?' Darj asked. Before I could answer, he passed me some bread and cheese.

I ate and told them what had happened in Jazmarda and the promise I'd made. I didn't mention the note I'd found and the reference to King Amaz; I wanted to talk to Darj about that without Alexia listening in.

They heard all I had to say with quiet thoughtfulness, and then Darj suggested I get some rest. 'I will keep lookout tonight,' he said.

I thanked him and lay down by Eva, whom Alexia had already tucked in for the night. The little girl gave me a drowsy smile before closing her eyes and succumbing to sleep.

I wished I could do the same so easily. Instead, I lay with my back to Darj and Alexia and found I could only watch the grass blowing in the slight breeze. My mind went over and over the events of the past few weeks, tormenting itself over Elhian, the deaths of Ival, Karlen . . .

'Here, take my cloak.' Darj's voice brought me back to the present as he spoke to Alexia some time later.

'Something's wrong with me, Darj,' she said.

He didn't answer immediately. 'You've been under a lot of strain . . . '

'It's not that. You know it's not that.'

I turned back towards them and saw Alexia picking at the grass near her feet. They were sitting next to each other and looking out over the river.

'Part of the reason I like archery is because it doesn't feel as much like you're killing someone's loved one. When you have a bow and arrow, they're just targets in the distance. But that soldier, at the camp that morning . . . He begged for mercy, and I killed him.' The cool breeze picked up, flapping the cloak around Alexia's shoulders and whistling over the grass. 'Do you think it's the Zalems doing this to me? Have they sent Anash to haunt me?'

'I don't know,' Darj said. 'It's not their way, or at least they've never done anything like this before. But when I think of the way you were when we first found you in the forest . . . You haven't been right since then.'

'Their way,' she said. 'How is it that you know so much about "their way"?' There was a suspicious tone in her voice that unsettled me.

'Does it matter?'

'It does if you feel you must keep it a secret,' she said, but when she continued, her tone softened. 'People are beginning to fear, Darj, to distrust, and I don't want them distrusting you.'

'I am not one of them, if that's what you think. See?' He pulled up his pant leg and bared his ankle, where the Zalems had all had their symbol tattooed. There was nothing there.

'I never thought you were,' she said. 'But how do you know?'

He tugged at his boot. 'It's a painful memory . . . I would not burden you with it.'

'Darj, please, I have burdened you many times over. Let me be a friend in turn.'

He was quiet for a while, and in the end, I got up and walked over to them. Sleep was still far off, and besides, I wanted to hear Darj's story. He saw me and sighed, knowing he was now outnumbered.

'Go on,' I said. 'I want to know, too.'

He cleared his throat. 'All right. It happened when I was just a boy, about Zavad's age or maybe a bit older. You know my father was a scribe . . .'

'No,' Alexia said. 'There's a lot I don't know about your life before you became involved with the army.'

'Well, he was, and he was also good friends with the lord of my town, Benne, who was, of course—'

'My father-in-law,' Alexia said.

I could well remember Lord Benne Lowelan. He'd always hoped Alexia would marry his son, Ethaniel, but not for love, the very thing that did bring them together. Benne had been a good man, but all he'd seen in the match was wealth and power and a regal name. Targian tradition dictated that any who married into the direct royal line took the surname Elryane.

'Yes,' Darj said, 'which is why Ethaniel and I also became good friends, the closest thing I ever had to a brother.' He paused as if wondering how to proceed. 'One night, my father and Benne were meeting in our house. I don't know what they were discussing—my mother had shepherded me out of the room to play with my sisters—but later, someone else burst into the house. There was lots of yelling, and a fierceness that was unnatural for my father and Benne.' He hesitated again, and when he spoke, there was a pain in his voice I hadn't heard before. 'My father was killed.'

'Killed?' I wondered why I'd never known that.

'Yes. I remember seeing him lying on the floor . . . Benne was still trying to fight the man off. Amidst everything, I saw the tattoo on the man's ankle, the crescent moon and eye. A few weeks later, after the funeral and once things settled down a bit, I remember overhearing my mother talking to Benne about the Zalems. I never forgot the term, and as soon as I was old enough, I found out what I could about them from the few stories that remained. Benne would never talk about it, not even for my father's sake. I resented him for that, but I suppose he was trying to protect me. At the time, part of the reason I joined the army was so I would learn how to fight and one day be able to exact my revenge.'

Darj shifted his position on the ground. 'My mother was never the same after that. It was left to me to be the man of the house, to look after my sisters. As you both know, one of them took her own life several years later. Then Ethaniel died . . .' His eyes glistened with tears, and he couldn't finish the sentence. 'I've never been good at protecting the ones I love, you see, so it's probably best if you put your faith in someone else.'

Alexia reached over and gently took his hand. 'You're not being fair on yourself,' she said, sounding more like the woman I knew and loved. 'I know you've lost loved ones, but as the general, you have saved thousands of people, all of whom are dear to someone, loved by someone.'

Darj looked down at her hand, holding his. I think in that one gesture, she had eased years of pain. 'But if I can't protect the ones I love, what kind of man am I?'

'A very good one,' Alexia said. 'Ethaniel gave his life trying to protect me. Just because it didn't work out like we'd hoped, doesn't make him any less of a man.' She squeezed his hand. 'The same is true of you.'

The ground was wet and spongy when we rode into Delya the next day. We were surrounded by picturesque farmland dotted with a few cottages, but I could also smell the swamplands Delya was known for.

The path we followed soon became a road, and before long, we came in sight of a small village. A sign told us it was Myrton.

'Well, we may as well change now,' Darj said. He tethered Guntar to a fence and lifted Eva down from Alexia's horse.

Alexia took out a common, green dress that Darj had bought in Fenellar and stuffed in her saddlebag. It was crinkled and thinning.

'It adds to the authenticity,' Darj said when Alexia frowned. He handed me a blue dress that was of similar quality, and the two of us walked to a cluster of trees to get changed.

Returning, we took off our rings. For Alexia, that included the signet ring that symbolised her position. She stored them in Guntar's saddlebag and turned back to Darj.

'Do we look common enough?' she asked.

Darj stepped towards her and removed the clip that held the rest of her hair back. Her ebony locks fell about her shoulders, giving her a more carefree appearance. A stray curl blew about her face. It made her look more like her old self, and I wanted to smile and laugh with her like we used to in the old days.

'You look fine,' he said.

Alexia put a hand on his arm. 'You need to take this off as well if we are to be convincing.' She undid the military band around his upper arm.

I helped Eva change into a plain, linen dress. 'Look!' she said with wide-eyed curiosity, pointing to a nearby paddock. 'Cows!'

'Yes, lots of cows,' I said. Eva was now my only link to a pure and simple world. I picked her up, and she snuggled into my neck and giggled.

The three of us hid our weapons underneath draped cloaks. By then, we looked nothing more than a poor farming family. I wondered if Darj felt like he was with his two sisters again but knew that in reality, the situation was very different.

We walked with our horses into Myrton. The streets were filled with people. They were talking to each other in short sentences and moving towards the marketplace. Caught up in the crowd, we were forced to follow. Alexia held onto her daughter's hand tightly.

Amidst rows of people selling fruit, fabrics, and livestock, there stood a small Delyan man holding onto something and crying. The villagers had surrounded him, murmuring amongst themselves. 'What is it, Alel?' one of them asked.

'There has been another murder,' the man said. 'My nephew is dead!'

He showed the crowd what he held in his hands.

It was a long, bloodied arrow, with gold-tipped, green fletching.

15
MESSAGE OF DEATH

We sat together in the local inn. A young woman brought Darj a mug of ale and slammed it on the table in front of him. I knew Alexia was resisting the urge to reprimand her. If only she knew who we were . . . But so far, almost every Delyan had treated us with the same contempt.

'They believe the Targian queen is personally murdering their loved ones,' Alexia said when the girl left. She leant over the table towards Darj. 'Someone has set me up! Why?'

The people sitting at the next table over glanced at us. Darj gave a weak smile and patted Alexia's hand. 'We'll talk about it later,' he said behind gritted teeth.

'Now we know why Lord Fenton insisted we come as commoners,' Alexia said. 'I would've been lynched as soon as I crossed the border.'

'You still will be if you don't be quiet,' Darj whispered. 'Now, for goodness' sake, one problem at a time!'

'What exactly are we doing here?' I asked wearily.

'We are just passing through on the way to Nirrana,' Darj said. 'I'm happy to continue travelling whenever you're both ready.'

Alexia sighed and took a mouthful of Darj's ale. She cringed and spat it out. 'How can you drink that? It tastes like dirt.'

Darj said nothing but took his mug back and drank the rest of it without flinching. Alexia rolled her eyes.

Apart from the girl who had brought us our drinks, Alexia and I were the only two women in the room. Four aging farmers sat across from us, talking about the quality of cow's milk. Two younger men were, from what I could overhear, discussing their chances with the girl. And then, in the far corner of the room, there sat a man in a dark cloak, watching us.

I recognised him as the one who had brought the High Zalem's marriage proposal to Alexia in Chettona. Alexia noticed the shock in my face and followed my line of sight. She stiffened when she saw him.

The man held her gaze and pulled an arrow out from under his cloak. It was one of hers—or made to look like one of hers, at least. He brushed the feathers against his cheek and smiled. There was blood on the arrowhead.

Alexia put an arm around her daughter. 'We have to go.'

'What is it?' Darj asked.

'We need to leave,' Alexia said.

I picked up Eva, and we hurried outside.

Alexia began walking to our horses but fell to her knees. I thought she had tripped, even though it was unlikely for her. It wasn't until she didn't move or get up that I knew something else was wrong.

Darj and I ran to her. 'Alexia?' he asked.

She wrapped her arms around herself and hunched over the ground like she had acute stomach pains. I could see the colour draining from her face. Darj grabbed her hand, and I bent down next to her. 'Alexia?'

She groaned as if someone had hit her. 'It hurts . . . '

'Darj, it is getting worse,' I said. I moved her hair to the side and checked the back of her neck, expecting to see a dart there.

There was nothing, not even a drop of blood. And yet she fell to the ground, unconscious.

I was sitting next to her when she woke the next morning. Her face was sweaty and her hair damp.

'Where are we?' she asked.

'In Alel's house—the uncle of the murdered boy. He and his wife Samela saw you collapse in the street and brought us here.'

'What?' Unsure of her strength, she slowly raised herself into a sitting position. 'They think their nephew has been killed by Targians, by me, and still took us in?'

'Yes, they are kind people, even though they are hurting, but they don't know who we are.'

We could hear laughter downstairs where Alel, Samela, Darj, and Eva were. Eva was giggling, and I saw Alexia's face soften when she heard it.

'Do you remember what happened?' I asked. 'In the street?'

Alexia frowned as she thought about it. 'No . . . I just felt unwell. I don't know what's going to happen to me, Adaliah.'

I brought her a glass of water, and there was silence while she drank.

'Alexia,' I said, taking the opportunity to talk while she seemed more like her normal self, 'there's a lot of unknown danger right now. You're right—we don't know what's going to happen, and I'm so afraid I'm about to lose everything I care about, especially Elhian.' A sob escaped, surprising me as tears ran down my face. 'That's why it's so important for me to know that you will, at least one day, forgive me for the awful words I said in Chettona.'

She gripped her cup. 'It's not you I am having trouble forgiving, Adaliah. It's myself.'

Darj came up the stairs, drawn by our voices. I quickly wiped away my tears. 'You're awake,' he said to Alexia with a soft smile. 'Good. I have some information. There have been several murders lately—they are convinced it's you because of the arrows. Alel said the only reason they let us in is because he thought our Targian presence would cause a riot and that enough innocent blood has been spilt already.'

'But we're not innocent, are we?' Alexia said. 'Not in the truest sense.'

'What do they know about us?' I asked.

'Almost everything but our identity. I wanted to keep things simple. They know Alexia's widowed and think I'm your friend. They believe you two are sisters. I told them you are from a noble family and I a mere soldier. That should explain my knowledge of warfare and any slips you have with . . . '

'Failing to be common?' Alexia asked with a raised eyebrow.

'Exactly. They don't have any children, which is why their nephew was so important. They adore Eva, and she seems to like them, too. I've told them false names for now. We have to be careful.'

It wasn't until later that day that Alexia felt strong enough to get out of bed. Now that she didn't seem to entirely hate being in my presence, I gave her a basin of water in a servant-like manner. Samela had given it to me with some soap. She was a shy sort of woman who, judging by the furtive looks she flashed us from time to time, was still unsure whether she and her husband had done the right thing in taking us in. After freshening up, Alexia began putting on the common, green dress again and reached behind to tighten the cords.

I threw the water out of the window and onto the garden below. When I turned back, my mouth dropped. The black-cloaked man was standing behind Alexia. I couldn't believe he had appeared yet again without either of us hearing or sensing him. Alexia didn't even realise he was there until he took the cord from her and pulled it tight.

She jumped with astonishment, and both of us were speechless.

The man slid his hand around her waist and pulled her up against him.

'Get your hands off me,' she said.

He put a hand on her lower back and, even though he didn't seem to be pressing hard, she let out a cry of pain.

'Leave me alone!'

'Not until you give me your answer.'

'How did you get in here?' Alexia asked.

'Never mind that,' he said, tightening his grip around her waist until she whimpered. 'Are you coming with me to meet the High Zalem or not?' He kissed her bare shoulder; she squirmed but couldn't get away.

'Under no circumstances would I ever consent to marrying a man renowned for such evil. I told you that already.'

'I'm very sorry to hear it. The High Zalem may now feel obligated to try and change your mind. He will send you a message very soon.'

The man pushed her to the ground and stepped towards her with a coarse grin.

I grabbed a candlestick from the small table next to Alexia's bed, stepped over her and struck at him.

He ducked and laughed. This made me even more determined. I flung the candlestick at his head and heard the thud when it made contact. He fell to his knees, and I kicked him in the stomach. The force of it pushed him to his side, and he groaned.

I saw a dagger belted to his waist. I grabbed it, but he took my wrist and bent it backwards so hard, I almost fainted from pain.

By this time, Alexia had risen from the floor. She picked up the candlestick and struck him across the head with it again. This time, he was knocked senseless.

I reached for the dagger again.

'No, Adaliah! Don't forget the promise you made.'

I retracted my hand. I *had* forgotten. It was only luck that my initial blow with the candlestick hadn't drawn any blood.

I knew I wouldn't be able to adhere to the promise!

'What are we going to do with him?' Alexia asked.

'I don't know . . . I just couldn't stand by while he treated you like that.'

Alexia closed the shutters at the other window across the room, presumably where he'd entered. As if to block out the outside world altogether, she picked up a thinning cloth that had been lying on the ground and hung it over the window frame as well. Then, she stood with her hand over her heart.

'The Zalem message is always death,' she said.

'What?'

'I remember that from somewhere . . . "The Zalem message is always death." He said the High Zalem would send us a message.'

'Where did you hear that phrase?'

'I was a child. I remember I was looking for Father. It was on his desk—that's right—a letter of some sort. I think there was the Zalem symbol on the back of the letter.' She said this with wonder at her own memory.

'We have to tell Darj,' I said. 'I know you don't want to put him in danger but . . . ' I gestured to the man lying at our feet.

'No, you're right. I should have told him already. He's more than capable of protecting himself. I was just worried about him. I don't want him harmed.'

We headed downstairs but paused when we heard Darj talking with Alel and Samela.

'Perhaps she's in the family way,' Samela said.

'No, no, I'm certain she's not,' Darj said. There was embarrassment in his voice. 'No, I think she's just overtired.'

'I wish it were that simple,' Alexia whispered to me as we descended the rest of the stairs.

The three of them were sitting around a table. Alel was a grandfatherly looking man with a long, grey beard and a bald head, but he was muscular from years of work on a nearby farm. His hands were calloused and gnarly and his skin browned by the sun. Samela looked about a decade younger than him, and she had the most intriguing eyes that I had still yet to determine the colour of.

Eva had been sitting on Darj's lap, but she launched herself off when she saw her mother and ran towards Alexia with outstretched arms. Alexia lifted her up and kissed her cheek. 'How's my little girl?'

'Good,' Eva said, burying her head in Alexia's neck. 'Mother better now?'

'Yes, darling, I am.' Alexia stroked her hair back from her face.

'You are looking better, Grace,' Samela said.

Alexia stared at her blankly, but I figured that was the name Darj was using for her and nudged her.

'Thank you,' she said. 'And thank you for taking us in. I know it must not have been easy for you.'

Samela said something in response, but I was looking intensely at Darj and wondering how we could talk to him alone.

Darj leant forward in his seat. I think he was about to ask me what was wrong when someone outside blew a horn.

'That's the sound of attack,' Alel said. 'It must be the Targians!'

'It can't be the Targians,' Alexia said, moving towards the window. Civilians were running down the street, yelling and pointing to something behind them. 'They have not been given orders to attack Delya; they have no reason to be here.'

'Neither did their queen have reason to kill my nephew,' Alel said. He hurried to a trunk and pulled out a sword. 'I have two,' he said to Darj. 'Take your pick, unless you don't want to fight your own kinsman?'

'They're not my kinsman,' Darj said as he took the first sword. 'And even if they are, they haven't been ordered to attack by the Targian monarchy.'

There was a scream. Swords clashed, and men started yelling to their comrades.

Alel whispered instructions to his wife while Darj hurried to us. 'Stay in the house. No matter what happens, stay in the house, both of you!'

Once more I felt the utter frustration of not being able to help.

Alexia shook her head. 'I need to get my bow and arrows—'

'You will not,' Darj said, 'or you will give yourself away. It's you they want. Stay inside and keep Eva safe.' He kissed the little girl's forehead.

'They already know we are here,' Alexia whispered, searching his eyes. 'They are attacking because I didn't do what they wanted. "The Zalems message is always death." They are attacking because of me.'

Darj held her gaze. 'I will not let them win, I promise.' He gently touched her cheek, gave me a strained smile, and then ran outside with Alel.

Alexia handed Eva to Samela and ran to get her bow and arrows anyway, telling me they were for our protection. I ran upstairs where there was a better view from the window. I stepped over the Zalem, who was still unconscious on the floor.

When I saw the attackers, I knew they weren't Targians—they didn't have the Targian black hair or blue eyes—but they were dressed in Targian armour. They even wore the iconic green sash around their waist.

One of the soldiers pushed a woman to the ground. Darj pierced his side and killed him. He checked the man's ankle, and I could tell by the maddened expression on his face that it was definitely a Zalem.

Only fifty or so of the Delyan men were armed. They had killed no more than twenty of the nearly hundred Zalems.

I saw a Zalem setting the inn on fire. The flames and smoke filled the air, and there was screaming inside.

'You there!' Darj yelled to one of the Delyans. 'Clear the inn! The rest of you—stand by me!'

There was something about Darj that commanded obedience. The armed Delyan men ran to him and formed a rough circle, shoulder-to-shoulder, with their backs on the inside.

One of the Zalems threw a dagger at the man standing next to Darj. It cut across his throat, and he fell down dead.

'Hold your positions!' Darj called. He glanced at the body lying on his foot. 'Let them come to us!'

The Zalems did just that.

Darj killed one, then another. He ducked when a sword swiped near his head and skewered the Zalem who wielded it. The other men, now with their backs protected, did the same. A further twenty Zalems fell.

The man Darj had sent inside the inn hurried out again with a young girl, the same one who had served us when we'd first arrived.

Just as they stepped onto the street, the inn collapsed behind them. The man lurched forward, but the girl was trapped by debris. Blood flowed from a head wound, and she didn't move.

'Get out of here!' Alel yelled at the man, who was staring at the girl's body, stricken. 'Get everyone out of here!'

The man tried to pull the girl free, but it was impossible. He left her and hurried to collect the other civilians. Running into the nearby houses, he yelled at the residents to follow him while the men in the street continued to fight.

Another Delyan was killed, and his blood splattered onto Darj's clothes. Alel fell next. He lay on the ground, gripping his side. Darj attempted to get closer to help him, but a Zalem hit his old arm wound with a sword handle. While the wound had completely closed up, I knew it was still tender. Darj dropped one of his swords and gritted his teeth.

Before the Zalem could strike again, however, an arrow landed in his chest, and he fell. Another three died in the same way before Darj could even turn around. I leaned out the window and looked up: Alexia was crouched up on the roof, shooting arrows with gifted speed.

A part of me was jealous that she was able to contribute, but mostly I was afraid she was giving herself away, that they would come for us, or that the Delyans would turn against us.

Even Darj wouldn't be able to save us then.

The Zalems were now focusing on lighting houses. More and more went up in flames, creating chaos amongst the people. Many were fleeing the town. A few women and unarmed men lay dead in the streets. The air became thick with smoke. Tethered horses reared and broke their ropes, allowing them to bolt. Darj was about to kill a Zalem when one of the horses knocked his shoulder, sending him sprawling to the ground.

It was at that point that smoke began to fill the room I was in, and I knew Alel's house was on fire, too.

'Come on,' Alexia said, suddenly appearing out of the smoke and grabbing my arm. 'We have to get out!'

I glanced at the Zalem lying on the floor and hesitated. Could we leave him there to burn?

We had no choice. If we tried to save him, our own lives would be forfeit.

I ran with Alexia towards Alel's stables, where Samela was waiting with Eva.

Alexia killed another two Zalems with a dual shot, and the remaining few began to retreat.

The villagers gathered around Darj. 'Thank you,' Alel said, struggling to his feet. 'You saved us.' The sentiment was repeated a few times amongst the men.

Darj gave them a quick nod and hurried to us. When he saw Alexia standing with her bow still loaded, he gave her a fierce look, and she returned it with a guilty defiance I'd seen more than once in Eva when she did something she knew she shouldn't.

He grabbed her arm. 'What do you think you're doing? Are you trying to get yourself killed?'

The loaded arrow fell at their feet, and it was only then that Samela made the connection. She started to cry. Alel came in behind us, and Alexia dropped her bow altogether.

Holding his side, Alel looked at his wife and then back at Alexia. He saw the bow on the ground and paled. 'You're . . . you're the Targian queen?' He picked up the arrow. 'And you,' he turned to me, 'the A'zyon Warrior?'

I could see the disgust rising in his eyes.

'I am,' Alexia and I said together.

There was a tense moment while Alel considered this. Then, he thrust his sword up against Alexia's throat.

Darj tried to pull him away, but Alel hit the wound on his arm violently, having seen him flinch when the Zalem did the same earlier. Darj groaned and gripped his arm again. It was bleeding.

'Mother!' Eva began to cry and wrestled her way out of Samela's arms.

'You killed my nephew!' Alel yelled, pressing the sword into Alexia's neck. 'We took you in, and all the time, you killed my nephew!'

Alexia shook her head and tried to back away. 'It wasn't me,' she said breathlessly.

Darj kicked Alel away from her, this time sending him down on his knees. 'Her Majesty did not kill your nephew or any other Delyans.' Alel attempted to get up but Darj pointed a sword at his chest. 'If she was against you, she would not have risked her life for yours just now!'

'She is the reason we were attacked. I'm sure of it!'

'You were also sure it was the Targians attacking, even though they are clearly Zalems.'

'Zalems?' Alel said. 'Well, if it was them, they still never would have come here if it weren't for her. Our whole village is lost because of that woman!'

'He's . . . he's right,' Alexia said. Eva was clinging to her arm. 'Darj, we both know he's right.'

Darj looked at her and at the burning houses in the street. He lowered his sword. 'If we had known we would bring such danger to your community, we would never have come,' he said, 'but this is not Queen Alexia's doing. It is the Zalems doing it in her name to spark hatred amongst your people against her and the Targians. It is information about them that we came to seek, information on how to stop them. You need to believe me, because if you dare hurt her again, I will kill you.'

16
TYDELL

The Delyans brought the bodies of their loved ones to the paddock we had passed on the way to town. Family members cleansed and anointed them with Delyan myrrh while others began the somber work of digging their graves.

We waited until they were all laid to rest, and once the priest had blessed them to Ru'ach and the last sod was pressed in, we abandoned the burnt village altogether. So far, Alel and Samela had not betrayed our identity to the others, but the way they kept their distance suggested we were not yet forgiven. We felt responsible for the loss of their village and determined to accompany them to the next town, Tydell, before continuing on to Nirrana.

That night, we made camp with the Delyans not too far from the swamplands. Alexia, Eva, and Samela fell asleep quickly, but I lay awake thinking of Elhian, wondering if he was seeing the same sky, the same stars as I was. Was he all right? Was he thinking of me?

Elhian, Elhian, Elhian . . .

Dear Ru'ach, keep him well. Keep him safe!

I blinked tears away and muffled a sob.

Elhian . . . I miss you so much.

'You said you came here to find out more about the Zalems,' Alel said to Darj as they sat by the campfire, interrupting my thoughts.

'Yes, particularly of their location. The Casmodian king is missing, and as far as we know, he is being held in Sharlard. Have you heard of it?'

'Yes, yes, I have. Most Delyans grow up hearing the story. But I don't know where it is, and even if I did . . . ' Alel folded his arms. 'I'm sorry, Darj, but it's a hard thing when a man saves my life one minute and betrays it in the next. I don't know what to think.'

'I didn't mean to betray you. Had you not invited me in when Queen Alexia collapsed, we would never have spoken. I'm sorry your kindness was repaid in such a way.'

Alexia was sleeping on her side next to me with an arm around Eva. She looked like a common woman in her simple clothing but beautiful, nevertheless.

'I have to admit,' Alel said, putting some tobacco in a pipe, 'I'm sorry I attacked her the way I did. Maybe she's just another tired mother trying to cope with everyday life. From what I've heard, she's had to cope with more than that. A witness to her husband's and son's brutal murders . . . No one should have to start a life like that.' He lit his pipe, inhaled a lung-full of smoke, and breathed it out again. 'But I've been surprised by people's characters before, and some of them can be very cunning. One day, we may be able to boast we housed you all, but that day won't be for a while yet. Someone has worked hard to make sure Targe is disliked in Delya.'

He sounded almost apologetic, but Darj was too busy gazing at Alexia to notice.

'You know,' Alel said, a smile in his voice, 'women like her need loving, Darj, loving by brave men. They won't admit it—they may even fight against it—but they need it.'

I held my breath. Alel had seen what I believed Darj refused to see because of Alexia's position.

'She is the queen,' Darj said, confirming my thoughts.

'Then the need is only ten times stronger.'

Darj ignored him. 'Is Sharlard in Delya?'

Alel took another puff on his pipe before answering. 'No. It's said to be a harsh place—'

'An underground city, I believe.'

'Yes. It houses all those who believe in the Zalem faith, which of course centres on power in all its forms, particularly the power of the evil spirit Anash. They seem to have set their mind on taking Alexia, and I don't think they will be stopped as easily as you might hope.'

The air was potent with the smell of mud and heavy with moisture as we continued towards Tydell. When night fell for the second time, we made camp in an open field, and the Delyans burned crystallised minerals found commonly in the nearby swamps. It lit up the night with a soft, yellow glow and deterred the thousands of insects that had otherwise been bothering us.

'This weather is unbearable,' Alexia said as she sat by Darj near a campfire. She rolled her sleeves up while Eva snuggled in her lap. 'I feel like I'm constantly sweating for no reason.'

I opened my mouth to agree—I had been longing for a creek or brook to wash in—but the most divine music started. Someone was playing a sort of flute, and everyone was up and listening. The tune was melodic and lovely. Another joined in, tapping on a drum. The people cheered and began dancing under the night sky.

Darj and I walked over to Alel, who was clapping the people on. 'What's happening?' I asked.

'It's what we do, we Delyans. Whenever we are sad, whenever we need hope, we dance! Samela! Let's go!' The two of them joined the others.

I don't know about Darj, but it reminded me of the dances at Liane Palace. It wasn't as grand, of course, but there was the same joy on the people's faces.

'Well, go on,' I said to Darj. 'Be brave. Ask her.' I nodded towards Alexia.

'Don't you want to dance?'

'Not without Elhian.'

I expected him to be unmoved, but he did look over at Alexia. Eva was chatting to her, pointing at the people with interest and smiling.

He meandered back to her in an uncommitted sort of way. I remembered what he'd said in Liane: that she hadn't danced since Ethaniel died. Was he thinking of that now? Or was he thinking about what Alel had said?

I watched as he held his palm out to her. Alexia glanced up at him and did a double take when she saw his hand inviting her. She stared at him with an open mouth.

They spoke, and I gathered Alexia was using Eva as an excuse. Darj bent down to the princess and whispered something. Eva smiled. When Alexia didn't move, she took her mother's hand and placed it in Darj's. I saw the word 'dance!' form on the child's lips, followed by a playful grin.

Darj tugged on Alexia's hand, and she finally responded by getting to her feet. Eva ran to me, and I picked her up and settled her on my hip. Darj led Alexia to the others and brought her around to face him. Even from where I was standing, I could see the resistance in her eyes and hoped I hadn't encouraged something that would ultimately set them both back.

But then he said something to her, and her gaze softened.

Darj twirled her like the Delyans were doing. They both stumbled trying to copy some of the other steps; the Delyans noticed and laughed in good humour.

'Show us how the Targians dance!' one called. The others stopped and echoed the request, as did I.

'Our dances are a little more formal,' Alexia said.

'Oh, go on,' Samela said.

The music changed before they could protest.

Alexia turned back to Darj.

They appeared to discuss which dance to perform, and then he put his hand around her waist, drawing her closer. She put her hand in his other one, and he guided her through a traditional dance I recognised as 'the Swan'. It was elegant and beautiful, and after the first few steps, Alexia was smiling.

The humidity, the insects, and the haunt of war seemed to fade, and we were back in the ballroom at Liane. I saw Alexia not in a tattered green dress, but in a beautiful gown with a diamond necklace sparkling in the candlelight. I imagined Darj wearing full military regalia and the people of Targe watching on. It was only the Delyans and I watching them in reality, but we were just as transfixed by the grace of their steps.

It was raining by the time they finished. I sheltered Eva with my cloak but kept my eyes on Alexia. The Delyans were clapping, and she was laughing. It warmed me to hear it, gave me courage and hope that the old Alexia, the one who had loved and enjoyed life, was still lingering. Darj brought her hand to his lips. She gave him a warm smile, and I knew then that in some way I could not name, he had made her feel safe. Safe from cold hands and vulgar promises. Safe from fear.

The Delyans began to copy their dance with impressive accuracy. Alexia and Darj joined in again, the rain running down their faces and washing away the grit of the day.

Alexia laughed again as they drew closer to me. 'I can't tell you how nice it is to hear that sound,' Darj said.

'I'd forgotten what it feels like,' Alexia said.

'Laughing? Or dancing?'

Alexia paused and looked over at the other couples. Like me, she saw how the music and dancing was easing their burdens. 'No,' she said. 'Happiness.'

As soon as she spoke the word, she fell as if something had hit her head. It happened so fast, Darj was powerless to stop her from dropping to the ground.

She put a hand to her forehead like she had a burning headache. The others saw her, and the music stopped.

I ran to her side. 'Alexia . . .'

'No . . .' She groaned.

'What is it?' Darj asked. He looked at me. 'I don't understand what's causing this!'

'Make . . . it . . . stop . . .' Alexia could barely form the words—she sounded like her tongue had been made limp.

She gripped Darj's arm and tried to pull herself up but slipped. Her dress muddied on the wet ground.

I put a hand on her forearm. She was cold to touch.

She pulled away from Darj and clasped her hands over her ears like she was trying to shut out an unbearably loud noise. I knelt behind her, holding her up in a sitting position until she fainted into my arms.

We hurried over a hill on the third day and came into a thick swamp. Bagred sloshed through the muddied water and sank a little. When he struggled to take another step, I hopped off his back and sank into the ground, too. The trees around us stood close together, thin and tall.

Eva had been riding with me, and as I glanced back to check she was all right in the saddle, I felt certain we were being watched. The trees' leaves were wispy but quiet. There was no breeze, just an unnatural stillness that made me uncomfortable. The sky was grey. 'I think it's going to rain again,' I said to Darj. I took Bagred's reins and trudged ahead of him and the others.

It was only an hour later—although it felt much longer—when I first saw a group of huts in front of me, a township built right on top of the fen. There were at least thirty or forty huts, and all were made out of mud and reeds. Smoke wisped out of chimneys and hovered in the air in a lonely but cosy way, and there were some platforms up in the trees—watchtowers, I decided—but there was no one on them.

When we reached the centre of Tydell, the small village was soon clogged with people. Alel explained to the leader what had happened to their town, and the two of them began to negotiate lodging. I took Eva from Bagred's back and tethered both him and Guntar to a post.

'Mother?' Eva asked.

Darj had been riding with an arm around Alexia, and I helped him get her down. Darj carried her unconscious body in his arms. It frightened me that she had been out for so long. She still showed no signs of waking.

One of the swamp-dwellers saw Darj and began to yell at him. I couldn't understand what he was saying but got the impression he was insulting Targe. He struck Darj across the face, and then everyone was yelling, including me.

'How dare you!'

If Darj hadn't had his hands full, I'm sure he would have felled the man. His face was red, and he was so stunned he couldn't speak.

'Leave him be!' Alel yelled.

'They killed our family!' the assaulter said. 'Why are you trusting them?' He raised a fist to hit Darj again.

Alel grabbed his arm. 'It is because of him that we survived at all. Stand back!'

He pushed the people away and directed us to a small, quiet hut.

I stood at the door for some time, watching as the Tydell villagers took in the refugees. The town was much more peaceful than it had been when we'd first arrived; the paths in between the huts were almost empty. I also noticed scouts now watched from the high platforms, armed with bows, arrows, and daggers. Others patrolled the perimeter, walking noiselessly through the watery bog. Their skin was disguised with a thin layer of mud.

'Get out of my way,' a voice said behind me.

I turned on my heel and came face to face with my cousin.

Her eyes were cold and hard.

'You're awake! Are you all right?' I wanted to hug her, but something told me not to. 'You collapsed again—'

'How dare you even come near me after what you said?' Alexia took a step towards me, and I moved back.

'What?' My breath caught in my chest. 'I thought we'd moved past that.' There was something in her face that disconcerted me on a deeper level. I'd never been afraid of her before. 'Please, Alexia, not this again. I know you loved Jeri—'

'Do not speak his name.'

I raised my palms. 'You are not yourself. You're ill, Alexia. They've done something to you. I don't know what, but you've got to let this anger go. I know we can't bring him back—'

'Do you honestly think that's what this is about? That I haven't accepted he's dead?'

I hesitated, trying to think why we were having this conversation. 'Well . . . No. I don't think you have.'

Alexia's eyes narrowed into a glare. She tried to step around me.

'No.' I put my arm across the doorway. 'You're not going until we sort this out.'

'Who do you think you are? I am the Queen of Targe, and I will not be dictated to by you or anyone else.'

'It is my cousin I'm talking to.'

'Your cousin is dead!'

My mind reeled as I tried to think of a response, but when Alexia pulled a sword out from Darj's things and pointed it at me, all words left.

'Get out of my way,' she said.

Having always favoured the bow, Alexia had never been an elite swordswoman, and I was fairly certain I could disarm her. But what if it went too far and I drew blood?

'The Zalems are doing this to you, Alexia. They must be. You must connect to Ru'ach, so he can help you. The Zalems have Anash on their side—his evil is pursuing you, and you need Ru'ach to protect you. The Zalems are playing on your grief and pain. You have to let it go. Forgive me, forgive Cades, forgive yourself!'

Alexia stretched her neck from side to side. I watched as something changed in her eyes, as she gripped the sword with both hands.

'No.'

17
REGENCY

'Don't do this, Alexia.'

She flinched as if a bug were crawling on her neck. 'You have no idea how much it hurts.'

'Do you think you're the only one who has suffered? That you were the only one touched by Cades?'

'Do you think I don't feel the weight of my kingdom's pain as well as my own?' Alexia raised the sword to shoulder height.

'Alexia . . .'

But she snarled and struck at me.

I sidestepped the attack and grabbed her wrist, but what I didn't expect was for Alexia to pull away from me. This one movement dragged me forward and sent me stumbling to the ground. I rolled over, but Alexia crouched on top of me and held the blade at my throat.

'I'm not going to fight you.' I lay unmoving on the ground, the cool blade resting on my neck. 'Do your worst, but I will not fight back. You're my family.'

Alexia pressed the sword into my skin.

'Mother?'

Eva, who up until that point had been outside with Darj, was now at the doorway. She sounded frightened, and I wondered how long she'd been watching. 'Mother?'

Alexia turned to her daughter as if in a dream. She blinked. 'E . . . Eva.'

Her face changed like a shadow had suddenly left her. Alexia dropped the sword and reached for her little princess. Eva wrapped her arms around Alexia's neck in an emotional daze.

Alexia now looked lost, confused. She kissed the top of Eva's head and glanced in my direction but seemed to find it painful to look at me. 'I'm . . . I'm sorry.' Her voice was rasping. 'I'm sorry.' She stood and walked out of the hut.

I spent an hour thinking over the whole event in detail, at times feeling more afraid, at others, more in control. The Zalems had to be responsible for her condition, and if they were, then there had to be a remedy.

I wanted to discuss this with Darj in hopes that we could come up with some sort of plan. I searched for him for a while before I glimpsed him walking into a shack used for food storage.

I planned to go after him but stopped when I realised he'd been looking for Alexia and had found her sitting in the corner of the shack. I circled behind, thinking I would find Alel and Samela instead, but I realised I could hear what they were saying through the walls. Without even questioning what I was doing, I paused to listen.

'Look, Da!' Eva said. I don't know what she was showing him, but she still sounded cheerful despite everything.

'Have you come to see the insane queen?' Alexia asked.

I peered through the cracks in the hut and saw Darj sit down next to her. Alexia looked like a small girl huddled up in the corner, hugging her knees.

'No daughter should have to go through this,' she said. There were tears in her voice, something I hadn't heard in many months. It made my heart constrict, and it took me a second to realise why. It wasn't that Alexia sounded sad or upset—she sounded defeated.

'She's still got you.'

'Everyone has a right to feel safe, and I can't even give her that—just as I couldn't give it to Jeri.'

Will she never forgive herself?

Darj attempted to respond, but she silenced him with a wave of her hand. 'I have something for you.'

I saw her pull a piece of parchment out of her bodice and hand it to him.

There was quiet while Darj read it. 'A regency? Alexia—'

'Darj, please. We both know that if things keep going this way, I'm likely to . . . ' I leant forward, desperate to hear whatever she was going to say. 'I will be unfit to rule. I trust you. Ethaniel did, too. I know if something were to happen to me, you would look after Targe better than anyone until Eva comes of age. Should the worst happen, I need you to promise you will protect her and her right to the throne, while acting as the regent until she is ready to be crowned. Can you do that?'

'Yes, but I will first do everything I can to prevent such an outcome.' Darj tucked the document under his shirt. 'You must know the Zalems have done this to you. I think they want you to become one of them, to join with the High Zalem or something. I think you already know that. You were sworn to secrecy, weren't you?'

'Yes. My choices have never been easy, but now . . . Either I give into insanity and illness to save the ones I love, or I stay true to myself, fight for good, and watch as you, Elhian, and Adaliah die, to say nothing of Eva. The only way out I can see is if . . . is if I were the one to die first.'

'Don't you dare speak like that. We will find another way. Just stay alive; the rest we can figure out. You must fight the evil with good. You must draw near to Ru'ach. He has protected us before; he has heeded your prayers before. He won't let us down now. You must have faith.'

From what I could see, Alexia was still hugging her knees, and I wasn't sure if she was listening. 'Adaliah received a letter that mentioned a pact King Amaz had with the Zalems. Does that sound familiar to you at all?'

'I do have a small memory of him writing to them about something, but no, not really.'

'Well, I've been looking into it these last few days. Some of the Delyans know about it because he came into this region to hide something—a treasure of some sort that the Zalems don't know about. They say he hid it around here in the North Fen. It might help to cure this . . . this illness they've given you before it gets any worse. The only problem is we don't know exactly where it is.'

Alexia said nothing.

'In Ru'ach's name, we will beat this,' Darj said. 'We conquered Cades, and we will conquer them, too. We will find a way to help you. Death will neither be the answer nor the victor, I promise.'

As Alexia was still incapable of travel, Darj and Alel spent two days looking for information in the surrounding villages and searching the swamps for Amaz's treasure, going further and further afield each time.

Still generally resented by the Delyan citizens, Alexia and I kept to our hut with Eva and only Samela for outside company. I tried to talk to Alexia numerous times, but she said less and less and only seemed able to interact with her daughter. She often refused food and was looking thin.

On the third morning, Samela came rushing into the hut with restrained excitement. 'There's a visitor for you,' she said. 'He's come all the way from Nirrana!'

Before either of us could respond, Samela stepped aside from the door.

A young man walked in behind her. He was topless but wore an impressive medallion around his neck and gold bands on his arms. Daggers were sheathed on his hips, their handles covered in precious jewels, and on his left hand was a signet ring with a yellow stone protruding from it like a small sun. It wasn't King Thane. But it was his brother.

'Prince Ren Markus,' Alexia said, standing. 'I haven't seen you since you were a boy.'

Ren bowed. 'Your Majesties.' He kissed our hands. 'It is good to see you both.'

'How is your brother, the king?' I asked.

'Safe and well. Thane sent me to find you, to tell you that while we respected our father, we admit he should not have sent men to fight with Cades in that last battle for Targe.'

'Because they all died?' Alexia asked.

'Because it was not an honourable cause.' Ren gave Alexia a significant look, as if determined not to be bullied. I admired him immediately. 'With the Zalems on the move, we Delyans feel partly responsible. We had the opportunity to eradicate them years ago, but the threat was thought minimal. So, when my contacts told us you were on your way to see us, searching for answers, I thought I'd meet you and offer my services.'

'Even though the rest of your people hate us?' Alexia returned his look with a stubborn one I knew all too well.

Ren remained unconcerned. 'The Zalems attempted to shoot my brother with one of your arrows to try and convince us that you were trying to kill him, but they forgot two very important things.'

'What was that?' I asked.

Ren pulled out part of the arrow shaft from his pocket and handed it to me, and I looked at it closely. Engraved just below the feathers was the Zalem symbol.

'What was the second thing?' I asked.

Ren's mouth curved in a small smile. 'I think we both know if it had been Queen Alexia, the shot would not have missed its target.'

I grinned, and even Alexia's face lightened at this.

'I knew then they were trying to turn our kingdoms against each other, which meant they must fear us uniting.' He took a step towards Alexia. 'I don't know about you, but I think anything that causes them fear is a good thing.'

'Well,' I said, 'I'm very glad you could come.'

Prince Ren met my eyes. There was softness in his expression but also a new strength that Alexia and I needed. 'Adaliah, I did not come alone, nor solely for this reason. I have something for you, but you must prepare yourself.'

If it weren't for the fact he was smiling so gently at me, I would have been afraid. I was only just able to follow him outside as it was.

Ahead of us was a hitching post. Guntar and Bagred were both there, but next to them was another new horse. Someone was dismounting, and he or she—I couldn't yet tell—was wearing a heavy overcoat that was too thick for the Delyan humidity. They were covered in mud, and I could see numerous trails of blood down the back of their neck.

When they turned towards me, I realised it was a man, but I didn't recognise him at first. When I did, I couldn't believe what I was seeing and stood gaping at him in shock.

'Adaliah,' he said, and I could no longer contain the sob rising in my chest.

'Elhian!'

18
RETURN FROM SHARLARD

There was so much I wanted to say to him, so many things I had rehearsed, hoped for, and imagined. But after uttering his name, no other words would form, so I ran to him and held him close against me.

I felt him shaking with the same emotions. He kissed my temple and my lips. No one had ever warned me about marriage, how they become a part of your soul. I wanted to melt into him.

'I can't believe it's you,' I said, cupping his face with both hands and kissing him again.

He drew back, and I could see the tears in his eyes. I brushed the hair away from his forehead, and it was only then that I was able to take in his appearance. He was much thinner than when I'd last seen him. His skin was a sickly grey colour, like clouds that bring soft rain, and there were wounds all over his body. I shuddered to think what he'd been through.

'Where have you been?'

He rested his forehead against mine. 'To the pit of Anash.'

'Alexia,' Elhian said, kissing her hand when we went back inside. 'I'm glad to see you.'

'I'm so glad you're safe.' Alexia was carrying Eva on her hip.

'As am I,' Darj said. The two men gripped each other's forearms. 'How did you get here?'

'With difficultly, and a lot of assistance.'

I had to help him sit down. I kept staring at his face, taking in every detail, trying to convince myself that he was really back, that he was safe. *Thank you, Ru'ach*! I pressed his hand against my lips.

'Samela, could you please get us something to eat?' Darj asked.

'Certainly.' She gave a complying curtsey and added, 'It's not every day I have the opportunity to serve six members of royalty.'

Darj glanced around the room. 'Five,' he said.

'No, six in my eyes.' Samela gave Darj a shy smile before walking out of the hut.

Alexia arched an eyebrow. Darj's cheeks flushed mildly.

While Elhian ate and drank, I peeled off the crude bandages that were on his arms. Samela brought me a bowl of water, and I cleaned his wounds as carefully as I could.

'Thank you for bringing him back,' I said to Ren for a second time.

'My pleasure, but I didn't rescue him, you know. He did that himself and is the only person I have heard of to escape Sharlard.'

'I had help,' Elhian said again, cringing as I tried to get some dirt out of a slash on his arm.

'I need to take your shirt off. It's torn to shreds anyway.'

'No, there's no need, really.'

At first I was amused, thinking he was being modest, but he pulled away from me. 'What is it?'

When he didn't answer, I reached behind and lifted up his shirt before he could stop me.

I gasped. Across his back were innumerable lacerations. 'Oh, Elhian . . .'

'You were flogged?' Darj asked, his mouth dropping as well.

'More than once.' Elhian pulled his shirt down again. 'They really wanted to make me pay.' He picked up a cluster of grapes and pulled two off with his teeth.

'Grapes for me?' Eva asked, crawling out of Alexia's lap towards him.

'Here you are.' Elhian gave her some after seeking Alexia's nod of approval. 'Alexia,' he said, 'have you been all right? I mean, have you felt unwell at all?'

If only you knew, I thought, but Alexia's expression betrayed nothing.

Darj had been pouring himself a drink of water, but he looked up at Elhian's question. 'What do you know?'

'Remember that night when we fled Liane and I went after that last Zalem? I witnessed him opening the Dark Orb. Bylon, his name was.'

'Opening the what?' I asked.

I knew by the look on Prince Ren's face that he understood exactly what it was, but Elhian explained it for the rest of us.

'It's a device that looks like an orb a monarch holds at coronations, but which contains a sort of virus that works its way to the brain. It makes people sick and confuses their emotions. They call it the Zalems' Bane. It's what controls the Ghosts. It actually sustains them, in a way. I read about it once in a book of Cades', back when we lived in Semanez, but I've learnt much more about it in the last month or so.

'When I found Bylon, he was taking the vial of the Zalem's Bane out. Alexia, have you noticed a cut anywhere on your body?'

Alexia ran her fingers through her hair. 'Yes.'

'Can you show us?' Elhian asked. 'I think I should be able to tell if it's infected with the Bane by looking at it.'

Alexia didn't move.

'Does showing us require you to be immodest?' Elhian asked.

'A little. It's on my back.'

'Please,' Elhian said, 'we need to know what we are dealing with.'

Alexia sighed. 'Adaliah, can you undo the back of my dress, please?'

I moved over to her and carefully pulled the cords away. As soon as her skin was visible, we all took in a sharp breath. Alexia's entire lower back was swollen, covered in small bumps, and streaked with a purplish-red colour. It was the worst rash I had ever seen. There was a small curve cut in the middle of her back, right on her spine. A crescent moon. The purplish-red colour extended from that.

'Why didn't you say something?' Darj asked with astonishment.

'I . . . I don't know.'

Darj rubbed his face in his palms. 'You knew all along what they were doing to you . . . '

'No, not at first. I thought it was just a rash. Then when I realised . . . I'm sorry, I just didn't see the point in causing concern when there was no obvious solution.'

'Is it painful?' Ren asked.

Alexia's mouth twitched. 'Yes.'

I tied up her dress again, too shocked to say anything.

'This virus is what gives the High Zalem power then,' Ren said. 'Nothing else.'

'Yes,' Elhian said, 'but I don't know what's in the formula, so I don't know what the cure is or . . . ' He gave Alexia a sad look. 'Or if there is one. Bylon implied that the dose they gave Alexia was particularly toxic, potentially incurable if not treated in time.'

Alexia stared back at him with tired, almost bloodshot eyes. She closed her eyes, and I saw a tear drip down her face. I guess before there had been hope that something less sinister was at work, but now that hope was gone. At least one thing now made sense—the fit she'd had in the forest was the virus first reaching her system.

'Why me, particularly?' she asked. 'Do you know?'

'No, I'm afraid not,' Elhian said, giving her a look filled with apology. 'There was a man by the name of Sirvan, a Zalem soldier who makes me think of Jag as the embodiment of goodness. He slit the throat of the guard who was with me. We'd lost the other guard, Karlen. After killing the only thing that might get in the way, Sirvan captured me. It was so simply done. I was disgusted with myself for days. They blindfolded me and beat me when I tried to resist. I was in and out of it for what I think was several days.

'When I woke properly for the first time, it was so dark, I thought I was blind. My arms were chained above my head, and my feet weren't touching anything. I had no idea what was beneath them. I thought I would go mad. In the end, the only thing that seemed to keep me sane was focusing on a positive memory. Usually, it was a picture of you.' This time, he took my hand to his lips and kissed it. I ran my fingers over his wrists. The legacy of the chains was still there.

'What happened next?' I asked.

'I was left for ages—no food or water and no light.' He picked at a chipped fingernail as he spoke, and there was no valour in his words. 'I wanted to die in the end. I felt nothing more than a wraith.'

'How did you get out?' Darj asked.

'Eventually, Sirvan and a man called Cordale released me, and I was taken to see Bylon. The three of them told me it was time to pay. They beat me. I couldn't even think why they were doing this to me. Something about my father—that I'd killed my own father. The same thought torments me frequently, but it wasn't until Sirvan's boot connected with my skull that I began to wonder what I could have done differently.

'They made me stand, but I could only just manage it. The pain was so deep, it almost seemed surreal, like it was all a bad dream and would end any second.

'The next thing I knew, I was being taken out of the building to a cheering crowd. I was somewhere in an underground city. It was huge, and I was amazed at how it had been crafted amongst the stone. But the crowd wasn't cheering because they were happy to see me. They were rejoicing in my downfall. Sirvan and Cordale made me walk through them. They spat at me, threw fruit and stones, yelled at me, but I couldn't understand what they were saying.

'Later, I was thrown into a cell. The next day, I was beaten again but by two common guards who took me outside a cathedral for their own amusement. It was then that something I didn't expect happened. Did you know Zavad was captured as well?'

'Yes,' I said. 'We had heard that. Did you see him?'

'It's because of him that I'm alive.'

'Zavad helped you?' Alexia asked.

'Yes, more than you know. I am sure he will tell you about it one day, but all I know is that he was taken in the attack on Liane Palace and made to work in the city with a team of slaves. They were building a tunnel, another exit out of the city. He told me he'd been so scared when he'd arrived but had made a good friend with an orphan boy a bit younger than him—Dayle. Dayle couldn't remember a time of not being in the city, so he was scared to leave. Even so, the two of them hatched an escape plan that outsmarted their guards. They were acting on it when I was outside the cathedral. They were going well, too—I could hear guards yelling somewhere in the city, but the boys were well ahead and would have made it, I think. The thing is, Zavad saw me being beaten and called my name, recognising me despite my wounds. But my two guards heard him as well.

'I knew what Zavad was trying to do, and I couldn't let him fail in his escape. I used what strength I had to knock the first guard down. I told the boys to run, but they didn't. Instead, they ran to help me.'

'Brave boy,' Darj said. 'He will do great things one day.'

'He's already begun,' Elhian said. 'Of course, at that point neither of us won. The guards grabbed us, and we were all dragged to a couple of cells. I was tied up and face-down in the dirt. I couldn't find a way to breathe that didn't hurt. Zavad and Dayle were in the opposite cell. They hadn't been harmed, but they were bound, too. I was fairly sure we'd be hung in the morning. A guard was walking back and forth between the cells like a restless lion.

'A woman came into my cell some time later. I'd never seen her before, so I was inclined to distrust her at first. But then, she was the first person who didn't seem determined to draw my blood. I didn't understand the language when she spoke; she must have realised this as she indicated for me to be quiet instead. She wanted me to sit up, but it was easier said than done. She fetched a bowl of water and tended to my wounds. I think she was about to leave when Bylon came in behind her. He saw what she'd done, and they spoke together for a minute or so. Then, Bylon asked me where my wife was. I had no idea, of course, so he asked me what I knew about you instead.' His eyes focused on Alexia.

'What did you say?' she asked.

'He wanted to know if you have a "supernatural immunity".'

'What?' Alexia asked, frowning at the peculiar question.

'From what I understand, most people are completely overtaken by the Bane immediately, but you've resisted it—a more potent dose—for weeks. I told him I know you have Ru'ach on your side, that you will not be easily defeated, and that if his plan relies solely on that, we will gladly see him dead.'

Alexia gave him a nod of thanks.

'Bylon kicked me in the stomach and assured me their plan did not rest solely on that at all, but I think he was lying, at least in part. Anyway, he left me with the woman.'

Elhian fell silent and looked around at us all. Alexia was sitting on the bed, while Eva was keeping herself amused with her doll. Ren and Darj were seated in front of Elhian on the floor, the former resting back on his hands and the latter leaning up against the bed. We were all watching Elhian, taking in his words and processing them in quiet wonder. I continued to knead his hand.

'I'm not proud of what happened next,' he said.

'I'm sure you have nothing to be ashamed about,' Ren said. 'Not after all of this.'

'The thing is, the pain of my new injury was overwhelming. My head was spinning. I thought of Adaliah, of all they had done to me. They hadn't even given me a reason for it. It all boiled up inside me, and I snapped. I wrapped my arm around the woman's neck—not tightly enough to hurt her, but she grabbed at my arm and panicked, and the guard rushed in. I told him if he didn't want her to die, he'd better get out of my way. He laughed. "Where would you go?" he asked. "You can't even stand!"

'I dragged my legs up under me until I was on my knees. I pushed myself off the woman, stumbled to my feet, and pulled her up with me. "They say you hated your father," the guard said, "and yet, right now, there's no stronger reminder of him".'

Elhian stopped talking and took his hand away from mine. We were all holding our breath. All of us, especially me, knew how such a comment would have cut him.

'A memory came to me of when I was a little boy,' he said. 'For a moment, I was back in Semanez. I saw my father throttling my mother after he'd caught her giving food to some prisoners who had defied him. I can remember every detail—how she shook in his grip, how I thought Cades would kill her then, and how she yelled at me to get away. I tried to pull him off her, but he just shoved me to the ground. She survived that time, but her neck was black for a week.'

The memory was a heavy one, and it moved us to silence again. 'What did you do?' I asked quietly.

'I released her and struck the guard across the face, hard enough to make him fall. I grabbed his sword and brought the hilt down against the back of his head. I took his keys, let myself out, and locked the woman in behind me. I told her I was sorry, but I don't know if she understood me. I went to free the boys but was feeling lightheaded by then. I leant against the bars of their cell, and Zavad had to ask me for the keys to release his shackles and Dayle's and to unlock the door. Zavad offered to be my crutch, and Dayle followed his example on my other side. They helped me past several guards and all the way through the tunnels. I could not have done that by myself.

'We came to a blocked doorway, where Zavad had been working with his team of slaves. There was a section where they'd nearly broken through to the outside. We threw the stones and clumps of dirt aside until the space was big enough for us to get out. The boys pulled me through.' Elhian looked up at the nearby window. 'All of a sudden, we were outside in the blinding light. Dayle was turning about, trying to take everything in. He couldn't remember seeing the sky at all. "I never thought it would be this big, or the sun so bright and hot!" he said. His wonder reminded me how lucky I'd been.'

'Lucky?' I asked.

'Yes, lucky—lucky to be free, lucky to have lived at all . . . It almost seemed worth it to give Dayle back his life.

'I surveyed the landscape but saw no woods or trees—we were looking for water at this point. Beyond the cliff, I could see the green Targian fields and knew that's where we needed to head. In the other direction, there was nothing but stony ground and rocky hills. Zavad aptly called it a wasteland. He told Dayle about Targe. "It's full of life and goodness. We have a queen who cares about everyone and a warrior who nearly died saving us all".'

Elhian went on to explain that they travelled on foot for several hours until they were attracted by the sound of men over a small hill. There, they discovered a large army of Zalems preparing for battle.

'How many?' Darj asked.

'Thousands. Possibly tens of thousands. I'm sure they've mobilised since. They could be in Targe even as we speak.'

Alexia and Darj exchanged glances, and I knew they would discuss it more later.

'We had an incident with a guard who saw us spying on the army, and we only evaded him by stealing two nearby horses. Dayle couldn't ride, but he was able to sit behind Zavad, who—thanks to your training, Darj—is quite the horseman. We hurried all the way back into Targe and came to Hunt.'

Alexia cleared her throat. 'Did you see Jeri's grave?'

Elhian met her eyes with sadness. 'Yes . . . yes, I did. I hope you don't mind, Alexia, but I met Captain Xander in Hunt, told him of the army, and encouraged him to evacuate the people. He said he planned to fall back to Chettona.'

'I am glad they will be safe,' Alexia said, though I think she was now anxious to get back to her kingdom.

'I left Zavad and Dayle in Hunt with Xander. It was Xander who told me you had all travelled to Delya, so I had one meal with him and rode on.'

'I found him semi-conscious in a swamp two days ago,' Ren said, winking at me. 'Completely by chance! He was lost, sore, and feeling sorry for himself, I think.'

Elhian laughed a little at this. 'Yes, I was.' He turned to me. 'But not anymore.'

19
No Choice

Later that night, after we'd discussed everything at length, I collected my things to move into a small room with Elhian, separate from the others. Alexia watched as I packed up but didn't say anything. Her words were becoming fewer and fewer, and I was deeply concerned about her—about the pain she was in—but I didn't know what to do.

As I was leaving, Darj arrived to pack his things up, too.

'I think it's best if I share a hut with Ren tonight. I don't want Alexia losing her reputation now that you won't be here.' He gave the queen a quick smile, but she didn't seem to hear him. 'Alexia?'

'Yes?' She rubbed her arm and looked out over the fen. 'Darj . . . Adaliah . . . You do understand that whatever I do, I only do it with the safety of my kingdom and loved ones in mind, don't you?'

'Alexia.' I searched her blue eyes. 'Whatever you're thinking, martyrdom isn't the answer. You must know that.'

'And you don't always have to be so brave, you know,' Darj said.

'That's the thing. Sometimes, I do.'

The following day, Alexia and I joined Prince Ren and the others in the search for Amaz's treasure. 'He hid it well,' Ren said as he led us through the swamps. 'My father was with him at the time and wrote about it in his journal after Amaz died. I suppose he didn't want the information to be lost.'

The air around us was still and heavy. Somewhere in the distance, a bird was making a sharp, irritating sound, like someone scraping rock against glass. We sloshed through the watery ground in a line, grabbing the tall, skinny trees to propel ourselves forward. Before long, we were all covered in mud, even Alexia.

'At least it keeps the insects off our skin.' I eyed the unusually large mosquitoes that were hovering near my face.

'Here it is,' Prince Ren said, stopping by one of the trees.

'Where? Alel and I came past here numerous times.' Darj put his hands on his hips and looked around again.

Prince Ren pointed to the tree and the Zalem symbol that had been engraved deeply into its bark.

'All right, but where's the treasure?' Darj asked.

'Under the water?' I pointed to the base of the tree, where the water was at least knee-deep.

Darj looked at Ren, who nodded. Darj and Alel kneeled and began to dig through the mud with their hands.

I studied Alexia while they waited. She was hot and pallid. I closed my eyes and prayed that whatever they found, it would bring my Alexia back. With Elhian by my side again, it was the only other thing I wished for. I touched her arm. To my surprise, she didn't flinch or pull away. She just gave me a tired look.

'There is something down here.' Alel shoved his hand further into the mud and grappled with whatever it was. 'It's metal.'

Darj furrowed his brows as he fiddled with the same object. 'There are handles.' He struggled with it until they both got a firm grip. 'Ready? Lift!'

It took a minute of them wrestling with it before enough air got in underneath, but it finally sprang free, and the two of them launched it out of the water.

The mud slowly fell away. Alel cupped some water in his hand and poured it over the object.

Underneath was a small box, heavily gilded. Alexia moved closer and wiped the mud off the top, revealing a green emblem with twelve stars. 'The royal seal.' She tried to open it, but it didn't budge. She ran her finger over six tiny holes that were beneath the seal. Closer inspection revealed a faint engraving there shaped like a butterfly.

'The Armoured Butterfly was the key,' she said. 'It was the key to ensure only one of the Ordained could open it.'

'But the Armoured Butterfly is gone,' I said.

Alexia turned to Prince Ren. 'My time just ran out.'

I woke the next morning and smiled to myself when I realised I was back in my husband's arms, just as I'd hoped and prayed, but when I heard Eva calling for her mother somewhere outside, the hairs on my arms prickled.

I held my breath and waited for Alexia to call her daughter in turn, but only silence followed. Eva started to cry.

I shook Elhian awake. 'What is it?' he asked groggily.

'Listen.' I waited for him to register the sound of Eva crying.

The two of us stepped outside and found Eva standing on a small, wooden bridge. 'Come here, darling,' I said.

'Where's Mother?' she asked with a sob.

I bent down. 'It's all right,' I said, opening my arms. 'We'll go and look for her.'

'Is she sick again?' Eva didn't move any closer.

I lowered my arms. Eva's blue eyes were brimming with tears, and she looked both tired and vulnerable. I could also see that the top of her hair was damp. I gave her a smile, stepped closer, and took her hand in mine. Elhian and I walked with her back to Alexia's hut.

The first thing I noticed was that Alexia's bow and arrows were gone. Her bed hadn't been slept in, and a note lay on Eva's bed. I clasped my hand over my mouth to stop myself from saying something that would worry Eva, but the dread of it filled me. All I could think of was the words she'd said to Darj: *The only way out is if I were the one to die first.*

'Where is she?' Darj asked, hurrying in behind us. 'I heard the princess . . . ' He noticed the absence of Alexia's bow and arrows and fell silent. I bent down to pick up the letter. 'Read it aloud,' he said.

I didn't appreciate his terseness but knew it was his fear speaking. 'She writes, "I have gone to do my duty. Return to Targe. Take the princess to Liane. Do not disobey me; it is no longer safe".' I turned it over. Hurriedly scrawled on the back were the words, 'I love you all.' Tears prick in my eyes as I held it up for Darj to read.

Ren entered the shack, too. 'She's gone, then,' he said.

'Yes.' I touched the top of Eva's damp head again and realised Alexia had wept a goodbye over her sleeping daughter before running into the darkness.

'You knew about this?' Darj's hand tightened into a fist as he turned to Ren. 'You knew she was going to throw herself into their hands?'

'What choice did she have?' Ren asked. 'She knew they were following her. If she hadn't gone, they would have assassinated you all. That is what the poem says.' He turned to Elhian. 'Why do you think they took you? Revenge? Yes, but you were also bait, a ransom for her. They didn't expect you to escape, but they used it to follow you to Delya, to her.'

Elhian faced paled. 'But I was careful . . . '

'You can never be too careful for them.' Elhian opened his mouth again, but Ren quelled his defence with a raised hand. 'She knew they were here and gave herself up instead. She has done this for you all, and she has bought Targe time. Now, if you are smart, you will use this time to figure out how to save her. She needs a cure. Here is what I suggest.'

Ren pulled out a square, flat piece of material from his pocket. He unfolded it and showed us a stitched map with the Targian land marked in green and Delya in yellow. Kest, Casmodia, and the edge of Jazmarda were all visible in their colours as well, with small, black dots marking the major cities. 'Where is Sharlard?' Ren asked.

Elhian pointed to the eastern mountains beyond Targe. 'Here, but it is well hidden. You would only know where to find it if you had been there before. Here is where we saw the army of soldiers.' Elhian moved his finger slightly in a southwestern direction. 'They will most likely follow the same path as I did with the boys; it is the only place smooth enough to carry so many horses and men.'

'Darj,' Ren said, 'I suggest I meet you here in four weeks.' He pointed to a blank space on the map, about one finger-width south of Hunt and near the base of the eastern mountains where Elhian had indicated the path. 'I will bring my best dagger fighters. You rally the Targians. Elhian, you may even have time to send for your army.'

Darj thought about this with folded arms. 'Why are you doing this?'

'Isn't it obvious?' Ren folded the map and put it back in his pocket. 'We must all work together to defeat them, or they will overtake Targe, then Delya, Casmodia, maybe even Jazmarda. We Delyans missed the opportunity to eradicate them centuries ago, and we are determined to learn from our mistakes. So, better we defeat them outside their lair than wait until they kill thousands of innocents, wouldn't you say?'

20
From Hunt to Chettona

'I will take Eva and Amaz's box to Liane,' Darj said as he threw his saddle on poor Guntar the next day. 'I will call up the army. Elhian, you should go to Casmodia to rally yours. Adaliah, visit Hunt and Chettona before joining me at Liane. See if you can find out where Alexia has gone.'

'Wouldn't she have gone to Sharlard?' I asked.

'Their army is in Targe,' Darj said.

'I will travel with Adaliah,' Elhian said. 'When I was in Hunt, I came across Casmodian soldiers who had been sent to search for me. I sent them back with instructions to bring the Casmodian army to Liane.'

'Good,' Darj said. 'I will see you there.'

'General?' a soft voice called. We turned and found Samela coming towards us. 'I know you must go, but I would like to give you a gift to thank you for getting us safely to Tydell.' She held out a small, hide bag secured with drawstrings. Darj took the gift, loosened the drawstrings, and pulled out a bottle of a honey-coloured substance. 'It's Delyan myrrh,' Samela said. 'It has many healing properties, and it may prove useful. I'd like you to have it.'

'Thank you,' Darj said, his tone softer. He put the bottle back in the bag and drew the strings again. 'I will keep it with me.'

Both Elhian and Darj had been right—Hunt was the first stop for the Zalems. I could tell they were already there as we drew close to the town almost a week later—not because it was forebodingly quiet, but because I could feel a darkness oppressing me as we rode through the outer fields.

Anash has made his home here.

'I think we should leave the horses here,' Elhian said, meaning the empty farm we were cutting across.

We walked into Hunt from there, hiding behind buildings and making our way to the town centre. It had seemed quiet from a distance, but now we could see it was full of people—and all of them Zalems. They were occupying the town like it was their own.

We hid in the back of one house for several hours, listening and watching for any sign of Alexia. From the only window we had, I could see Jeri's grave split in two and desecrated with the Zalems' crescent moon and eye, just as Xander had told us. It was a painful sight. I hoped Alexia would be spared from it.

I turned to Elhian. 'I'm so glad you're here with me. I'm no longer afraid somehow.' I gave him a kiss.

'I know. I feel the same.' He kissed my forehead.

A few minutes later, the Zalems began to file past us towards Jeri's grave. Around three hundred gathered there, and a man seemed to be in the centre of them all. 'That's Bylon,' Elhian whispered to me.

Bylon gestured to someone, and I knew before I saw her it was Alexia. 'What's she doing?' I asked, instinctively reaching for my sword.

'Wait,' Elhian said. 'Just watch.'

Bylon put a hand on Alexia's shoulder and pressed down until she lowered herself to her knees. Her hands were tied behind her back, and it was Bylon who carried her bow and arrows now. Behind her stood a half-circle of men and women with hooded faces, each of them holding a burning torch in their left hand. None of them spoke, and I knew they were waiting for their king.

When he first appeared, I somehow understood he was the High Zalem. It must have been the presence he brought with him, for it certainly wasn't his appearance. I had expected him to be ugly and deformed, but he was breathtakingly handsome—tall, tanned, with well-toned muscles and a thick crop of fair hair that made him look more youthful than I think he was. His eyes were deep set and attractive. It was only his smile, thin and lustful, that looked untruthful, like a moon lingering in a blue sky.

I felt an overwhelming power rise up within me.

The Jazmardian blessing.

This is the man I have to kill.

The High Zalem walked towards Alexia and cut the ties that bound her hands. He pulled her to her feet and planted his mouth on hers before she could protest.

I moved towards the door, pulling out my sword.

Elhian grabbed my arm. 'No.'

'Let me go! I can't stand by and watch him touch her like that. He's the one I need to kill!'

'Yes, but not now! You wouldn't even reach him with all those Zalems out there!'

The men and women standing around Alexia and the High Zalem unsheathed their swords and bowed their heads. Bylon approached the High Zalem and uncovered the Dark Orb. He set it on the ground, and segments of it opened out like orange pieces separating from each other.

The sun was already setting, but now its rays were entirely diminished as the sky darkened with an edgeless storm. Black clouds billowed across the expanse, blocking the first stars and the rising crescent moon.

The High Zalem watched the clouds form with satisfaction. He sneered at Alexia, who had fallen to her knees again. Everyone watched as she stood and met his eyes with a menacing smile. Her eyes were icy blue, the only colour visible in the dark night. The High Zalem smiled to see them, and I knew then the Zalems' Bane had done its work. The virus had completely taken her over.

She was his.

I felt a physical pain in my heart as Elhian and I snuck out of Hunt and back to our horses. The old Alexia had faded, but she had still been good. I knew she had done this for us, to save us, but it didn't make it any easier. I'd grown up with her. She'd always been a part of my life. It was her loving guard over Targe that inspired so many men to fight for their kingdom, for her. It was her faith in me that made me feel I could do anything. How could I feel that now?

'We should have done something,' I said to Elhian.

'Adaliah, you know we would have been quickly overpowered,' he said, but his voice was shaking a little. 'This is dreadful, but if we remain free, we can still do something to save her.'

We rode on to Chettona and, in so doing, gradually escaped the dark cloud the High Zalem had caused to form over Hunt. By the time we'd ridden past Mount Dennell, we could see the night stars again. We stopped and slept for about three hours but were woken up by calls in the night.

I raised myself into a sitting position, Bagred standing behind me with his ears perked and his eyes alert.

'What was that?' Elhian asked when another call echoed around us.

'It's a different language . . . ' I scanned the flat plains around us. I saw them, and a lump grew in my throat. 'There.'

I pointed at an army of men marching through the grass. They were armed for battle: archers, cavalry, and infantry. The calls seemed to be from commander to commander.

Elhian counted their battalions. 'It's not all of them,' he said. 'The ones I saw outside Sharlard, I mean. But there's still a few thousand of them.'

They were setting a steady pace and were diligent in their march. Their unified steps pounded the ground with unnerving resolve, and I knew then we would see the same resolve in battle. These men were not the drabs of a dying kingdom or a rabble of militia. They were focused soldiers. With this sort of devotion, they could easily make the High Zalem king of all and set my cousin as the queen by his side. Until then, I had not embraced the thought as a real possibility. I had underestimated the enemy and assumed that, despite everything, we would be victorious.

I'd taken far too much for granted.

'They're heading to Chettona,' I said.

Elhian stood and grabbed his things. 'We need to ride. Now.'

Five days later, we came to the eastern gate of Chettona just as dawn was breaking.

'Let them in. Hurry!'

I couldn't see who the voice belonged to, but the gate began to lift. One look around the town and I breathed a sigh of relief: they had prepared for battle. Soldiers lined the walls and the streets, all of them armed, quiet and ready. A division marched past us as we rode to the stables at the barracks. There, Elhian found Leuk and greeted him with a quick pat.

'This way, Your Majesties,' a soldier said. He led us to the top of the wall.

There, Xander and Raggin stood shoulder-to-shoulder, looking out over the plains in front of them. Xander's hair was tied up, and Raggin looked like he was carrying less weight.

'Captains?' I whispered, for speaking out loud in such a tense atmosphere seemed inappropriate.

The captains turned and nodded their greetings at us.

'You know the army approaches?' Elhian asked.

'Yes,' Xander said, 'our scouts spotted them yesterday. I sent for men from the nearby villages. They joined us this morning.'

If the army kept up the pace I'd seen that night, they would only be a few hours behind.

'I cannot fight,' I said, 'but I can help the wounded.'

The sun was rising over the Targian countryside. I couldn't help but notice the deep blue of the sky or the thick scent of spring flowers on the wind. The beauty of everything seemed to be accentuated.

'Do you ever wonder how we get to this point?' Raggin asked. 'How it is we live our lives peacefully one minute and face battle the next? Who are these people that think they can come and steal our peace? We shouldn't have to spend our lives fighting to keep it.'

Xander turned to Raggin, disbelieving. 'Isn't that a bit deep for you, particularly at this hour of the morning?'

Raggin rolled his eyes. 'I just restrain my intelligence around you, so you don't feel too much of a lesser being. That's how kind I am, you see. Besides, we wouldn't want Jacinth to find out the truth about you now.'

'Captains!' Elhian said, pointing out into the distance.

Raggin, Xander, and I all looked up. In the far distance stood a long line of soldiers—the frontline of the Zalem army.

They came closer and closer, and I could feel the tension in the men around me increasing. 'There's too many,' Xander said.

'Well,' Raggin said as they stopped just out of range of our archers. 'I guess we should go and talk to them.'

But before any of us could take a step, a catapult arm flipped into the sky and launched a heavy projectile.

'Get down!' I yelled.

The soldiers around me ducked behind the wall. It shook from the impact.

I leant over the wall and checked the damage. There was dust everywhere, and stones had fallen to the ground. 'They're going to break their way in.'

'We can't defend against heavy machinery,' Raggin said. 'Why didn't our scouts see them?'

'I don't know,' Xander said.

'They didn't have them with them the other night.' Elhian looked at me as if seeking reassurance he hadn't been completely blind. I shook my head. I hadn't seen them either.

The wall trembled as it took another hit.

One of our archers shot at the catapult. The arrow curved into the sky and fell short.

'Get my horse,' Xander said. 'Get the other horsemen. We will hit and run.'

'Have you lost your mind?' Elhian asked.

'What are we supposed to do? Let them destroy the town and its people?'

I could see Raggin thinking, a rare, serious expression on his face. 'Wait,' he said. 'Oil. We need fire and black oil. And archers.'

'What?' Xander asked.

Raggin ran towards the stairs. 'Xander, come with me.'

It took me some time to understand Raggin's plan. Once I did, I knew it was doomed to fail, but nothing Elhian or I said had any impact on his decision.

'As captain, I only answer to General Darj and Queen Alexia,' he said. 'And they're not here.'

Within the hour, he and Xander rode to the eastern gate of Chettona with fifty horsemen. Twenty of the horsemen were mounted archers, and one was a torchbearer.

'Are you ready?' Xander asked.

'Yes,' Raggin said. 'Open the gate!'

A catapulted rock hit the gate and broke through altogether, filling the air with splinters. A piece of wood landed in Raggin's leg. He pulled it out before the pain registered.

'Open the gate!' he yelled again, affronted.

The doors opened, and the fifty horsemen rode out while Elhian and I stayed on top of the wall. We were to send out more men in ten minutes to rescue them if Raggin's plan didn't succeed.

'This is a death ride,' Elhian said.

The Zalem army had drawn closer to us, but the infantry and cavalry stopped again. It seemed they were waiting until the catapults brought down the gate and walls before attacking the town itself.

'Oil ready!' Raggin called as the broken gate closed behind him and his riders. He reached down and pulled out a small, leather bag from his saddle. It was full of black oil. Xander and the horsemen grasped one each as well. They rode towards the enemy, towards the first of three catapults.

Arrows flew past them as they drew closer. Two soldiers fell. I closed my eyes, expecting them to be dead within minutes.

How will we explain this to Darj?

I heard Xander yell something, but they were already too far away for their voices to be clear. The mounted archers loaded their bows. The torchbearer, who up until that point had been riding at the back of the unit, now came up on their right side. The archers held out their arrows, and the torchbearer lit them as he passed.

'So far, so good,' I whispered to myself. I hadn't dared to hope. I shot up a quick prayer to Ru'ach.

Protect them, please.

The Zalem army sent their two front lines to attack. Xander yelled at his men again, ducking an arrow.

The unit dug their heels into their horses and trampled the men in front of them. They threw their leather bags at the catapult, and the archers followed with their fire arrows.

The result was much grander than I'd anticipated. Flames engulfed the wooden catapult. The men who had been operating it caught on fire, too. Screams filled the air; I could hear them from the wall.

The unit didn't stop. Raggin drew ahead as they rode along the front of the Zalem army towards the second catapult.

The Zalems were charging at them from all sides now. The Targian horsemen unsheathed their swords and slayed those within arm's reach, making the most of their height and speed.

Two Targians fell down dead as they neared the second catapult. Xander reached for the next leather bag and threw it as soon as he was close enough. The others did the same. The torchbearer lit the second round of arrows, and the archers released their shots.

This time the catapult exploded altogether, sending wood flying in all directions. It took at least ten men with it and burned a large circle of grass. The fiery oil spat through the air and landed on some of the Zalems' clothes.

A volley of arrows rained on the unit, killing six or seven of them, including two archers. Xander and Raggin yelled and pointed ahead of them. They didn't want their remaining men to hesitate.

The third catapult pitched another rock towards us.

'Brace!' Elhian called. I ducked for cover next to him. I thought it was going to go straight through my middle this time. Dust and bits of stone fell over us like rain. I clasped my hands over my head and felt the noise of it shaking me.

Three men died within a few steps of me.

Raggin flung his last bag of oil at the final catapult. Xander did the same, and then the others. They veered their horses away and began to ride back to us. We cheered them on.

But seconds passed, and nothing happened.

I glanced back at the catapult. There was no fire, no hint of smoke. A minute passed. Still nothing.

Raggin had noticed by then as well. 'Archers!' he yelled.

They shouted back at him, and he turned to see what was going on.

They were riding after him but pointing to something further back on the field. I followed their gestures and realised there lay a fallen Targian. The torchbearer.

The torch was still burning in the dead man's hand, but the archers had no fire to light their arrows.

Elhian banged his fist against the wall.

I don't know what I thought they would do. I just wanted them to reach Chettona and the safety of the walls. Raggin's plan had succeeded in part. That was enough and much more than I thought they'd achieve. They were riding away from the army, but the Zalems would soon catch up and engulf them like an army of ants engulfs a piece of meat. 'Hurry up,' I said under my breath.

Raggin hesitated and slowed his horse.

'What's he doing?' I wondered aloud.

He turned and rode back past Xander.

'What are you doing, you idiot?' Xander yelled after him.

Raggin didn't answer. Xander began to ride after him, but his horse stumbled over some uneven ground and skidded into the dirt. Xander's lower body was trapped beneath the horse, its leg surely broken.

While the last soldiers rode to help Xander, Raggin galloped back to the dead torchbearer and jumped off his horse. He raised his sword against the cluster of Zalems that quickly surrounded him. He kicked and fought them off, slaying as many as he could as fast as he could.

It didn't take long for him to tire, and then one of the Zalems pushed him down. Raggin fell onto the torchbearer's body. When one of the Zalems kicked his sword away, Raggin held his arms out.

'What's he doing?' I asked again.

Elhian didn't answer; I turned and realised he was gone. A moment later, I saw him galloping out of Chettona, he and Leuk a white blur as they rode hard towards Raggin.

I put a hand over my heart. *No!*

'It's been eight minutes,' a soldier nearby said, pointing to a time glass. 'If they don't get back inside these walls now, you must send more men out.'

I didn't answer.

Come on, Raggin! Get up!

The Zalems were pointing at Raggin and laughing.

Leuk tore up the ground as he and his rider thundered towards them.

'Your Majesty?' the soldier asked, more urgently.

'Just give them a minute!'

I held my breath.

Ride, Elhian!

The archers had nearly freed Xander.

'Come on, come on,' I muttered.

A Zalem near Raggin fell down dead. Elhian had somehow procured a bow and arrows. He shot another Zalem, and a third. Now with some space around him, Raggin scrambled to his feet and impaled another two Zalems. Elhian rode down several on his horse, now fiercely slashing them with his sword. He reached Raggin, grabbed his outstretched forearm, and wrenched him up onto Leuk's back.

Raggin had the torch.

Across the field, Xander was freed. The archers remounted and began riding to Raggin and Elhian, shooting the Zalems on Leuk's heels as soon as they were close enough. Then, the archers changed their arrows back and rode by Raggin to light them. One of them was forced to shoot his fire arrow at a large man who stood in their path. The Zalem fell to his knees in flames.

Only four fire arrows remained.

Elhian and Raggin charged towards Chettona, while the archers rode back towards the catapult. One of the horses was stabbed through its chest and fell to its knees, taking another archer with it.

The final three rode around him and fired.

The arrows hit their mark. The catapult was immediately covered in flames, and the blue sky was soon overtaken by swelling plumes of smoke.

21
A FIELD OF SPIRITS

Our celebrations increased when the Zalems began to move away from Chettona and Elhian, Raggin, Xander, and the surviving riders returned to safety inside the walls.

'See,' Raggin said shortly afterwards, all of them once again on the wall, 'they're running with their tails between their legs!' He laughed heartily, but I could hear nerves in the sound more than anything. One of the men handed him a drink. It shook in his hand.

Elhian watched the Zalems and listened to them call out to each other. They were moving into formation again, marching in that same cold manner we'd witnessed on our travels from Hunt.

'Elhian?' I asked.

'I don't think they're running,' he said, still catching his breath after his rescue. 'They could still easily defeat us if they wanted. I think something else has drawn their attention.'

My mind filled with possible scenarios: perhaps Darj was bringing soldiers for us, or Prince Ren, or Lord Fenton and the queen's council . . . But how could any of them know we needed aid? Elhian and I hadn't had time to send a message, and while one of Xander's men had ridden for Liane in the morning, there was no way he could have reached the city already, let alone brought back reinforcements.

'Send a scout or two to follow them,' I said to Xander, who had just staggered up to the top of the wall. 'In the meantime, let's strengthen the eastern gate.'

We instructed some of the Targian soldiers to escort the civilians from Hunt and Chettona to Liane. With the battle so close by, it was important they were well out of the village, and now they had time to reach clearance. It was two hours later, as we lifted another heavy bar up against the gate, that the scout returned.

'You were right,' he said to us, grinning. 'They were drawn away by something else.'

'What?' Xander asked.

'The Casmodians. King Elhian's men! As I was leaving, the Casmodians were riding to engage with the Zalems.'

The effect on Elhian was instant—pride rose in his face, and it warmed me to see him so encouraged. 'How many do you think there were?' Elhian asked.

'Quite a contingent, but not as many as the Zalems. They will need help, sire.'

'Of course,' Elhian said. 'We will ride out to join them at once.'

We left a few soldiers on the wall and inside the village. While I knew I had to stay out of any fighting, I was determined to ride with Elhian and the others, at least to the edge of battle. I could help the wounded on the plains, which could be the difference between life and death for them.

We rode for over an hour before we reached the battleground. But there was no battle to join. There was no fighting, no army, no men. At least, no men still alive.

Instead, hundreds of bodies lay ahead of us, lying like battle-worn dummies across a field stained with blood, mud, and death. We stopped and stared. The air was ripe with butchery. We could smell it.

At first, there were no words. Elhian dismounted and walked to one of the soldiers. He picked up a Casmodian banner, now sullied and torn. The blue material flickered in the wind as he held it up. 'They were destroyed,' he said. 'We're too late.'

He looked back at me, but there was nothing I could add. It was all too simple: the Zalems had run to meet these soldiers and killed every one of them.

I also knew that news of it would reach Casmodia, that Elhian would be held responsible for the wanton death of so many Casmodian soldiers. *You let them die for Targe.* I could hear the Casmodian council's voices ringing in my ears even then.

We guided our horses between the dead. The Casmodian blue tunics were still visible underneath the blood and dirt stains. We split up and surveyed the field of men, sifting through them in hope of finding life, but not one gave breath. I stopped Bagred near an older man with a nice face. A spear protruded from his middle.

Raggin shivered at the deathly silence. 'The air is filled with spirits. Ru'ach is drawing them to him.'

I was struck with a thought and turned back to Elhian. 'Where would the Zalems have gone?'

Elhian gave me a panicked look when he realised what I meant. 'Chettona!'

We saw the smoke before the town; it billowed into the sky like a volcano had been disturbed. Red embers circled around in hot wind and fell on our clothes as we drew close to the charred walls. Every house had been set alight, and the few Targian soldiers who had remained to defend the village were now bodies burning in a heap at the town centre. The stench was overwhelming. Some of the men vomited. A couple of horses reared and threw their riders.

Raggin rode ahead of us, dismounted, and kicked a burning piece of wood with a yell. He pulled a dagger out of his belt.

'What are you doing?' Xander asked.

'Ival would never have let this happen,' Raggin said. 'Darj certainly wouldn't have.' His eyes were reddening with tears and the smoke. 'Her Majesty trusted me with Chettona. I knew it was a mistake.'

'These are just houses,' Xander said, dismounting, too. 'They can be rebuilt. The people were sent to safety, and our army still stands. That matters more than this.'

'Assuming the people make it to Liane.' Raggin eyed the dagger, tears rolling down his face.

Xander snatched it out of his hand. 'This is as much my fault as it is yours, but I will not see more blood shed over it.'

'This is my fault, too,' I whispered to Elhian. 'I should have stayed here instead of following you onto the plains.'

'I shouldn't have let so many men come with us.'

'We were over-confident.'

'We assumed we were doing the right thing.'

'We didn't stop to ask, to pray . . .'

'But . . . but it was a reasonable risk, wasn't it?' Elhian ran his hands through his hair. 'We couldn't let the Casmodians face the Zalems alone . . .'

'And yet they died anyway.'

I thought of Alexia and looked down. A tear dripped onto the ash at Bagred's hooves.

I'm sorry, Ru'ach. I'm sorry, dear cousin. We have failed you both in every possible way.

22
THE TARGIAN ORB

I hoped when Liane came into view that life would make sense again, that I would feel more in control than I had since the loss of Chettona.

But I only felt alone.

The people came out of their houses when we entered the city. They pressed around us, and the crowd seemed to grow and grow by the second. Some of them were residents of Chettona and Hunt, searching for their loved ones amongst our soldiers.

'Save us, A'zyon Warrior!'

'Where is our queen?'

'What happened to Chettona?'

'Is she dead?'

'Are we at war?'

The public voice grew louder and louder, and it was all I could do to not show emotion. I did not want to panic them. They would find out soon enough how dire our situation was.

The palace loomed in front of us, still wounded and blackened from the first attack on the princess' birthday. I raised my eyes in search of the royal ensign. It was gone, marking Alexia's absence.

I found Darj sitting with the princess in her chambers, several of the queen's maids in attendance. Eva ran to me when I came into the room but paused, like she'd thought I was her mother but then realised I wasn't. 'You're back,' she said, and I felt desperation in her embrace when I picked her up.

'Yes, darling.'

'Where's Mother?'

'She'll be back soon, my princess. She loves you very, very much.' I kissed her cheek, hoping it would make her certain of it.

I carried her towards Darj. He looked like he hadn't slept since the last time I saw him. I squeezed his shoulder affectionately, wishing I had the words to bring him comfort or hope. Instead, all I had to tell him was what we'd seen in Hunt and how we'd lost Chettona and a battalion of Elhian's men. How we'd failed.

'The beginning of the end, then,' he whispered when I finished. 'Anash's power is strong.'

'Not as strong as Ru'ach's. And I will not be defeated, not while there is still breath in Alexia's body or Eva's. And I know you will not either, whatever you might say now.'

I heard a growing noise outside the princess' window and stepped towards it. 'You must speak to them,' I said, pointing at the hundreds of men and women walking towards the palace. The royal guards were trying to hold them back, but the people were pressing against them. 'They deserve to know the truth as much as anyone.'

Darj walked out onto the queen's balcony with Elhian and me behind him. The people below us were yelling, begging for attention, but they stopped as soon as Darj appeared.

He didn't know what to say. The queen had always been much loved, particularly after the Northern Invasion, and the kingdom had endured more than enough pain in recent years. Almost everyone knew someone who had been killed as part of Cades' rampage, and both Darj and Alexia had declared they would do all they could to stop it from happening again.

'General, tell us what's going on!' one of them yelled when he hesitated. 'Will we have to abandon Targe?' The people began to call out again with similar sentiments, and the palace guards yelled back at them in turn, trying to keep them in order.

Darj raised his hands to silence them. 'Her Majesty has been taken by a sect called the Zalems.' He paused as a hum of concern and disbelief spread across the crowd. 'These people seek to swallow her and Targe in their evil. Because of this, we are at war.' Darj spoke each word carefully, so there was no misunderstanding him. The concern amongst the crowd was now replaced with stillness. 'But we will not leave Liane or Targe until there is no hope. This is your home, and you must help us defend it. Chettona and Hunt have fallen, and we will soon face battle again. Every man who can fight will be asked to take up his sword or bow and do whatever is required to help the queen return to her throne, to help vanquish this evil. Your strength and faith helped us defeat Cades and many other villains in the past. We have done it before, and we will do it . . . ' He stopped.

'Darj?' I asked.

He was focusing on something beyond the crowd, something in the sky. I followed his line of sight.

'The High Zalem's storm,' I whispered.

Elhian gripped my hand as we watched the dark storm billow across the sky. The last light of the day was quickly bested, and black clouds hung close to the earth.

The reach of his evil is spreading.

The people began to panic. Some ran away from the palace; some screamed. Others said nothing but stared at the phenomenon with open mouths.

'Adaliah, get your sword—the Armoured Butterfly sword,' Darj said.

'The butterfly is gone.'

'The High Zalem's power is growing by the minute. Just get it. We have to get into Amaz's box now!'

I ran along the palace gallery towards the guest chambers Elhian and I were staying in. I passed portraits of the royal family, including one of myself when I was a lady of Targe. At the end of the hall was Alexia's most recent picture. Despite Darj's urgency, I paused to look at it. She had been painted wearing the Targian crown and the white gown she'd worn upon returning to Liane after Cades' defeat. She held the sceptre in her right hand, a symbol of her authority over the people.

My eyes fell to her left hand. There, the queen held the Targian Orb, a golden orb with thin, gold-leafed waves wrapped around it, which actually represented the breath of Ru'ach. The orb was held in recognition of the monarch's care over the realm's faith. It was only used for formal occasions, and I hadn't seen it since Alexia's coronation.

'Of course.' I tried to remember where it was kept. 'The Jewel Room.' The room was near the palace chapel, the royal family's private place of worship used to pray for strength and guidance. Alexia had spent much time there leading up to the Northern Invasion, but I knew she hadn't frequented it much since, despite making peace with Ru'ach just before Eva was born. I hurried past, reached the Jewel Room, and grabbed the golden door handle.

It was locked.

I rattled it and then slammed my hand against the thick, wooden panels.

'That room is only accessible to myself and the Queen of Targe,' a voice said. I turned and saw a man walking towards me. 'I am Archbishop Dennear,' he said, though I remembered him well enough from the princess' birthday party, when he had told Alexia to marry again.

'Then let me in! I need to look at the Targian Orb—it may help us save Her Majesty!'

The archbishop scoffed. 'There are no clues for anything on the orb. It is merely a ceremonial piece.'

'No, you don't understand.'

'If Her Majesty had married when she had the chance, she may not be in this predicament.'

'What? What do you mean?'

'If she had married, the High Zalem would have less reason to pursue her now. She has put us all at risk.'

I thought about this and noticed that Dennear was avoiding eye contact with me, as if he'd said too much. 'I don't imagine that would be enough to stop the High Zalem,' I said. 'He would just kill whomever her husband . . . ' My mouth dropped. 'Ethaniel . . . Is that why Cades killed Ethaniel?' I stepped to the archbishop and pushed him up against the door of the Jewel Room. 'Why?' I shouted in his face. 'Why does the High Zalem want to take her as his own? Tell me the truth!'

Dennear pushed me hard. I fell to the ground, landing on my wrist. It didn't break, but I felt my muscle weaken. Dennear tried to get away. I put my foot out to trip him. He sprawled onto the floor and kicked towards me.

I felt his foot connect with my calf. I launched myself towards him before he could get away, and the two of us wrestled on the ground. He pulled at my hair, but I soon had him pinned to the floor with both hands above his head.

'You are supposed to be a man of faith! Now tell me the truth—why her and not any other woman? Why were they so desperate for it to be her that they murdered her husband?'

'Maybe you should have asked her father before he died,' Dennear said.

Then, he spat fully in my face.

I resisted the temptation to slap him, wiping the spit off with one hand instead. A ceramic vase was sitting on a table next to the Jewel Room door. I grabbed it before Dennear could move, swung it back towards him and hit him on the side of the head. He was knocked senseless, and yet, no blood had been spilt.

I put the unscathed vase back and searched Dennear for the key. He had a ring of them tied to his belt. Most were gold, and only two were silver. I started with the largest gold one and tried eight keys on the door before I came to the smallest. It slipped inside the lock, and the door opened.

The Jewel Room was dark. I opened the curtain near the single window and was confused when I was confronted with darkness there as well, but the sight of the storm reminded me of the importance of my mission. I turned to light one of the torches on the wall with a nearby piece of flint.

It caught fire. My eyes adjusted, and I could see the room more clearly. Inside a massive, glass-topped table at the centre of the room was the most important jewel—the Targian crown. Alexia had many tiaras, diadems, and crowns, but no other announced her power and authority as impressively as this one, with its twelve gold stars and interwoven strands of precious metals. In another cabinet lay a range of the royal family's most valuable jewellery, and in another, the sceptre. I studied it for any hints, but there was only the old Targian adage carved into it: 'Remember those who died, but fight for those who live.'

The next thing I found was the Targian sword. By stealing it, Cades had officially started the Northern Invasion, yet now it looked no more consequential than the red cushion it lay on. The word 'Love' remained engraved just above the handle.

I continued my hunt for the orb. It wasn't in any of the glass-topped cases; I double-checked them to make sure. I started opening cupboard doors, revealing more ancient jewellery and weapons that dated back to Targe's formation. In one was a beautiful diamond necklace that I recognised as belonging to Jenethea, Alexia's mother. I knew that having lost her mother so young, Alexia had deemed it too precious to wear.

I was close to giving up and returning to Darj when I realised there was one more cupboard. It was underneath the crown—a special compartment. I fiddled with Dennear's keys until the securing padlock clicked open.

Inside was the orb.

I breathed a sigh of relief but frowned when I realised it was glowing. I reached out to pick it up, and the engraved patterns on the outside of the golden orb lit up with purple light.

It opened at my touch. Inside, a small, mechanical butterfly was hovering.

Another Armoured Butterfly.

It was almost exactly the same as the one that had been in my sword, but smaller, thinner, more delicate.

I reached out to touch it.

It sent a bolt of energy through me, and I collapsed to the ground.

23
KING AMAZ'S LETTER

When I woke up, I felt drained of all energy, like I hadn't slept for a week. I couldn't even lift my head. Opening my eyes took so much effort, it was almost painful.

I was tucked in bed in one of the guest chambers. Elhian was holding my left hand. My other hand felt hot and thick. It was burnt.

'Thank you, Ru'ach,' Elhian said, reaching over and placing a hand on my forehead. 'Adaliah, I thought you'd . . . that you'd . . . ' He swallowed.

'What happened?'

'I don't know, but you've been unconscious for two days.'

'Two days?' It felt like barely a second had passed since I touched the orb.

'How do you feel?' That was Darj. I hadn't even noticed he was in the room, but he was standing on the other side of my bed, looking ever concerned.

'Exhausted. Thirsty.'

'Here.' Elhian passed me a goblet of water. I gulped it down.

'What were you doing with the orb?' Darj asked. 'I sent you for the sword.'

'I know . . . but I had an idea. I think the Targian Orb is the dichotomy of the Dark Orb, the good to its evil. I thought maybe . . . I thought it might help.'

'It nearly killed you,' Elhian said.

'No—it has the butterfly inside!'

'What?' Elhian moved to the only desk in the room, where the orb was lying on a cloth. He picked it up, and it began to glow again. 'It's alive . . .'

Darj moved closer to inspect it. 'It didn't do that before.'

We watched as the orb opened again. The Armoured Butterfly—or its lesser twin—was still there, shining and beautiful.

Elhian reached for it. I yelled at him to stop, but I was too late.

Nothing happened. It fluttered harmlessly in his hand, as if waiting for instruction.

I stared at it in bewilderment. Darj reached for my hand, the one I'd used to touch the butterfly. 'This burn . . . It looks like what happens to someone when they touch something reserved for the Ordained.'

'But Adaliah is ordained,' Elhian said. 'She would only lose that honour if Alexia had a second living child.'

Darj considered this. 'Perhaps we were wrong to assume that because of Jeri's death, Eva was considered the first child, in line to inherit her mother's crown and sword . . .' He paced the room. 'Perhaps Eva, as the second-born and only living child, is ordained to take both. Think about it—we would never have known the difference. Adaliah ended the swords' dark powers on the night Eva was born, and we all assumed the power of the Ordained was made redundant that night, too. But maybe it was not—not entirely.' Darj pointed at the small butterfly.

'But tradition and the prophecy always talked about two living children,' Elhian said. 'King Amaz inherited the Targian sword. His brother inherited the Kestian sword—two living children. Adaliah was ordained to touch the Kestian sword and the Armoured Butterfly because Alexia was an only child and had yet to have two children herself.'

'But when Jeri died . . . ' Darj sat on the edge of my bed and rubbed his forehead. 'Something must have changed when he died or when Eva was born. Otherwise, why couldn't Adaliah touch it?'

'Perhaps all the Ordained have lost their power,' I said.

Elhian studied the butterfly in his hand. 'But I can touch this, and you can't. That has to mean something.'

Darj said nothing for a while, but I could see he was thinking. He paled. 'There is only one explanation I can think of . . . Cades always wanted Alexia to bear him a child, remember? What if . . . What if the High Zalem is now after the same thing? What if Alexia has conceived a child? To him?'

I stared at him, too repulsed by the idea to even speak. I hadn't told him how the High Zalem had kissed her. Of course, I'd felt that was just the beginning of the High Zalem's desire, but I hadn't wanted to think on it.

'It makes sense . . . ' Darj continued. 'When a monarch's second child is born, time immediately starts ticking for the Keeper of Kest. They have sixteen years before the second child inherits their position. Over that time, they gradually lose their protection as one of the Ordained. They lose their ability to use the swords from other kingdoms first, but they can normally still use the butterfly to send messages, as that is their role.' He folded his arms. 'It must be different for Adaliah because she was the Keeper's daughter, not a monarch's second born. That must be why her position as one of the Ordained is transitioning so quickly. Unordained people die when they touch something reserved for the Ordained. This child would only just be conceived. That must be why Adaliah is still alive, but its existence must also be why she was harmed.'

We looked at each other, trying to come up with another suggestion, all unwilling to admit that Darj's words fit the situation almost perfectly.

'If she has conceived,' Elhian said, 'the child will be her second living child, destined to inherit the Kestian sword. The Life Sword.' He looked back me. 'It seems the transition of authority has already begun.'

They left me to rest and, even though I wanted to process all we had talked about, sleep came swiftly.

When I woke up, I guessed it was morning. The storm still lurked outside, and it was difficult to tell whether the sun was up.

I rolled over and saw Darj by the window, holding Eva in his arms. The window gave a good outlook of the city. To the right was the city's cathedral—tall and imposing, but breathtaking. In front and to the left were hundreds of houses stretching out into the distance. Some of them were formed from beautifully hewn stone, others of wood. They were built closely together, allowing for as many residents as possible to live within Liane's protective walls. Tall, aging trees lined the streets, some covered in fading spring blossoms.

'See there, Eva?' Darj asked, pointing down to Ethaniel's stone figure. 'He was your father.'

Eva wrinkled her nose and pressed her little finger into Darj's chest. 'You can be my father.'

Darj laughed, but I think it was only to keep his emotions in check. I felt my eyes smart. Darj kissed her temple, and she leant her head against him. Then, he turned around and saw me watching him. 'Oh, you're awake,' he said, but before he could be embarrassed, Elhian walked in.

'Darj? Adaliah?' He was holding both the new butterfly and King Amaz's box. Standing in the doorway, Elhian didn't look like himself. He was slouching. His eyes were red, and some of his bruises from Sharlard were still visible. I wondered if he'd slept at all while I'd been unconscious.

He readjusted his grip on the box. 'I figured it was time for us to see what's inside. Alexia won't be able to hold on much longer.'

'Yes.' Darj took Eva out into the hallway, where he called for and gave her back to one of the maids. He and Elhian drew up chairs beside my bed.

Elhian set the box on his lap and placed the butterfly over the seal. It adjusted itself so each of its little feet slipped into the six holes Alexia had first identified. It pressed in, and the box clicked open.

There were two objects inside. Darj pulled them out. One was a letter addressed to Alexia. The second was a large, round object hidden under a small, green blanket that Elhian pulled away.

Underneath, there was a third orb.

It was the same size as the Targian Orb, but white instead of gold. It was alight, too.

'What is it?' I asked, looking at Elhian.

'I'm not sure. Should we read Alexia's letter?' He held it up.

Darj gritted his teeth. 'Usually to do so would be treason, but . . . ' He waved his hand dismissively. 'Open it. If anyone asks, I'll tell them it was your idea. You cannot be demoted.'

Elhian forced a smile, but it was crooked and weak. He took the letter and read it aloud.

My dearest daughter,

That you have come to find this package means my greatest fears have been realised. You are on the run from the Zalems and are probably doing all you can to save our beloved kingdom from their grip.

By now, you most likely know I was forced to make a pact with them. Please do not think ill of me, daughter, for I did so for your sake.

I think it is best if I tell you everything I know. These people are a sect that came into existence through a Delyan prince known as Mors Zalem, third son of the Delyan king. This was long before Delya was formed as the kingdom we now know it.

Envy for his older brothers consumed Mors. He had been a monk, a servant to Ru'ach, but his lust for control over his brothers corrupted him. At first, he explored the dark arts of Anash in the most remote of places—not an uncommon thing at the time. It gave him power to raise an army against his own family and kingdom, and he killed his father the king as well as his eldest brother, Markus, the crown prince.

His other brother, Dan Zalem, fought back and defeated his army. But when it came to facing Mors, Dan saw in him his brother the monk and could not make the kill. Dan forgave him. Mors took the opportunity to retreat to the eastern mountains, where he founded Sharlard, the city of the Zalems.

It was at that time that Dan, now King of Delya, changed the surname of the royal house to Markus in honour of his murdered brother. He met with the Jazmardian queen, Cazine, King Hazaka's ancestor. Together, they forged the four swords as protection against evil and as symbols of an alliance between our kingdoms. The swords had been designed to be wholly good, blessed by Ru'ach. But somehow, Mors and the Zalems corrupted them and gave them

Anash's evil as well as good. Because of that, leaders would forever have to choose what they wielded.

The fourth sword, the one we call the Kestian sword or the Life Sword, was actually destined for Delya, but Dan refused it. He felt that as his kingdom had birthed the evil, the sword would only be used for its cause—for death. Our ancestor Jovan won it in a challenge, and that, as you know, began the fracture between the Jazmardians and us.

One source of the Zalems' power is located in what is commonly known as the Dark Orb, which Cazine locked away with the power of the four swords. In it is a virus, a pestilence that can be put into a person's blood to confuse their brain. They call it the Zalems' Bane.

The world returned to peace, and no one heard of the Zalems again for a long time. Then, one night not long after your mother died, I was confronted by a group of them in my chambers. Among them was the current Zalem Servant, better known to you as Cades, King of Casmodia. He said, quite practically, that the Zalems needed a successor. For this, he required a 'pure shell', something so good, so untouched, that he could pour himself into it and mold it to his will. You were his target, but for another reason as well.

Mors the monk had a son, and by him, a long line of descendants that still lives today. Somewhere along the line—once they forgot their heritage—his descendants bred with the Targians.

The Zalems went to great lengths to track down Mors' heir. That night, Cades showed me that my dear Jenethea had been his direct descendant. But as she had died with only one child living, the dubious honour was now yours.

But do not let this deter you—remember, he himself admitted that you were pure, good, untouched, just as your mother was. However, it was upon this discovery that they decided you were the key to bringing the Zalems back to power. The fact that you are in line for the Targian crown only made them more desperate to secure you, as such a powerful alliance would ensure their survival and dominion forever.

As you can imagine, it was inconceivable that I would let my only child and heir live to bear his children, no matter what her maternal heritage may be. He couldn't even offer you marriage without first dispensing of his current wife, which he did most cruelly.

But they seized me and produced the Dark Orb. They put a cut on the back of my hand and rubbed in some of the Zalems' Bane before forcing me to your room. There you were, sleeping soundly with one of the soldiers holding a knife at your throat. One flick, and I knew my princess would die.

Already ill and under the influence of the pestilence, I was made to promise that you would one day bear a Zalem child—good and evil bred together, the Zalems reborn.

That was the pact I made, and I am sorry for it. But it bought you time, and with that, I hope you can find a way to defeat him.

I have provided a tool to help you, as I did not make the pact uncompromisingly.

At that time, I had a Jazmardian healer working for me by the name of Erran. I employed him to try and find a cure for your mother. But even after she died, I funded him to experiment with new medicines, hoping we could use some of his concoctions to prevent others dying as your mother did. Still infected by the Zalems'

Bane, I approached him after my visit with Cades and the Zalems and begged him to help me find a cure.

It took him a few weeks, but he did it after talking to Lord Benne Lowelan and Naythan Ryder, both of whom had made a study of the Zalems. I was almost mad by then, but they created a balm that drew out the virus and cured me immediately. It is in this box within the White Orb. The Zalems are not aware of its existence. The White Orb is a holy artifact, one that has been consecrated before Ru'ach.

Sadly, soon after the orb and balm were created, Benne was attacked. While I believe he and Ethaniel were the targets, Naythan died defending his friend instead, leaving poor, young Darj fatherless. Despite this tragedy, I can only hope they think they got what they came for.

That's why I'm now going to hide it in Delya with the help of their king, who truly understands the need for its existence. Its use is not limited to the Ordained, so it must not fall into the wrong hands. I won't always be able to guard it personally.

At the time of writing this, you are married and in love with Ethaniel. I am watching you through the window, walking with him through the gardens. He is making you laugh. I suspect you are with child, even though you may not know it yourself. You look as your mother did when she was expecting you. I am very proud of you both. I see how you have flourished and am relieved you will have him to protect you after I am gone.

I hope and pray you never come to read this, that your marriage to Ethaniel and any subsequent children will ruin the Zalems' plan. But I fear they have been discontent with your marriage ever since

Lord Benne and I first discussed the potential of it when you were both young.

Whatever happens, stay strong. You must remain connected to Ru'ach at all times. Remember what you are really fighting against. If you have endured grief and hardship, pray, forgive, and let it go. The Zalems are powered by Anash, who feeds off misery, and the virus can use your misery to draw you into their trap much faster. It was my grief for your mother that made me vulnerable.

But remember, they were subdued before and can be again.

Never forget who you are.

Your loving father,

King Amaz the Second

When Elhian finished reading, he scanned through the letter again and gave it to Darj to do the same. Darj nodded at Elhian, encouraging him to get the White Orb out. It was bright, as if a star had been trapped inside.

'I thought my father was involved with the Zalems,' Elhian said, staring at the orb. 'But I never thought he was the Zalem Servant. That is the role Bylon now plays.'

'Reinforcement that you did the right thing the night Eva was born,' Darj said. 'Now we know why he really wanted a child from the queen. With that child, he could have challenged the High Zalem, taken his position, and raised a true successor. That must be why Jeri and Ethaniel . . . were targeted . . . '

'It not only got them out of the way,' I said, 'but created a pain in her for them to draw on.' I watched as Elhian ran his hand over the smooth surface of the White Orb. 'I am glad Cades is dead, but I now think we were naïve to believe the evil was vanquished with him.'

Darj grunted in response. 'So the Targian Orb is not the dichotomy of the Dark Orb. It is just the holder of the small butterfly. This White Orb is the Dark Orb's enemy.' He looked over Amaz's words again. 'The cure must be inside it.'

Elhian found a small latch. He opened the tiny door and discovered a secret compartment, where a vial had been carefully placed. Elhian pulled it out. It was full of a golden liquid.

'It reminds me of holy oil,' I said, thinking of the sort of thing a monarch is blessed and consecrated with when they rise to the throne. 'Maybe to cure someone of the Zalems' Bane is to re-consecrate them or reconnect them to the Great Spirit and goodness.'

'Maybe. Either way, we have the cure.' Darj leant back into his chair. 'If only she were here now. This whole nightmare would be over by dinner time.'

That night we ate dinner at the table with Eva and discussed everything we knew about the orbs, the Zalems, Erran, Alexia's new heritage, and my lost position as one of the Ordained. I told them what had transpired between the archbishop and me. Dennear had since woken up and locked himself in the palace chapel, or so one of the guards said when Darj asked for him to be found.

After dinner, we met with the queen's council in the War Room. Darj took off his sword belt and put it on the table. Raggin, Xander, and some other soldiers stood around the walls of the room, watching and waiting. No one was talking. All eyes were on Darj.

He cleared his throat and recounted to them what had happened in Delya. 'I think you all need to know that Queen Alexia gave herself up to the Zalems willingly, and I can only assume this was to buy us time or to try and influence the Zalems from the inside.'

'That is not what you're afraid of though, is it?' Lord Fenton leant forward in his chair while the others exchanged glances.

I could tell Darj was trying to decide whether or not to answer him.

'No, it is not,' he said. He grasped his hands together and rested them on the table. 'I am afraid the queen will sacrifice herself for Targe—that if it comes to it, she will see her death as the only answer.'

'Well, we have an heir—'

Lord Bannard was interrupted by an uproar from the lords.

'That borders on treason!'

'We must fight for the queen!'

'How callous!'

'Silence!' Darj called. He glared at Lord Bannard. 'How dare you imply such a thing when the queen is risking her life for us.'

The others grunted their agreement, and Lord Bannard slumped back into his chair.

I wondered if Darj would tell them about the regency, whether he would claim the monarch's power. His hand moved towards his pocket, and I think the thought crossed his mind, too, but he hesitated and rested his hand on the table again.

'Of course, we must fight for the queen,' Lord Fenton said carefully, 'but that is not our only problem. That storm outside tells us this. This evil must also be conquered, for all of Targe.'

The other men around the table nodded.

'I understand that, Lord Fenton,' Darj said, 'but I see it as my duty to protect both the queen and the kingdom, and I will not consider it a victory unless we secure both.'

'I agree,' Lord Fenton said. 'What do you suggest then?'

'We will meet them in battle to the southwest of Hunt, in the shadow of Mount Dennell. Prince Ren has agreed to meet us there, but I must have your support. We don't know how many Zalems there are or how strong their power is. The truth is, I may be sending men to their doom. If we lose, if we need to fall back, every man from the south of Delya to the north of Casmodia will need to join the militia, even you.'

The men began to fluster. 'We are lords, not warriors!' one said.

'And what is the point of that if there is nothing left to be lord of?' Darj asked, standing. 'I cannot do this on my own! Liane has already been attacked. Hunt and Chettona have been sacked.' Raggin flinched at this. 'Our queen has been subjected to the Zalems' Bane. How long until we are all infected? We cannot sit here and watch as Targe is taken over for a second time. I will not see Fenellar, Jasteria, or Liane filled with Zalems, or any other town for that matter. Now, I am asking you in the name of Ru'ach: if you really care about your city, about the people you govern, and about the queen who governs you, stand and fight with me!'

Raggin, Xander and the other soldiers cheered, and I think it was this that finally compelled the council to agree.

24
PREPARATIONS

I wanted to speak to Darj alone before bed and found him in the empty throne room, sitting in the chair reserved for him. He was hunched over as if he'd been hit in the stomach and resting his face in his palms. The room seemed larger and colder, now that it wasn't filled with the usual bustle of people and the throne was vacant.

I made my way to him across the marble floor, carrying a goblet of honeycomb. 'Darj?' I placed a hand on his shoulder.

His eyes were glazed and red.

'Here, I think you need this.' I passed him the goblet. He took it but didn't drink. 'You did well just now. I know you're worried about her—'

'Of course I am. She is the—'

'Queen. I know. But I still think you love the woman behind the crown even more.' I rested my hand on his forearm to stop him from escaping.

Darj swished the honeycomb around in the cup. 'She's as stubborn as a deep-rooted tree. Unpredictable, like a storm. She's living more and more inside herself every year, yet she still doesn't hesitate to argue with me if the mood takes her . . . ' He saw me grinning at him. 'What?'

'Are you describing Alexia, or yourself?'

Darj opened his mouth but closed it again with a small smile. 'We have to get her the cure as soon as possible.'

'Yes, I know that . . . ' I knelt beside him. 'But I'm asking you right now, as a friend, what is in your heart?'

He glanced at me. 'Duty and war, as it should be.'

'Darj . . . '

'I know what you're thinking, what you want, but this is the real world.' He made a sweeping gesture towards the throne. 'She is the reigning sovereign; I am the son of a scribe.'

'This isn't about what I want. You two . . . You both get so caught up in "duty" that you forget it's love that makes life worth living. Unless you can see that, you will both spend the rest of your lives even lonelier than you already are. We are Targian, remember? Love is at the core of who we are. It's what we fight for.'

Darj shifted in his chair. He seemed to fall back into one of his silences, so I gave up and turned to go. Perhaps he wasn't ready to know his own heart. But then, he put a hand on my arm. 'Wait.' He stood and took a step towards the throne. 'Look. If you must know, the truth is . . . '

'You're in love with her.'

He turned back to me and put his hands behind his head. 'Adaliah,' he said, 'I've been in love with that woman almost from the moment I met her.'

I put my hand over my heart.

I knew it!

'But Ethaniel was like a brother to me. I was happy for him when he loved her and she loved him. I knew I had no right to her or even a chance—I am a commoner by birth—so I learnt to admire her from a distance, to see her as "the queen", as his wife. I think I have loved her more in these past few years, but even now, her heart is still his.

I can't compete with that. I am grateful for her friendship. How I truly feel is my secret, my burden, buried so deep I'd forget it was there if it wasn't for your persistent nagging.' He wrung his hands together while he waited for me to say something. 'You think I'm ridiculous, don't you?'

I blinked away tears. 'You are a good man, Darj,' I said, hugging him. 'And I do think you're ridiculous, but not for the reason you imagine. The son of a scribe? A commoner? Darj, you are the grand commander of all armies, a man who has led Targe to victory in many battles. Those men out there don't just fight for Alexia. It is every young man's dream to follow in your footsteps, to say they "fought with General Darj Ryder". You're so busy being a "commoner", you forget your position in this palace. You are the queen's most important confidant, and her council is ready to act on your words! And you know what? I think she loves you more than either of you realise.'

'How can you say that? You know she lets no one but Eva near her heart.'

'I saw how she changed when you danced with her, and I was with her when she was afraid. It was your name she called.'

'All that means is she's used to me being around. It's not the same as—'

I took his hand. 'It means that in her darkest hour, she trusts you to be there for her. She hopes for you.'

I sat on the edge of the bed in the morning while Elhian put on his armour and fastened a blue sash around his waist. His sword hung from his right hip, sheathed but sharp. I reached for my leather armour, too. I was going with Darj to meet Prince Ren on the field, and Elhian was travelling to Casmodia to face the Casmodian council and bring more soldiers down to help us.

'Adaliah, do you ever wonder if I have the same evil in me as he did?' Elhian asked as he put on his boots.

'As Cades, you mean?'

'Yes. I know I wasn't chosen to be a part of the Zalems, but I still wonder what lies within me.'

'You weren't chosen because they'd discovered Alexia was the direct heir. Cades was never one of them by blood. That's why he wanted a child with her so much. To retain power in the face of a restless Zalem community, he had to make use of her blood. When he couldn't get it, he waged war against Targe.'

'There were other reasons he did that, though. He lusted after Alexia in his own perverted way. And he wanted more power, more land, more money . . .'

'Of course.'

'I just . . . I can't stop thinking about that woman in Sharlard. I spend time praying to Ru'ach every day because I want to be a good person, a good king. But I was capable of killing her, and I'm scared there might be something in me that could hurt you, like Cades hurt my mother.'

'Oh, Elhian,' I said, moving towards him. 'You were capable of killing her, but you chose not to. That's what makes you the man you are. Besides, if you even tried to hurt me, I'd have you pinned to the ground in a second.'

Elhian laughed. It was deep and warm, the sort of laugh that relaxed the soul. 'True. Though that might not be an unpleasant thing.' He winked at me, and I couldn't help but grin back.

We finished getting dressed, and I picked up the Life Sword, which I had cleaned and laid out to take, just as Erran had instructed. I looked at the word 'Life', which remained clearly etched into the handle. I felt the weight of it. Could I really stop the High Zalem?

I slipped it into the sheath that was on my left hip; the tree-blade was on my right. When I saw myself in the mirror, I knew the transformation was complete. Secured in leather armour with a sword on either hip and a dagger in my left boot, I was the A'zyon Warrior again. I just wished I felt as brave as I looked.

'My Armoured Butterfly,' Elhian said, reaching an arm around my waist from behind. 'Beautiful and clever, but fast and dangerous, too.'

'Do you think we'll be all right?' I asked.

'Well,' he said, resting his chin on my shoulder, 'we are riding out to face an army that nearly tore me to shreds. My love alone must kill their leader, the embodiment of all evil, and her cousin is probably planning to sacrifice herself in the middle of it.'

'So you think we'll be all right then?' I smiled.

He laughed again, but more softly. He kissed my shoulder. 'The outcome of the next couple of days will determine both our history and our future. I am worried that we will fail and that the world we leave for our children will be tormented with evil.'

'Our children . . . ' I said, looking down. Would I survive long enough to be a mother? What kind of mother would I make? 'At least we will know we did everything we could to fight for it, to fight for good.' I searched his face in the mirror's reflection. 'Sometimes, I think the willingness to do that is more important than the outcome. You and I, Darj and Alexia—we must fight, or we will regret it forever.'

Elhian turned me around so he could kiss me. 'You are right, of course.'

'I always am,' I said, and kissed him again before he could protest.

'I must find Leuk and ride to Casmodia. I will join you on the battle-field as soon as I can. Please arrive safe and unharmed. I love you, Adaliah.'

I watched Elhian ride away from the palace until he disappeared into the city. My heart constricted with a familiar longing, as if a part of myself was riding away with him. Behind me, the palace courtyard was filling with men as was the yard before the barracks. The air was noisy and tense.

I could see the golden statue of King Phylip and Prince Jovan reaching above the soldiers' heads. I wondered if they ever felt as hopeless as I did sometimes, if Targe would have been a different place had Jovan not won the Life Sword in a challenge or if King Amaz had lived a bit longer. He would have been mortified to know his daughter had given herself up to the Zalems. Proud of her honourable motives, but heart-broken. I thought of her bidding her daughter farewell and tried to imagine the pain she must have felt. Why did she do it? We could have found another way, surely.

I could see the general astride his red horse just outside the palace courtyard, overseeing the organisation of the men. Some final food rations were being sold and distributed, mostly rye and bean flour bread, dried meat, salt, and olive oil. Carts were filled with grain and hay to sustain the warhorses. I also saw a cart of live hens. The soldiers who managed their pay well and survived the battle would be able to enjoy roast chicken.

I peered up at the palace, where we were leaving the princess without any family at all. I questioned whether we were doing the right thing for the hundredth time, then turned away before I lost my courage altogether. We couldn't take Eva with us, and there was nowhere else for her to go.

Watch over her.

I glanced up at the black sky and wondered if my prayers could penetrate such a gloomy barrier. I longed for the sun again, for warmth and colour. I walked through the gardens as I had done with Alexia not so long before. It wasn't lush and full of fragrances now. I sat down on the garden bench and couldn't help but notice how lonely it felt without her. I could see the statue of Ethaniel and Jeri beneath Alexia's window.

Would we soon be making a memorial to her?

There might be one for me instead. There's no guarantee I'll see this city again either.

I returned to Darj, and a stable boy brought Bagred to me. My horse nudged me as I patted his head. I checked the White Orb, which I had packed in the saddlebag. It was secure and safe.

'Darj,' Raggin said, riding to him with Xander. 'About Chettona . . . I need you to know how sorry—'

'Stop,' Darj said. 'From what I've been told, you were both heroes on that field.'

'Elhian saved my life,' Raggin said, 'and then his men all died. They—'

'Should have come straight to Liane as they were instructed. From what we know of the enemy, you should be proud you were able to evacuate the people.' Both Raggin and Xander tried to speak, but Darj raised a hand. 'Captains, to your men. We ride out now.'

The soldiers carried the Targian ensign high on poles as we rode through Liane. The flags flapped noisily in the morning breeze. Families and well-wishers lined the streets and threw flowers at our warhorses' feet.

'Darj!' Zavad called, pushing through the people towards us. Another boy was with him. 'Adaliah!'

'Where have you been?' Darj asked, waving him over. Zavad and the second boy broke through the crowd and walked alongside us.

'We've been in Liane ever since Captain Raggin sent the people away from Chettona. Before that, we were in Hunt.'

'You were in Chettona?' I asked.

'Yes, we left with the people.' Zavad rested his hand on Guntar's neck and gestured to the boy next to him. 'This is Dayle, the friend who helped me escape Sharlard.'

The boy's hair grew thickly over his forehead, and he looked down so I couldn't really see his face. I did notice how thin and pale he looked. It was sad to think he had spent so much time in darkness.

'We want to come with you,' Zavad said. 'My eldest brother, Landor, is going off to war. Why can't I?'

'You're too young,' Darj said, 'and you've had more than enough adventures to last a lifetime.'

'But you taught me to fight. What is the point of that if I don't use it when it matters most?'

Darj studied the boy's determined face. I wondered if he saw himself in Zavad. It was how I imagined Darj as a boy: determined to fight and hard to deter.

'You are a good fighter, Zavad,' Darj said, 'but I need you here. You must protect the princess. I want you both to stay up at the palace and look out for her. Can you do that for me?'

Zavad took a deep breath and saluted Darj. 'Yes, sire.'

'I'm counting on you.' Darj leant down and shook the boy's hand.

'Take care, Zavad,' I said, 'and thank you both for what you did for Elhian. I will never forget it, truly.'

25
NEW LEADER

The ride across the Targian plains took more than a week. It rained often, and some of the men began to get colds. This only added to my worries: what chance did we stand against the Zalem army if our men couldn't stop coughing? We couldn't afford to lose men to disease before we even reached the battlefield.

It was difficult to light fires in the evenings, and I felt like I was never quite dry. We only had the clothes we carried on our backs and, if we were lucky, a spare pair of woollen socks squeezed into our saddlebags. With no heat or rest for comfort, our sick men had no choice but to keep marching.

Darj and I were glad to see Ren Markus' men waiting for us as arranged. He had brought almost five thousand soldiers from what I could see as we rode towards them.

'Set up camp,' Darj told Xander, who turned back to address the soldiers. 'We are close to him,' Darj said to me. He pointed towards the stormy atmosphere, which seemed particularly low and thunderous.

'Then we are also close to her.' I inspected my burnt hand. Thankfully, it had mostly healed, except for some dry skin and lingering redness. 'If we can find her early enough, we may be able to stop all this.'

'Yes, provided it isn't too late. Either way, we . . . well, you still have to defeat the High Zalem.'

I grimaced. 'Yes.'

We found Ren drinking a glass of wine alone in his tent. In the time that had passed, his brown hair had grown over his forehead and below his ears, giving him a boyish look. I couldn't help but wonder what his ancestors would think of him, leading the Delyans onto the field of battle.

'We have a tough fight ahead,' he said when he saw us. 'I have fifty of Delya's elite dagger fighters with us, and yet I fear we will lose every one of them unless you can kill the High Zalem first.'

I wrapped an arm around myself. 'Thanks.'

'A lot rides on your shoulders, yes, but the quicker he dies, the more lives that can be spared. Darj and I will keep the men distracted by battle and give you as much time as possible to find him.'

'He must be in Hunt,' Darj said. 'That's where the sky is darkest.'

'Yes, in Hunt,' Ren said, 'because that's also where the queen's pain is darkest.'

The sound of a great horn rang out through the night.

I looked at Darj. 'What was that?'

Prince Ren pushed past us out of the tent. Darj and I followed.

'It's . . . It's them!' Ren said. 'They're here!' He pointed to the horizon, towards Hunt.

A hundred or more torches burning on poles had been thrust into the ground, throwing a faint light on the innumerable soldiers that stood behind them. I tried to speak, but the words caught in my throat.

They were shouting. They were rallying for battle.

'They intend to fight now?' I asked.

Our soldiers aren't ready! I'm not ready!

'Blow the horn!' Prince Ren called to one of his men.

The sound of the Delyan call to battle echoed across the field, and the men in Prince Ren's camp began to stir. 'You have to go, Adaliah,' Ren said. 'You have to find him.'

I put a hand over my heart, trying to keep it under control.

Ren began to yell further instructions to his men, but Darj and I didn't stay to hear them. We rushed back to the Targian camp, where Xander was already sounding the call to battle.

I heard the first sword clash against another and turned to see Darj ahead of the army, making the first kill. I hadn't even had a chance to say goodbye to him; he had simply handed me the reins to Bagred and told me to ride. Watching him, I wondered how he had so much courage, how he never seemed to flinch—whether it was because he was confident in what he did or if he had seen too much death to be fearful of it.

Men were dying already; I could hear it in their screams. I tugged on Bagred's bit, turned him away, and began galloping towards the township of Hunt. The White Orb was still in my saddlebag. Even though I carried a dagger in my boot and two swords, I did not feel ready to kill a lamb, let alone the leader of all darkness.

The battle sounds faded behind me as I rode on, scanning the path ahead of me and directing Bagred accordingly. Hunt rose on the horizon much more quickly than I'd hoped. I still didn't have a plan.

There were no guards on the wall. That was my first bit of luck. I tied Bagred loosely to a hitching post and decided against taking the White Orb in with me in case the worst should happen. I felt sure I could bring Alexia back to it, should I be lucky enough to save her from the High Zalem.

I hurried inside the gate and came face to face with a head on a spike. The first thing I realised was that it was a Jazmardian. The second, Erran.

I clasped both hands over my mouth to stop the scream I could feel creeping up my throat. I turned away, fell to my knees, and threw up my last meal. The image of the head, of its numbed expression and blood-covered skin, seemed imprinted on the back of my eyelids.

I took a deep breath and forced myself to stand. This was a man I'd met and dined with, who gave me the Jazmardian blessing that was supposed to help me defeat the High Zalem. Had he died for that? I gulped. It didn't matter. What did matter was that if my mission failed, there was no one else to help me defeat the High Zalem now.

Without looking in the direction of the spike again, I hurried towards a nearby house and hid behind it. The town was quiet, but I felt like someone was watching me. The dark clouds above thundered, and rain began to fall, lightly at first, but then fast and heavy. I was drenched within minutes, and the streets of Hunt turned into muddy streams.

'Come, my love,' a voice said. I felt my skin prickle at the sound. *It's him.*

I peeked around the corner of the house but could only see his back, which was shirtless. He offered a hand to Alexia, who was standing at a doorway of another house. She wore black armour over her dress, but the bow and arrows on her back were hers.

My worry doubled at the sight of her. She didn't look like Alexia at all. There was no warmth, no strength in her face. All that was left was a shell vaguely reminiscent of the queen but no longer beautiful as it had once been.

I took the dagger from my boot. My hand was shaking.

The High Zalem turned suddenly. His very gaze caused me to drop the dagger. I tensed like a startled deer.

'You're the one they call the A'zyon Warrior,' he said. 'Fearless.'

I grabbed the dagger again, held it with both hands, and pointed it at him. There was something unnatural about his face. His smile was unnerving, and his black eyes were hard. They made him look like a beast, and I found myself both entranced and repulsed by him.

Alexia remained a few steps behind him. Her eyes, I noticed in comparison, were a fading blue.

'Alexia,' the High Zalem said. He flicked two fingers forward. 'Shoot her.'

Alexia reached for her bow as if in a trance.

I acted on instinct and swiped at him. The tip of my dagger nipped his collarbone, and I was relieved to see blood, to know for sure I could defeat him as I had many other enemies. But then he reached out and snapped the dagger like it had been nothing more than a dry piece of grass.

The broken blade clanged to the ground, and my head filled with voices. They were whispers at first. One of them even sounded like my father. I couldn't see or hear anything else, and losing my balance, I fell to one knee.

The High Zalem struck me across the face. I fell onto my back in shock. He attempted to impale me with the snapped dagger; I rolled out of the way just in time. I unsheathed my Life Sword, deflected his next strike, and pushed him back. The High Zalem growled with anger. The sky seemed to echo him with a grumble of thunder and lightning.

Alexia loaded an arrow.

I knew what that resolute look on her face meant.

She's going to shoot.

I struggled to my feet and began to run.

I only made it a few steps before I felt a piercing pain in my left calf. I stumbled a few steps more until my leg gave way and I went sprawling to the ground. The shaft of Alexia's arrow stuck out of my leg.

I began to tremble but forced the horror and pain out of my mind and dragged myself away from the High Zalem, away from Alexia. Impeded by the rain and mud, I didn't make two steps before the High Zalem grabbed my ankle and pulled back on it, aggravating my wound.

It was only then that I screamed.

I quickly snatched up a nearby piece of the broken dagger. I wrestled against the High Zalem's grip and stabbed him in the leg. He released me, and I took the chance to drag myself away.

Another one of Alexia's arrows landed in the mud next to my face, almost grazing my cheek. I shuddered and glanced back at her. Her eyes were empty.

'Did you think you could save her?' The High Zalem pulled the broken dagger out of his leg without any indication of pain.

I let my head flop to the wet ground and closed my eyes. I heard someone cantering towards me and feared I was about to get trampled on as well.

But the horse had no rider. It was Bagred. He stopped just in time.

I saw the bulge in the side of the saddlebag and remembered the White Orb. I grabbed the stirrup, pulled myself up, and ripped at the buckles. I took out the orb. It glowed.

The rain above me began to slow, and a patch of blue sky became visible. I lay on the ground again but held the orb up.

The High Zalem shielded his face and looked at me with dismay. He took a step towards me, but I thrust the orb at him. He stepped back. It was as if the consecrated power of the orb offended him.

'Alexia!' he shouted. 'Kill her!'

But Alexia had lowered her bow and was staring at the White Orb.

'Use your knife, like we discussed!'

Alexia still didn't respond.

Incensed, the High Zalem stumbled towards her and thrust the broken dagger up under her throat.

'Cover it up, or I will kill her.' His blood from the dagger smudged on her skin.

'You don't want to kill her,' I said quickly. 'You want her as your heir, as the mother of the next heir.'

'We can easily wait for her child to grow up instead.'

'Eva is her mother's daughter. She will fight against such a thing!'

Alexia looked up at the mention of Eva's name.

'It wasn't Eva I was thinking of.' He ran his hand around Alexia's waist.

Darj's words rang in my head: *What if Alexia has conceived a child? To him?* But if she was pregnant, surely he couldn't kill her until the child was born.

It doesn't make sense!

The pain in my leg was reaching a new level of excruciation, and I could feel my body shutting down. I couldn't think clearly. My eyes were insisting they close, and all I knew was I couldn't risk Alexia's death, no matter how much I needed to kill the High Zalem.

I lowered the orb.

The High Zalem began to laugh, but Alexia betrayed no emotion.

I gave into the pain and fatigue and closed my eyes. The High Zalem's laugh filled my head. I listened as it rambled on and on, as it drowned out the sounds of rain, bellowed in my mind, as it suffocated.

I opened my eyes. The first thing I saw was a dark arm wrapped around the High Zalem's throat from behind. The second was the knife in his neck, grasped by a thick hand. The third, the High Zalem's eyes rolling backwards. The fourth, the face of a Jazmardian I remembered well—Odavan.

'What are you doing?' I asked, my mouth dropping.

Odavan gave me wicked smile. 'Time for a change in leadership, yes?'

'What?'

The High Zalem fell to the ground.

'Erran said only I had the power to kill him! What's going on?'

'I was there,' Odavan said in his thick accent. 'What Erran did not realise was that just being present at the ceremony gives you the blessing. Karlen received it, too. That is why he had to die.'

I struggled to keep up. 'Karlen . . . Why didn't you tell me this?'

'Because I knew you would not like the second half of my plan. Besides, Erran would never have given me the blessing without you there.'

'What plan?'

Odavan's wicked smile returned. 'I am not here to save the world. My only intention is to give it a more powerful leader.' He rested his foot on the High Zalem's chest.

'What, you?' My hand gripped the White Orb, and I began to raise it again.

Odavan laughed at me and called for Bylon. He appeared behind him like he'd been waiting there all along. He had the Dark Orb in his hand, which he opened at Alexia's feet. Then, he handed her the High Zalem's sword.

'Finish it, Alexia,' Bylon whispered in a serpentine voice.

Alexia turned the blade down and impaled the High Zalem, killing him instantly. At first, I thought she'd done it out of empty obedience, but there was anger in her eyes. I was relieved to see she still knew something of emotion. Emotions could be persuaded, used to communicate. It meant part of her heart was still alive and that I might be able to reach her.

The sky thundered. Alexia withdrew the sword.

I wondered how much the kill had been about her own revenge. Perhaps she had wanted to do that all along and had just been waiting for the chance.

But I thought it could only be done with the Life Sword . . .

Odavan and Bylon dropped to their knees. 'Long live the High Zalem!' they shouted as they lifted their arms up.

Alexia's eyes grew hard like the High Zalem's had been. Tears rolled down my face as I watched.

'Well done, my servants,' she said, her voice stern and detached. 'You will be rewarded in due course. Now, it's time for us to join the battle.'

'What about her?' Odavan asked, nodding towards me.

Alexia met my eyes. A coldness filled me.

'Leave her, for now.' Alexia turned and walked away with Bylon.

Odavan leant down to me. 'The best part is you are still bound by the Jazmardian blessing—cannot fight, cannot join the battle, cannot spill blood without risking the boy's life. You can do nothing, and the only way out now is to murder your beloved cousin.'

26
SURVIVOR

I lay in mud—insensible, drenched, and sallow. When I finally woke some time later, I tried to drag myself towards a small house but stopped after only a minute. My entire body was too exhausted from the pain.

Bagred lowered his head and sniffed me.

'I need your help, old friend.' I reached for the stirrup again and wrapped my fingers around it. 'Walk on.' Bagred took one step and dragged me a little. 'Walk on.' This time, he dragged me across the road. Instead of going closer to that house or any other, he brought me to a stable, distracted by a bucket of feed.

I let go of the stirrup and fell on a pile of hay. I was glad to be out of the rain but began to shiver. The shivering got worse when I saw the arrow lodged all the way through my flesh. With no apparent soul left in the township, I knew I had no choice but to tend to it myself.

I touched the arrow, and it immediately irritated my wound. I bit my hand to stop myself from screaming again. I grabbed Bagred's leg for support. He didn't move, even when I snapped the tip of the arrow off and dug my fingertips into him.

A new stream of blood flowed down my leg. My hands were trembling. I took hold of the shaft, feathered with the gold-tipped, green fletching. I held onto Bagred again and drew it out of my leg. Sweat beaded on my face as I gritted my teeth and looked away. It finally came free, but before I could check the wound, I collapsed in an unconscious heap.

When I woke up for a second time, there was a small fire next to me. My clothes felt dry but were still caked in mud. The pain in my leg had faded a little, and I almost felt comfortable.

'Welcome back, old friend,' a voice said.

I opened my eyes, wondering if I'd dreamt it. 'Kadram?' I saw the Jazmardian sitting at my shoulder, sat up, and threw my arms around him. 'Kadram! I am so glad to see you!'

The Jazmardian chuckled and then waved at me to lie down again. 'I am glad to see you, too, and alive.'

'Only just.' My leg was now bandaged.

'That's what they said about you at Kest River, but you lived.' Kadram's eyes sparkled.

'Only because you were there to ask Ru'ach to save me.'

He smiled, and I gave him a fond look. His face was older than it had been during the Norther Invasion but filled with the same warmth and wisdom that reminded me of his late brother, Lezan. His eyes were more wrinkled, and his shoulders rolled further forward than they once had. But my eyes welled with tears at the sight of him.

'Did you see what happened? I am so afraid, Kadram.'

'I know, Adaliah.' His Jazmardian accent made my name sound enchanting, as if Erran was speaking it. 'Darj and his men are still battling. As soon as you have eaten, we will ride out to join him.'

I longed for that, but I knew I would be of no help to Darj in my condition. 'How did you get here?'

'I have been following Odavan. Erran joined me, but he was sadly caught. I suspected Odavan was up to something. King Hazaka favoured him at first, but after he left without bringing you to Etarbelec, even he began to suspect something amiss.'

'Etarbelec? So I was supposed to go there?'

'That was Hazaka's instructions, yes. He wanted to make sure you were equipped to face the enemy, even if that was only because he did not want to face him himself. But you were gone before we knew you had even made it to Jazmarda. It was all I could do to leave that note for you in the cabin. I later tracked Odavan down into Kest, by the river, where he met with his woman again. She was not a Zalem. When she would not join him then, he drowned her.'

I remembered the woman, how serene she'd seemed. I also remembered the letter I'd found pinned to the board, telling me of the pact and the danger Alexia was in. 'It didn't do much good, I'm afraid. I didn't save Alexia from the Zalems.'

'No, but it is not over yet.'

'The Zalems did this on purpose,' I said. 'They didn't want me to have the blessing just so I would stay out of battle, like I thought to start with. No, they planned this all along. Now in order to end it, I can't kill anyone but her, and they know I would never do that. They've trapped me. I can't kill her, Kadram. Elhian killed Cades, and it has haunted him ever since. He didn't even love him. I adore my cousin. And yet I can't see any other way out of this!'

Kadram leant over and laid his hand on mine. 'There is always another way.'

I rested a little longer while Kadram searched for food. When he finally returned, he helped me into a sitting position. My leg felt like a dead weight, and I had to lift it up with my hands so I could move.

'Try and eat,' Kadram said, handing me a plate of over-ripe fruit and a piece of salted beef. 'I found it in one of the houses.'

I chewed on the meat, willing my body to feel stronger and better than it did. Piece by piece, I finished everything on the plate, except a slice of apple that I gave to Bagred. Kadram put an old tankard out in the open until it was overflowing with rain. He took a mouthful and gave the rest to me. I used some of it to wash my face, but it was cold.

'Do you think you can go back?'

I nodded with a frail, forced smile. 'No' was not an option, so I tried not to let myself falter, even though I saw Alexia shooting me whenever I closed my eyes. I trembled, wishing I could rest in front of a warm fire with a hot drink of honeycomb.

Perhaps Elhian will reach us with the Casmodians soon.

Kadram was about to help me stand when we heard voices. Kadram indicated for me to lie down again and rested himself beside me.

'Who was that man on the field?' a voice asked. It was not one I recognised. 'The one with that interesting band around his right upper arm?'

'General Darj Ryder,' the second voice said. 'Slayer of Captain Hae, rescuer of Cades' prisoners in Semanez, and fierce protector of the queen. He has only ever lost one battle—the Battle of the Yellow Forest, when Cades first attacked Targe in the Northern Invasion and cast Alexia out of Liane. Rumour has it the general later played midwife to her when the princess was born.'

'So he was there when Elhian Edangard murdered his own father?'

'He was, Sirvan.'

Sirvan. Elhian had spoken of this man, had said he made Jag Warhin seem like the embodiment of goodness. I looked at Kadram. He put a hand on my arm, instructing me not to move.

'He was also close to the late Prince Ethaniel,' the second voice added.

'What town is Darj from?' Sirvan asked.

'It wasn't Chettona, no . . . The same town Ethaniel came from.'

'Levanna?'

'That's it!' The man chuckled at his own forgetfulness. 'Do you know it?'

'Yes. I think I was acquainted with the good general's father.' He gave a humorless laugh, and I heard a sword being drawn. 'I never thought I'd have the honour of meeting his son after all these years. Hurry up, Cordale. Let's get Alexia and return to the battlefield.'

Kadram helped me onto Bagred's back, but I couldn't put my injured leg into the stirrup. When I tried, the pain seemed to shoot right up to my head. I had to hold it out from Bagred, as it stung whenever it bumped against him.

This meant Kadram and I had to ride slowly. It had taken me less than an hour to reach Hunt from the battlefield, but it took twice the time to return.

I searched the field for Darj. I wanted to tell him all that had happened, but I also feared for him as well. I was not at all at ease with the interest Sirvan was taking in him or the insinuations he was making about Darj's father.

Kadram and I came to a small ridge and stopped. I spotted Darj ahead of the men, spitting out a tooth and a mouthful of blood.

The field was plagued with fighting men for as far as I could see. The Zalems continued to pour on our soldiers like an ever-flowing river. Our men were only just holding on, and many already lay dead with spears protruding from their stomachs. There was no sign of Elhian and the Casmodians yet.

Xander and Raggin fought near Darj. I could tell by the way they were gasping for breath that they were tiring. Our men hadn't had a chance to rest after the long journey from Liane. Many were still sick, and they had been fighting for hours. I glanced at the horizon, hoping Elhian would arrive with the Casmodians. We expected him at any time.

Xander ran to Darj and gestured towards the many bodies lying over the field.

'He's asking him to retreat,' Kadram said.

They exchanged several words before Xander gave him a short nod and ran back to his position on the field. Darj pushed towards the Delyan prince, killing several Zalems as he passed.

'And he won't call for a retreat without Prince Ren's agreement,' I said.

Darj was drawing close to Ren and had attracted his attention with a wave, but was unexpectedly pushed to the ground from the side by a man dressed in fine armour and knee-high steel boots. He was a head above everyone else on the field, even the general, and took long strides.

'That's Sirvan,' Kadram said.

Darj rolled in the grass a couple of turns before Sirvan's foot landed in his back. Sirvan pressed a sword point into the nape of Darj's neck.

'Stay away from him, Sirvan,' Kadram called as we rode closer.

I held a sword, but I couldn't get off my horse. I knew I wouldn't be able to stand.

'I never would have thought Naythan Ryder's son would be so easily caught off guard,' Sirvan said.

Darj tried to catch his breath. 'You knew my father?'

'I knew him very well. I tried to recruit him to our cause, but . . .' Sirvan shrugged. 'He refused.'

Darj narrowed his eyes at him. 'Who are you?'

'Sirvan, a messenger of the High Zalem.' He grinned. 'Naythan of Levanna's slayer.'

Darj turned over and knocked Sirvan's sword away with the back of his hand so quickly that even the Zalem was surprised. Darj's hand bled as he clambered to his feet, but it didn't stop him from dodging Sirvan's strike and kicking him in the knees. Sirvan stumbled. Darj kicked him again, and Sirvan fell over.

Prince Ren reached us. He and Darj pinned each of Sirvan's shoulders down while Sirvan wriggled and struggled against them.

'Why did you kill my father?' Darj asked.

Sirvan chuckled to himself. '"Why" is always a complicated question . . . '

A deep horn sounded somewhere in the Zalem army. It was so loud and low, I felt the earth move beneath us. Sirvan stopped struggling, and his chuckle became an outright laugh.

'What is it?' Ren asked.

The horn sounded again. The fighting began to cease, and the Zalems parted to let someone through. That someone appeared on the small ridge, mounted on a horse. Two others were riding behind the figure, one on either side.

Darj stared, his mouth open. 'No. No.'

'What?' Prince Ren asked.

'It's the queen. It's Alexia.'

Her hair was blowing in the wind, and she was armed with a sword. She stopped and raised her black blade.

The Zalems broke into a cheer. 'Praise the High Zalem! Glory to the Black Spirit Anash!' They began to reform their line. They were preparing for a fresh attack, an attack led by my cousin.

'No,' Darj said again.

The Targians were staring at Alexia, too. Many dropped their weapons.

'Retreat!' Ren yelled at the Delyans. 'Fall back!'

Sirvan grabbed Darj's wrist. 'Now what do you have left to fight for?' He elbowed the side of Darj's head so hard that Darj fell away from him. Sirvan stood and ran.

'Darj,' I called. Bagred was restless beneath me. 'We have to go!'

Ren and Kadram pulled Darj to his feet.

'We have to get out of here!' I said.

Darj's face was ashen, and his eyes remained on Alexia. Instead of inspiring confidence and hope, she now inspired fear. She had been caring and warm; now she was cold and inhuman. She had been a servant of the Great Spirit Ru'ach, the giver of all life. Now she was bound to Anash, the Prince of Death.

'Darj!' Kadram yelled. 'Let her go!'

'Retreat,' Darj said, his voice rasping. He cleared it and tried again. 'Retreat!'

27
TO TARCRAIG

I rode behind the men as we crossed the battlefield away from the Zalems.

'Hurry up,' Xander yelled at Raggin, who was struggling to maintain the pace. 'In case you haven't noticed, they're hunting us down!' Xander gestured back at the Zalems chasing us across the plains like wolves scattering sheep. I glanced at Darj; I'd never seen such despair on his face.

Many of the men had abandoned their weapons so they could run faster. Others were slowing already, tired and injured from more than a day of battle.

The Zalem horn sounded again. It was Alexia blowing it this time, but she was inflecting the sound so it was more high-pitched. The Zalems began to slow and turn back but not before yelling insults at us and even laughing.

'Oh good, I can catch my breath,' Raggin said, leaning on his knees.

Alexia was just a dark figure on the hill now. She watched the scene a moment more and then turned away.

'We're too far from the camp, and it's not safe to go back,' Darj said once the men had all come to a stop.

'I know, but we have no food or supplies,' I said.

'Most of the men carry rations in their saddlebags,' Darj said.

'Many of the horses are dead.' I could see their bodies littering the field.

'There is water at Tarcraig,' Darj said. 'We will spend a night there and send men out to hunt and fish. It won't be enough, but we'll have to make do. We will continue back to Liane . . . '

'There are thousands of us,' Prince Ren said. 'How—'

'Do you have a better idea?' Darj unsheathed his sword again. He seemed taller and more formidable than ever.

Ren swallowed. 'To Tarcraig, then.'

I wasn't sure how long we travelled, but it felt like two lifetimes before I saw the stark cluster of rocks that Tarcraig was. I knew by the silence of the men around me that they were tired and hungry.

'It's not just that,' Raggin said when I mentioned it. 'Seeing their queen like that has knocked their hope and patriotism all at once, as it has mine.'

Darj heard him, and I saw how it pained him. But he said nothing.

Later, Xander, Raggin and some of the other senior soldiers organised a hunt. Kadram tended to some of the wounded, assessing their injuries and healing them with what limited materials he had.

Darj and I found we had a few minutes alone. We returned to the cave we'd hidden in during the Northern Invasion. Alexia had been very ill then, too. At the time, we'd attributed this to her grief, not knowing until much later she was also pregnant. I smiled at the thought, wishing I could see the little princess again, hold her small hand, and enjoy her uncomplicated view of the world. 'Stay safe, Eva,' I whispered.

Darj slumped to his knees. I limped in beside him. 'Did you know about Sirvan before?' I asked. 'About his connection to your father?'

He shrugged his shoulders. 'I don't remember . . . I wasn't that old. Or maybe I just blocked it out.'

'Maybe that's what the poem was talking about, the thing you need to recall,' I said. 'We need to know everything we can about these men.'

He closed his eyes, focused but tormented. 'I'd been playing with my two sisters on the floor. The door opened behind me, so fast and hard, one of the pins in the hinges bounced out and fell to the ground. A man—Sirvan—he walked straight inside and into the room where my father and Lord Benne had been talking. I hadn't been allowed in, but I followed Sirvan then. I saw my father and Lord Benne leaning over a table. I can remember the astonishment on their faces when they saw Sirvan.'

He stopped and took a deep breath. I put a hand over his. 'What happened?'

'Sirvan unsheathed a long, curved, black sword. My father raised his hands and shouted. I threw myself at Sirvan's leg, trying to pull him away. Somewhere behind me, my mother screamed. Sirvan shook his leg hard, and I fell on the floor. My father said something to me.'

'What?' I asked gently.

Darj rubbed his face in his hands. '"We have a cure in sweet, holy wisdom".'

'Sweet, holy wisdom?'

'Lord Benne pulled out a shiv. He held it up to Sirvan but didn't say anything.'

'What was your father doing?'

'I . . . I don't know. There was a fray, and he was killed.'

Darj opened his eyes and let the memory fade. We sat in silence for a while, both trying to think what it meant.

'What happened to you?' Darj asked, indicating my leg. 'I should have asked before, I know. I was just . . . '

'It's all right.' My leg was swollen. 'She shot me.' A vision of the arrow piercing my leg passed through my mind, and my chest tightened.

'In the leg?' Darj asked with a frown.

'As you see.'

Darj's frown faded, and he let out a deep breath, like he was relieved.

'I don't see what's good about that.'

'You know Alexia never misses a target, no matter how small, fast, or difficult it might be. If she wanted to kill you, that arrow would have pierced your heart or landed in your forehead. The fact that she shot you in the leg means she didn't want you dead, that there is still some part of her that has some control over the darkness.'

I thought about this. 'She shot another just past my face. It landed in the dirt, even though the High Zalem told her to shoot me.'

'It was a warning shot,' Darj said. 'She probably saved your life!'

I scoffed. 'I don't think I'm ready to feel grateful yet.' I went on to tell him what had happened afterwards, repeating what Odavan had said to me about having to kill Alexia to end it all. 'They declared her the new High Zalem. If there was any goodness left, I'm sure it was taken then.'

'But she still walked away, leaving you alive?' Darj asked. 'Leaving you holding the White Orb?'

I met his eyes. 'Yes, she did.'

Darj reached into his pocket and pulled out the regency paper Alexia had given him back in Delya. It shook in his hands. 'Even so, I never suspected I might need to act on this. But after seeing her with the Zalems, after seeing the low morale of the men . . . '

He handed me the paper.

> I, Queen ALEXIA JOANNA GRACE ELRYANE, hereby authorise General DARJ NAYTHAN RYDER to rule the realm of Targe as regent in the event that I become unfit to do so myself or succumb to death before Her Royal Highness, the Crown Princess EVA JENETHEA ADALIAH ELRYANE, comes of age.

I read the rest of it and turned the page over. Alexia had written something on the back, so faintly I had to squint to read it. 'Look, Darj!'

I handed it back to him, and he read the sentence aloud. '"Have courage yet, my friend. While ever my heart beats, I will not give up".'

28
MAKING PLANS

We slept for a few hours until a Targian lookout asked for Darj. Darj climbed up the rocks to join him and looked out across the plains.

'Is it Elhian?' I asked from below. 'Has he arrived?'

'Yes, it's him with an army of men.'

I dragged my bad leg part-way up the rock until I could see the men coming through a small crevice. 'There isn't as many of them as I would have expected,' I said.

Darj climbed back down. Kadram grabbed his arm before he could take another step. 'Don't be hard on him,' Kadram said, and I realised with surprise that Darj was angry with Elhian. Elhian was later than we'd hoped, but delays where armies and distances were involved were not uncommon.

The king's men stopped outside the rocks, but he rode straight to us, his pants wet and dirty from horse sweat. Some of his wounds from Sharlard looked raw again, and a few more had been added since.

'What happened?' Darj asked as soon as Elhian had dismounted.

'Tiathi was attacked,' he said. 'We came as soon as we could, but they were deliberately trying to delay us.' I limped forward to embrace him. 'What happened to you?' he asked.

'Come.' Darj put a forgiving hand out to Elhian. 'We all have much to catch up on.'

Elhian had a quick meal with us and later took the bandage off my leg. I winced when the last piece stuck to my skin. 'It's a clean wound, if that's any consolation. I guess you're lucky Alexia didn't shoot you through the bone.'

I paled at the thought. Without warning, tears dripped down my face.

'Adaliah,' Elhian whispered, placing a tender kiss on my head.

'It was horrible,' I said. 'I love her so much . . . and it's such a mess . . . and I wish you had been there.'

He wrapped his arm around me. 'I'm sorry,' he said, tilting my head up so he could kiss me. 'We will find a way to save her, you know. This isn't over.'

He opened the bottle of herbal medicine Kadram had made for me, put his finger into the green-brown cream, and applied some to both sides of my wound.

'It mustn't get infected,' Elhian said. He wiped the excess cream away with his finger and began to reapply a clean cloth as a bandage.

'What was the damage at Tiathi?' I asked.

'The south section looks like a wasteland. I don't know how we will be able to afford to repair it. Our castle was untouched, though, and many of the townspeople were in the forecourt there when I arrived, in makeshift tents. I organised for the displaced people to seek refuge inside the castle until their homes are rebuilt or we can sort something else out. One of them told me the soldiers had attacked the night before but because the greater part of the Tiathi-based army was fighting in Targe, where they died, their defence had been weak.'

'You weren't to know,' I said.

'No. The Zalems are not playing fairly. They reappeared, too. I was just getting what men I could together—had sent for more from neighbouring villages—when the Zalems attacked again. We'd thought they'd gone back to Targe by then. But then I understood.'

'What?'

'They had been sent to delay me, so I couldn't aid Darj. We fought back from the castle, but the only reason we had victory was because the soldiers I had sent for arrived and were able to defeat them from the outside in. I took what soldiers were left and rode on to find you. Thankfully, it had only been a day and a bit lost and not weeks.' He let out a big breath, his shoulders sinking.

'What is it?'

'Casmodia is just a shadow of what it once was. Cades may have been evil, but our kingdom was great under his reign.'

'Great, but not good, and not the kingdom you believed in. Sometimes, it's like a broken arm that doesn't set right. You have to re-break it so it heals better. Casmodia is being broken again so it will grow to be a kingdom our children and their children can take pride in. A kingdom you can take pride in.' I cupped his face with my hand. 'But I know it breaks your heart to see it like this, as it does mine to see Targe shrouded in darkness.'

I leant forward and gave him another kiss. He put an arm around me and drew me closer, his kissing suddenly impassioned. I pulled away after a while and smiled. 'We shouldn't get carried away. We've already been through one war with a pregnant woman to look after.'

'Alexia is not generally a woman I would consider as needing "looking after",' Elhian said, 'and it may be too late after what happened in Delya anyway.' He grinned at me.

'It's not. Besides, I wasn't thinking about consequences then; I was just so glad to see you alive.'

'And you're not now?'

I cupped his face with my hand. 'Of course I am.' I kissed him again and happily yielded to his warm embrace.

Later, Darj, Elhian, Ren, Kadram, and I spent a long time discussing what to do once the Zalem army caught up to us. We'd managed another sleep and were all starting to feel like we could face the reality of war again. There was a part of me that wanted to go back to my normal life, as if I could ride back to Tiathi then and there and nothing would be different. I kept dreaming about nice things—Elhian's coronation, our wedding, the hopes and plans we had for the future . . . Memories were so important to me now. They sustained me through the times of despair. I hadn't had that comfort in the Northern Invasion.

'I would still prefer to go back to Liane,' Darj said, interrupting my thoughts. 'Tarcraig provides little shelter, and we still have limited supplies.'

'Respectfully, Darj, I don't think we'll make it back to Liane,' Ren said. 'They were ready for battle as soon as you joined me on the field before. I think they will be here any second. In fact, I'm surprised they haven't arrived already.'

'What do you suggest then?' Darj asked.

'I think we have to make the best of a bad situation,' Ren said. 'Our goal isn't victory; it's survival. And I think the only way we are going to be able to do that is if Adaliah . . . '

'If I what?'

'If you deal with the new High Zalem, one way or another.'

'I can't kill her.'

'Then, the White Orb,' Ren said. 'Get her the cure, if it's not too late.'

I looked at Darj, trying to read his thoughts. I couldn't.

'He is right,' Kadram said. 'Not only will they be here before long, but time is also running out for Alexia. Elhian said she had been given a particularly damaging dose of the Bane. I believe the virus will alter her brain and drive her irreversibly mad. She is already halfway there.'

I couldn't help but fear she was already beyond saving, but I refused to say so out loud, as if the words spoken would make it true.

'Fine,' Darj said. 'We will defend our position here as long as possible to give Adaliah time. I suggest that once we see the army, you go after Alexia. If she's not with the army, she'll be at their camp. It will be the best opportunity. Do you think you can do it?'

A horn sounded outside.

'I guess I'm about to find out,' I said.

29
THE CURE

A sea of Zalem soldiers rolled towards us—calm, methodical men marching on orders they didn't question, to kill people they didn't know, to overcome a kingdom that wasn't theirs.

In response to this, our allied soldiers began to flood Tarcraig. They stood both on the rocks and in front of them, armed with bows, daggers, and swords. Many didn't have enough armour. Others were already injured but continuing to fight despite the pain. I saw the determination in their faces but knew it was weakening under the ongoing assault of fear. No one wanted to admit it out loud, but we all understood that our position was a weak one. We were risking everything, and there was no certainty of victory.

And if we failed on the field, the Zalems would march on and take Liane. Alexia would lie in madness until death. Targe would be theirs. History would change. Our race would be lost. Casmodia and Delya would be next, and one day our world would be nothing more than an unread chapter of a history book.

I realised then that despite our titles and previous victories, Elhian, Darj, Alexia, and I were still so small in the course of history. In another hundred years, or even less, our struggle at Tarcraig would be of little everyday importance. No one would remember how much we loved each other, how passionate we felt about our kingdom, how much we grieved for the ones who died. All they would know was whether we survived or not.

'I will not retreat a second time,' I heard Darj mutter to himself as he unsheathed his sword.

Something happened then I didn't expect. A breeze picked up, and Darj began to sing. It was a song I hadn't heard since I was a child. Some of my father's men used to sing it at the Kestian keep, but there'd been only five or so of them. The soldiers joined Darj until there were thousands of them singing, and they sang so loudly it seemed to lift me off the ground:

Today when the falling sun sets

And the nightingale sings its last,

Today when darkness rides forward,

Tell them the sun rises—night shall pass.

Today as we unsheathe our swords,

Tell them we fought for all that's good.

Today as the green fields turn red,

Tell them we fled not—our ground we stood.

Today if I'm called home too soon,

Tell them I stand beside them still.

Today if they ask where I am,

Tell them I never left—never will.

Today Ru'ach is in the wind,

Tell them not to fear loss or strife.

Today we bare our teeth at death,

The last battle will be won by life!

Soon the men were cheering, roaring. The breeze grew stronger. I felt their strength, and the fear faded.

Be with us, Ru'ach.

'Is she ahead of them?' I asked Elhian.

He shook his head as the men began the song again. 'I can't see her. Sirvan is there.' He eyed the man leading the army.

I wasn't sure whether to be grateful or worried by Alexia's absence. 'I'll have to go and find her.'

'Go now then,' Elhian said. He called for one of the soldiers to get Bagred. 'Go out the back of Tarcraig and circle around the battle.'

Elhian helped me up in the saddle. With the assistance of Kadram's medicine, I could lift the toes of my injured leg into the stirrup but still couldn't put any weight on it.

Darj put a hand on Bagred's reins, stopping me. 'Do whatever it takes to bring her back to us. But should the worst happen, do your duty, too.'

'But I love her. You love her.'

'Yes.' His eyes reddened. 'But it may be too late.'

I took a deep breath. 'This is it then.'

My last chance.

I had to bring Alexia back or die trying.

My mind flashed back to a time when the two of us were children. My father had brought me to Liane to celebrate King Amaz's birthday.

As an eleven-year-old—not much older than Zavad—Alexia told me all about how she'd had a disagreement with her father the king. He'd chided her for rolling her eyes at an ambassador from the White Isles in an important meeting, but she'd insisted he'd deserved it for patronising her father. I hadn't even known what that word meant, but she made it sound like a terrible sin.

The same ambassador later made a rude remark to her at the dinner table, and I stomped on his toe with all the protective anger I could muster. Alexia couldn't help herself—she burst out laughing. Everyone looked our way and saw a crown princess and a lady behaving in a very improper fashion.

Seeing the rising colour in the ambassador's face, Alexia grabbed my hand, and we ran into the hallway. By then, I was laughing, too, now believing it all to be a joke. It wasn't until our fathers found us that we stopped, shrinking beneath their ireful looks. But when my father put his hands on his hips, about to lecture me, Alexia stepped in front and declared it to be her fault. She turned to me and whispered, 'You were there for me, and I'll be there for you always, all right?' It had been such an earnest promise, and I'd agreed to it with all the solemnness of an almost-six-year-old, like I was making a pact for life.

And so I had.

A pact more important than any other I'd made since.

Darj shouted 'Arjla divala!', and the men began to charge.

With Ru'ach we stand.

I rode north out of Tarcraig and then circled around the Zalems until I was heading southeast on a road I'd once called the Path of the Dead. Mount Dennell was already visible in the distance. On either side of me stretched the long-grassed Targian plains. Instead of their usual peacefulness, though, a wind was ripping over the undulating hills, fueled by an angry sky and ongoing storm. Hard raindrops began to pelt my face, and before long, I was cold.

The almost-deserted Zalem camp was set up just out of sight of Tarcraig. It was an insulting reminder that my homeland had been invaded, and I couldn't help but feel violated at the sight of tents. How dare they wage war on our soil! We didn't invite them; we didn't do anything to provoke war by attacking them or behaving in an aggressive way. What right did they have to be here?

Someone shouted. I didn't understand the word, but I knew I'd been discovered. I spotted the lone soldier; he turned on his heel and ran.

I dug my heels into Bagred and rode after him between the tents. It didn't take long for me to draw close, and once he was within a few steps, I launched myself off Bagred and landed on him. The air rushed out of his lungs. He tried to call for help but had no breath to form the words.

Bagred had gone a few steps further before realising he no longer had a rider, but he came back to inspect what I was doing. I grabbed a worn rope from my saddlebag. I tied the man's hands behind his back and a cloth between his teeth. 'Luckily for you, I promised not to spill blood,' I said, though I wasn't sure he could understand me. 'Otherwise, you'd be dead.'

He looked up at me. For the first time, I saw the utter fear in his face. I wasn't sure whether it was because of me or because he felt he'd failed the Zalem cause. Either way, it surprised me. Perhaps their men were just as afraid as ours. Perhaps they knew their lives depended on their victory just as much as ours did.

I wanted to drag him to somewhere less conspicuous, but I was struggling to walk and had to rub my leg for a few minutes before I could go on.

How am I supposed to face Alexia like this?

I took the White Orb out of the saddlebag.

I saw another Zalem up ahead with a man I recognised as Bylon. I left Bagred in the grass and, crouching low, limped behind Bylon and the other Zalem. I followed them to a larger tent. There, I was able to peek around the flap and lean on the frame for support.

Bylon sat behind a desk. The Dark Orb was in front of him.

'Something's wrong—something we weren't prepared for,' the Zalem said to Bylon in the common tongue.

'Yes, Cordale, and I am certain it is to do with the orb Adaliah had. We should have taken it from her—'

'But Alexia is the High Zalem now,' Cordale said. He had a scar down the centre of his chin. I could tell by its redness that it was relatively new. 'It's in her blood. If we didn't obey her, we would be dead. She must know what she is doing.'

'No, no, I don't think she does,' Bylon said. 'I don't think she understands her role as the High Zalem at all. Why else would she call the men back when we could have finished it once and for all on that field? She's agreed to send them now, but if she had done so earlier, we could be marching on Liane as we speak.'

Alexia walked into the tent from the opposite side, a knife in her hand. 'Are you questioning my will?' She flicked the knife up.

'Of course not,' Bylon said, but without any fluster. 'I am merely trying to understand it.'

'It's not for you to understand, only to do as I say.'

Bylon pushed her up against the desk. The sudden aggression surprised me. 'You are just a piece in this game to be played like all the rest, including the High Zalems before you. And let me tell you, unlike Cades, Sirvan and I will not be beguiled by your . . . ' he twisted a piece of her hair around his finger, ' . . . beauty. Besides, if you were truly powerful, I would not even be able to touch you as I am now.' He clicked his tongue. 'And to think Odavan thought you would be more commanding. To me, you will only be more useful.'

Alexia struck him across the face with the knife. It slit his skin, leaving a claw-like cut across his cheek. He covered it with his hand, but the blood flowed between his fingers.

'Never underestimate a woman,' she said. 'Especially not one who has grown tired of being used.'

She left, and I moved around the edge of the tent so I could keep her in sight. She paused in her step. She seemed disorientated, then tearful.

It was like she was changing temperaments by the second. At first, she looked like a little girl, hugging herself and wiping tears off her cheeks; the next, she looked angry and violent, gripping her knife and turning about as if seeking something to kill. Then she blinked a couple of times and gazed around at the camp like she was seeing it for the first time and didn't know where she was.

She gathered herself and hurried away with a new determination.

I followed her again but at a slow and tedious pace. I was still holding the White Orb, hoping I would be able to use the cure soon. But my leg was unforgiving and sore; I only just managed to keep up with her.

Where is she going?

I started to wish I had the means of getting back on Bagred, but I'd left him at the camp. Besides, he would have given me away.

Soon, Alexia and I were away from the camp altogether and out in the plains. Mount Dennell was looming ahead of us, its peak missing in the dark clouds. I continued following her until she stopped and pulled her knife out again. She knelt in the grass.

I hesitated. Was she hunting? Did she know I was there? Or was there someone else she was about to kill? I only understood what was really happening when she brought the knife up to her neck.

'Alexia! Don't!'

'Leave, Adaliah.'

She didn't turn. She must have known I'd been following her the entire time. I limped towards her. 'Adaliah . . . ' she warned.

I took a few more steps. She groaned in anger and stood. Before I knew what was happening, she ran back at me, knocked me over, and pinned me to the ground. The orb slipped from my hand and rolled out of reach.

I pushed her off. 'Stop!'

Alexia was back in a second. She wrestled with me until she was able to get the knife at my throat. 'Stop what?' she asked with a mad grin.

'This!' I grabbed her hand and twisted it back, forcing her to let go of the knife. I sat up and pointed it at her. 'I don't want to kill you.'

Alexia laughed shrilly. She pinched the knife's blade with two fingers and pressed it into her stomach. 'Why not? Just one push and I'm gone. All your problems solved. I would have done it. One more minute of this insanity and I would have done it!' Alexia pushed herself up against the blade point.

'Is there any part of you left? Any part of the woman I looked up to?'

Alexia kicked my sore leg, causing me to cry out in pain. My eyes pricked with tears. The sting of the blow lasted for several seconds. I gritted my teeth, willing it to pass.

She leant down to my ear. 'No, no, no. She's gone, gone, gone.' She reached over to my hip and unsheathed one of my swords.

I pushed her back and forced myself to my feet, despite the pain in my leg. I stepped towards the White Orb, but Alexia ran at me with the sword.

I pulled out my second one and slashed her blade down. I took a swipe that cut a few strands of her hair. She bared her teeth at me like an annoyed lioness. She dropped the sword and went for my throat with her hands. She was stronger than I expected, and I fell backwards, losing my blade. I began to choke and tried pulling at her fingers. I couldn't see anything of my cousin in her face.

I focused on bringing my leg up. I kneed her hard in the stomach. She let go. I coughed, picked up my sword, and pointed it at her. She fell to her knees with her arms open like a martyr.

'Go on then,' she said with great drama. 'Kill me. I am evil after all, responsible for many deaths.' She ran her tongue over her upper lip like she was enjoying the taste of her words.

I pointed the sword at her heart. My leg was throbbing.

Alexia remained kneeling with her arms spread. 'Go on. It will make you feel better.' She winked at me. 'I promise.'

'Yes. Eva can reign in your stead once she is grown.' I watched for her reaction to the princess' name.

She opened her mouth and closed it again, but I saw the change pass over her face.

'No. I will not kill you.' I dropped the blade. 'There is still something of my cousin left in you, and that is worth saving.'

Alexia laughed again, but instead of fighting back, she stood and began to run away across the plains.

I didn't go after her. I hurried to the White Orb. It took only a moment to open—a few seconds, five heartbeats—but it felt like forever.

Finally, it locked in place. I opened the compartment where the vial of balm was kept and took it out.

The orb's light got brighter, and Alexia fell into the grass mid-stride. She held her head like it was about to explode. I limped over to her with both the orb and vial. By then, she was lying on her back, wilting like the last leaf of autumn.

I took her hand. It was clammy. 'Alexia, can you hear me?'

She arched her back and fell flat on the grass again, her face contorted as if invisible instruments were torturing her.

I rolled her onto her stomach and ripped her dress back. The rash on her skin was much worse than when I'd last seen it, her skin black and hard. I moved her hair out of the way and saw that it also spread right up to her neck and into her hairline. It looked raw and excruciating.

'Oh, Alexia . . . '

I braced an arm across her shoulder blades to keep her from moving, brought the vial to my teeth with my spare hand, and unscrewed the cap. I tipped a few drops of balm out. I was aiming for her lower back, where the original cut was, but she moved again and it fell on her shoulder.

'I claim you for Ru'ach and for good. You are cured of this vile disease of Anash.' I poured the rest down her spine.

She shrieked as if it were acid. I screwed the cap back on with my teeth and put the vial back in the orb to keep it safe. I rubbed the balm into her skin, the rash bumpy against my palms. Alexia continued to elicit agonising cries. Once I'd completed the job as thoroughly as possible, I turned Alexia onto her side and took her hand again. The sky grumbled, and it started raining.

'You have to let your pain go, or they will have a grip on you forever,' I said.

Raindrops trickled down her skin. The colour was draining from her face. It was only then I realised I might still lose her.

She's . . . she's fading.

The idea that the queen was dying seemed surreal, like I was watching a play on a stage.

The White Orb continued to shine brighter and brighter. It shot a white light up into the sky, and the rain above us stopped.

'You deserve to be happy, Alexia.' Tears were dripping down my face. 'What Cades did to you was unforgiveable, but you must forgive him. You must forgive yourself, or they will always have power over you.'

Her eyes, which had been opening and closing, focused on me for the briefest of moments. 'Yes,' she whispered.

Her movements began to slow. Her eyes closed, and her breathing sounded strained. Blood bubbled out of her nose and mouth.

She's not going to make it.

'Alexia. Alexia!'

She didn't respond.

'Don't you give up!' I yelled at her, shaking her shoulder. 'Don't you dare leave me!'

Nothing. She stopped breathing.

I was too late . . .

'No.' I kissed her forehead and bent over her, praying and crying all at once.

Please, Ru'ach, you are the King of Life. Do not let Anash claim her. Spare her, please.

Still nothing. My beloved cousin was gone.

Several more minutes passed before I pulled back, now feeling forsaken in the plains. Ahead of me, an eagle swooped in the dark sky, screeching in its strong and piercing way. It saw something and dove down but missed its prey and returned to the sky in an elegant turn. It gave another cry before leaving me with nothing but the ghostly sound of the breeze in the grass. I took a deep breath and tried to stop crying. My mind flittered between worries, and I began to wonder what I would tell Darj.

I will have to tell him I failed. We will have to collect Princess Eva before the Zalems get to Liane. He will have to act on the regency. Our chapter in history will close. My cousin is dead.

But then, something started happening to Alexia's back. I moved her hair out of the way again. The red rash was beginning to withdraw from her neck. It retracted from her shoulder blades and her sides and disappeared back towards the cut. The swelling of her muscles lessened, and the colour of her skin began to return to normal. Her veins, which had stood out as inflamed lines, settled down again. I put my hand on her lower back; the feverish heat had gone out of her. After a bit longer, the only thing left that spoke of her ordeal was the small crescent moon incision the Zalems had made, and it was soon nothing more than an ordinary cut that, in time, would heal, too.

I'd been holding her hand the whole time, but now it grasped mine in turn.

30
My Cousin

'Alexia?'

She blinked and looked at me with eyes that were blue and lovely, like I remembered. 'Adaliah?' The light in the White Orb faded. 'What happened?'

'Alexia . . . ' I was so relieved, I couldn't hold back my tears. 'You're free!'

'Free . . . ' She looked around, trying to remember. 'Free.'

She lay on the grass, taking slow breaths. We didn't say anything for a while. She was dazed, like she was waking from a deep sleep.

She saw the blood on my leg. 'I'm so sorry,' she said, gesturing towards it. Quiet tears began to stream down her face, too. 'I am so sorry for everything.'

'Don't distress yourself.'

Alexia pulled herself up in a sitting position and leant her head on my shoulder. 'I thought . . . I thought it was over.' She looked at the orb, and then up at the sky, like she was seeing the darkness for the first time. 'You were right, Adaliah. All this . . . What you said about me not having accepted they were dead . . . About being cold-hearted, the Zalems working on my pain . . . You were right, particularly about Jeri. But he was just a boy, Adaliah, my boy. His death was so horrific, and I never got to say goodbye; I never got to tell him one last time that I loved him. Ethaniel died in my arms, and somehow, that made it a little easier. I got to tell him how I felt, how sorry I was, how I would never forget him . . . ' She sobbed. 'It was all so unjust.'

'I know,' I whispered.

'I thought by sacrificing myself to the Zalems, I could pay back my debt. They died because of me, and I have to live with that forever.'

I hugged her close. 'No, you don't. No one blames you, least of all them. Do you really think they are looking down on you with anything but pride and love? I can't begin to imagine what pain you've been in, but we have survived many things, you and I. We will survive this, too, and we will see them again.'

Alexia drew back so she could meet my eyes. 'I don't know why you look up to me when time after time it's your strength that gives me courage. I have known nothing but death and darkness these past few weeks. I have known nothing but grief these past few years. I hung onto it because I was scared of who I would become without them. I pushed you and Darj and Ru'ach away because I didn't want to be helped and I didn't want to let them go.' She wiped away her tears. 'But I want to be free of the darkness inside me. I don't want to forget them, but I do want to be happy. I don't think they will resent me for that.'

I kissed her cheek. 'I have missed you, the real you, so much.'

She squeezed my hand.

We stood, and Alexia looked around at the plains and Mount Dennell. The air smelt of rain and grass. She took a slow and deep breath, and for the first time since Cades, she looked peaceful. 'I want to forgive them properly. Cades, Jag, Sirvan, Bylon, the High Zalem . . . '

'Yourself?'

Her mouth turned in a smile. 'Yes, I think I'm even ready to do that.'

Not for the first time that day, she did something that surprised me. She knelt in the grass, closed her eyes, and tilted her face towards the dark and foreboding sky. 'Pray with me, Adaliah.'

I knelt down beside her. As she bent her head and began to pray, a white ray of sunshine peered through the storm towards us.

Once she'd gained enough strength and balance to walk, we went back to the Zalem camp to collect her bow. We searched a tent Alexia identified as Cordale's, who, according to her, was Bylon's secretary, the one in charge of non-combatant matters. He must have still been with Bylon. His tent, like most of them, was empty of people. The door was tied down, and I didn't have the patience to untie it, so I pulled out my sword and slashed an opening in the side.

'I'm sure he'll appreciate the new view,' Alexia said when I finished.

My blade proved its usefulness again when we uncovered five chests; I wedged it between the locks and forced them open. One was full of wine, which we left untouched, and another was packed with meaningless scrolls. The third held armour—steel vambraces, which Alexia accepted for her arms, and a breastplate that the Zalems must have made for her. It was almost a perfect fit. The green skirt on her dress hung down under it, but she looked more equipped for battle than she had before.

The fourth chest contained her dark wooden bow with its gold grip and her quiver of arrows. The fifth one was empty.

Alexia turned her bow over in her hands. 'I sent the Zalems after my own people, didn't I?' Her voice was quiet and ashamed.

'Everyone knew you weren't yourself.'

'Even Darj?'

'Especially Darj.'

'Did he act on the regency?'

'No.'

Alexia bit her lip. 'I'm not sure what to think of that.'

'He is still fighting for Targe, for you. He always will.' I didn't mention that he'd given me his blessing to kill her if it came to it, but I did notice how Alexia relaxed a little at my words. I thought of Darj's declaration in Liane. *Perhaps if we somehow survive this,* I thought, *they might have a chance.*

'What's that?' Alexia asked, moving to the new tent flap.

We walked towards the sounds of shouting and people marching somewhere close by. We hurried over a small hill and saw a battalion of men and women walking six abreast in what seemed to be an endless line.

'Who are they?'

'It's the Ghosts,' Alexia said. 'The men and women who occupied Sharlard. They have been infected and overcome by the Zalems' Bane and are slaves to the High Zalem, like I was. Sirvan did say they would come to speed their victory.'

My heart sank. We'd been outnumbered as it was at Tarcraig, and now they intended to obliterate us.

'They're coming to the camp,' I said.

'They must intend to rest here before joining the battle,' Alexia said. 'Come, we must get back to Darj.'

When we came in sight of the ongoing battle, I slowed Bagred to take in and understand the scene ahead. The Zalems were crashing against the rocks of Tarcraig like waves of an ocean. From where we were, the wave looked like a blur of black, as if it were polluted. We could see some of the bloodied men who fought on and those who lay dead in the grass. There were many bodies. Our men had been pushed back into Tarcraig.

'What's that?'

Alexia, who was sitting on Bagred behind me, pointed to something on our right.

I couldn't see anything, but someone called our names.

I recognised the voice. 'Zavad?'

The boy and his friend Dayle rose out of the grass.

'What are you doing here?' I asked, raising my voice. *Don't they know it's dangerous?* 'You're supposed to be looking after Eva!'

'She is surrounded by royal guards, who won't let us do anything! We wanted to help.' Zavad held up his palms. Alexia dismounted, and Dayle backed away from her, more frightened of being in trouble than Zavad.

'Adaliah!' Alexia pointed to a Zalem soldier riding up behind the boys.

'Isn't this a happy chance,' the man said as he drew closer. He swung at Dayle, but the boy managed to duck in time. Dayle rolled on the ground, grabbed a handful of dirt, and chucked it at the man's eyes. While the man was rubbing his face and cursing him, Dayle ran back to us.

I pulled my sword out and lifted it to throw, but Alexia released an arrow before I could. It was a clean shot that hit his heart.

'We don't know if you're still prevented from spilling blood,' Alexia said when she saw me staring at her. 'I don't want to take any chances.' She glanced towards Zavad.

I nodded. If I spilt blood while I was still under the Jazmardian blessing, it was Zavad's life that would suffer for it.

'Come,' I said to the boys. 'It's not safe here. We will take you to the caves of Tarcraig. Darj was planning to put the wounded there. You can run errands for the healers.'

They agreed, and Alexia helped them up onto the Zalem's horse.

We rode around the edge of battle, Alexia shooting arrows from behind me. I could hear them whirring past my ear and prayed her accurate aim wouldn't fail now. Zavad and Dayle rode close to my right; I was between them and the fighting.

It took us about half an hour to find Darj. He saw us coming. Even from a distance, I could see the utter amazement on his face as he watched us riding towards him.

'It's Queen Alexia returned!' a soldier yelled. 'The A'zyon Warrior has brought her back!'

'Arjla divala!' the Targians yelled as one, making it a fierce war cry. They shouted it again and again, but it soon transitioned to, 'Blessings upon the queen! Blessings upon the queen!'

Elhian helped me down, but Darj continued to stand motionless, as if he'd forgotten how to breathe and speak. The men were cheering so much, we may not have been able to hear him anyway.

'Darj?' Alexia called. She dismounted Bagred and walked to him. I think she was afraid he'd been injured because of the way he wasn't moving.

He came alive again at the sound of his name. He stepped forward and embraced Alexia with both arms. She wrapped hers around his neck—a particular display of affection, I noticed.

'I saw the light in the sky,' Darj said as he held her. 'I thought you were dead.'

'Adaliah brought me back.'

Darj met my eyes over her shoulder. *Thank you*, he mouthed to me. I gave him a knowing smile.

Elhian kissed my cheek. 'Well done,' he whispered to me. I leant my head against his chest, needing his strength again.

'Where are we up to?' Alexia asked as she drew away from Darj. We huddled near a gap in the rocks.

'Prince Ren took some men to the east and is supposed to come back now to flank them,' Darj said.

'He won't be late,' Raggin said, joining us with Xander.

'There are more soldiers coming, Darj,' Alexia said. 'Sirvan has called for the Ghosts.'

Darj nodded and looked to the east. He needed Ren to be punctual—the men were tiring, dying, and the mass of Zalems seemed impenetrable.

I wondered what he would do, what I would do if I were in his position. Run, and we would be hunted and killed. Stand, and we would still be killed—it would just take longer. The men were revived in seeing Alexia returned, but in real terms, there was still very little hope.

A contraption appeared on the horizon. A catapult, bigger than any I had ever seen. The others turned and saw it, too. 'That will break the rocks,' Xander said.

Before we could decide what to do, Ren Markus and his men flanked the Zalems as planned. The Zalems turned to face them, which took their focus away from Tarcraig. There was a moment of relief, but then the catapult was released. A heavy stone flew through the air, coming straight for us.

Raggin stared at it with an open mouth, frozen. 'Move!' Darj yelled. Raggin didn't hear him. Darj pushed him out of the way just in time. The rock hit the ground and rolled, killing several men.

Another one followed. It hit one of the crags, and a large chunk of rock fell to the ground. It was Elhian who had to get out of the way that time.

'Any ideas?' Elhian yelled over to Darj.

'We have to bring it down!'

'How?'

The blank look on Darj's face indicated he didn't have an answer. The field in front of us was clearing as the Zalems ran to meet Prince Ren's soldiers, and some of our men were already taking the opportunity to drag the nearby wounded further into Tarcraig.

Another rock flew through the air, this time killing several archers that stood on top of the crags.

Elhian looked at me and then at Raggin. I remembered what Raggin had done in Chettona.

Raggin noticed our interchange. 'Right,' he said. 'We need oil. Black oil and fire arrows.'

'If you take on a catapult of that size, you're an idiot,' Xander said.

'Now's not the time to compliment me.'

'Do you have oil?' I asked.

'Ah . . . ' Raggin hesitated, but I could see him thinking it through. 'Egra is the nearest city that would have some, and that would be a three day return trip at best.'

'I can do it,' I said. 'I don't know if I can fight yet, and I want to be useful. Bagred is fast and strong, and I can make the trip quicker on my own. I'm sure Lord Fenton will help us.'

I could tell by the look on Elhian's face that he didn't want me to go. But he held my hand, and I knew then he wouldn't stop me. He understood me enough to know I had to do something while the others fought, even if I had just brought the queen back. Alexia, familiar with her own determined streak, said nothing either. In the end, it was only Darj who asked me not to go.

'We can think of something else,' he said to me aside.

'Good, I hope you do. But in the meantime, I will get the black oil in case and speak to Fenton. I'll leave you here to look after Alexia.'

I took Zavad and Dayle to the opening of one of the caves. 'You will see unpleasant things in here,' I said before letting them in, 'but you will be safe.' *At least while we can hold the Zalems off.* 'Do you think you'll be all right?'

'Yes, we can help,' Zavad said. 'That's why we ran away from Liane, to help.'

'Does your mother know you're here?'

The boys exchanged guilty looks.

'We wrote her a note,' Zavad said.

That poor woman. I promised myself I would visit her once it was all over.

We walked inside, where the shell of the cave was glowing orange from the torches. It was warm. The air smelt of medicines, olive oil, dirt, and something else that seemed to make Dayle feel sick. I realised it was the scent of burning flesh. Healers were sealing off wounds to stop infection. When I turned to see if Dayle was all right, he was vomiting.

'Don't worry,' I said once he'd recovered. 'Plenty of grown men and women have fainted from such sights and smells. All you will need to do is fetch water and bandages for the healers.'

Dayle nodded, and Zavad stood at his shoulder, ever determined.

'Zavad? Is that you?' A young soldier had been cleansing a man's arm wound with olive oil, but now he hurried over to us.

'Landor?' Zavad rushed into the soldier's arms. 'It's my brother, Landor!'

'What are you doing here?' Landor asked, holding him close. 'Don't you know what it'll do to our mother with us both gone? You should have stayed with her.'

'I couldn't . . . I couldn't stand by and do nothing.'

They parted, and Landor ruffled his hair. 'Just like our father, you little imp.' They laughed. I could see that the sight of a family member, even that of an exasperating little brother, had encouraged Landor. 'Thank you for bringing him in,' he said. 'I will look after him, and he can help me.'

'Good,' I said. 'We need all the help we can get.'

31
TO EGRA

I was about a quarter of the way to Egra when I suddenly realised how overwrought I was. I stopped Bagred in the forest, my heartbeat drowning out all other sounds. A breeze sifted around me as I stared ahead. I felt numb, brittle, like the last piece of ice floating on a melting river. The Casmodian soldiers called it 'sword shock', a battleborn anxiety I'd once seen in Alexia one lonely night in the Northern Invasion. I took several deep breaths and tried to calm my worn nerves.

To my right, a doe was eating grass with her spotted fawn. She saw me, flinched, and moved in front of her offspring. The little fawn gave a bleating sound before they both turned and flitted into the forest.

I forged a fire with kindling from the forest floor and spent at least an hour kneeling before it, hugging myself and trying to get my heart to beat normally. The dark sky seemed lower than usual, and the lone light I had was from the flames.

I ate some flat bread—the only food I'd been able to find before leaving Tarcraig—but my hand shook as I brought it to my mouth.

I began to weep. It had been a constant strain: Elhian missing and not knowing if he was alive. Alexia dying on the plains, trying to pay a debt she didn't owe. I thought about Erran's head on the spike and Karlen's death in the southwestern mountains, the arrow in my leg, and what I still had to do. Only a few months earlier, I had been looking forward to starting a new life free of Cades and the scars he had left. Thankfully, no one was around to see me as I cried in the forest like a lost child.

But then the deer and her fawn came back, and I hoped it wasn't just because the patch of grass near me was the lushest. The mother perked her ears towards me, checking for danger, but then lowered her elegant head and began to graze again.

I didn't want to scare them a second time, so I forced back my tears and took several more deep breaths.

I can do this.

The breeze picked up more strength. *I can do this.*

Arjla divala.

With him I stand.

I put the fire out, limped to Bagred, and climbed up on his back.

The few people outdoors in Egra scattered out of the way when I came charging through. The surprise in their faces and the shouts of my name were mixed with joy and dread. They must have feared I was coming to warn them they were next, but I didn't stop to address them.

Instead, I rode around Egra's lake to Lord Fenton's residence: a formal building perched on a hill under a large oak tree. He must have seen me coming; he was already hurrying down the front stairs of the Royal Manor when I arrived and dismounted.

'Your Majesty,' he said as he doubled over in a bow before me. 'What news?'

'The queen is safe from Zalem hands. She's back with Darj and the army.'

Lord Fenton clasped his hands together with relief. 'The Great Spirit is with us.'

'But we need your help.' A servant took Bagred's reins and began leading him away. 'Feed him, but bring him back soon,' I said. 'I cannot stay.'

'What is it?' Fenton asked.

'We are battling at Tarcraig, but we will be defeated. They have a catapult bigger than I've ever seen, and it is destroying the very rocks at Tarcraig. They will all die if we don't bring it down.'

Fenton put a hand on his hip. 'They should retreat. The queen shouldn't even be there!'

'They can't retreat. They are outnumbered, and the Zalems would hunt them down if they tried. We have to destroy the catapult, and while I'm here, let me ask you to bring what militia you can—'

'Your Majesty . . . '

I raised a hand. 'You cannot fail the Queen of Targe now. Remember what Darj said? Even the lords must fight if Targe is to survive.'

Lord Fenton gave me a patient look, and I knew I was about to get some well-meaning but patronising advice. 'I have the greatest respect for Darj, but he is a military man. In such matters as these, I feel he lacks the broader political understanding needed to make well-rounded decisions.'

I couldn't help but groan. 'Do you think I care about political understandings right now? All I know is our men are dying at Tarcraig and that they will continue to die if they don't get the help they need! Darj, Elhian, and the queen will die with them. The Zalems will claim Targe as theirs. What political impact do you think that will have?'

Lord Fenton looked across his town. It was very Targian with its small, white, stone houses and slated roofs. In Casmodia, the houses were built a bit bigger, usually with a second storey and high-angled roofs designed to cope with the additional layers of snow from the long winters. Here, the houses represented a land used to stricter seasons. Around Egra's lake, there were thousands of flowers that would have been beautiful on a sunny day, but they were wilting in the darkness.

'Don't you see? Even Egra will be lost to them.'

Lord Fenton began to nod. 'I will do what I can, but first I must hear from the rest of the council.'

'Fine,' I said, 'but remember: every minute you delay, another son of Targe gives his life for his kingdom.'

We ate later in Fenton's dining room, and I explained to him about the oil and how it had worked in Chettona. He sent one of his men to assist me while he wrote to the council, and I soon found myself in the back of a stable, watching as the assistant loaded two barrels of oil into a small cart. I wished there was another way—the cart would slow my return considerably—but there was nothing else I could do.

'Are you sure you don't want to rest before returning?' Fenton asked when he came to see me off. The pigeon carrying his message to the council had already been released. 'You look exhausted.'

'They're expecting me as soon as possible. I cannot delay.'

I climbed into the front of the cart. Another horse was tacked and ready to go, while Bagred was tethered to the back. He deserved what rest he could get. Fenton's men locked in the oil. 'I hope to see you on that field, Lord Fenton—for the queen's sake, if nothing else. Please send food and medical supplies. I see intelligence in your eyes. Please use it.'

'I cannot promise you anything more than I already have, but please don't doubt that I know the gravity of the cause. The black sky is a constant reminder, as is my people's fear.'

The ride back to Tarcraig was slow and uneventful. When we stopped halfway, I brushed both horses down as thoroughly as I could and gave them what was left of my flat bread and an apple each. Lord Fenton had stocked me up with some to take back, and I relished the fruit as much as the horses did.

By what felt like the end of the day—I was still largely unaware of the time due to the storm—I could hear the battle ahead of me again.

When I came in sight of Tarcraig, I saw that Darj and the men had dug into the ground in front of the rocks, giving them a little more protection. I also saw that we'd lost a lot of soldiers but hoped they were in the caves as wounded men. Better that than dead.

I couldn't pass through the men with a cart unnoticed, so I unhitched the horse and left it with the cart just beyond Tarcraig under a tree. I saddled Bagred and rode him the rest of the way. I found Darj at the foot of the now-shattered rocks in the trench. Several trees had fallen from the crevices they'd called home for hundreds of years and lay in the battlefield like fallen soldiers. Darj had used a couple of them to build a rudimentary wall above his trench.

'I think they're running out of stones for the catapult,' Darj said when I arrived. 'They're slowing down with their attack, but my scouts tell me they've sent men to get more.'

I explained where I'd left the cart. He told Raggin and Xander. The two of them, along with several helpers, went out to put the oil into throwable bags, which they had sewn together in my absence.

'Darj, I will lead them,' Raggin said later as Darj and I attached bags of oil to Guntar's saddle. Six archers stood nearby, filling their quivers with fire arrows. 'I've done it once before, and you're needed more here.'

Darj didn't say anything at first. A stone crashed against the tops of the crags, flicking a burst of stone shards into the nearby soldiers. 'It's a death mission.'

'They said that last time, and we survived. Besides, if it is, better I do it than you.'

'No man is more valuable than another on the field of battle,' Darj said.

'No, I just meant . . . I need to do this, Darj. For Ival, for Chettona.'

Alexia had joined us in time to hear Raggin's last words. 'Captain, you have nothing to prove to anyone,' she said.

'Perhaps not, but I'd still like to do it all the same.' Raggin waited for our blessing.

Darj took the bags of oil off Guntar's saddle and handed them to Raggin. 'Ru'ach be with you, soldier.'

32
FIVE TURNS

Alexia helped me climb to the top of the rocks. 'I need more arrows,' she said.

'Here, Your Majesty,' an archer said, passing her a pack of them, 'but we're all running out.'

'Perhaps I could fight,' I said as she put the arrows into her quiver. 'You're not the High Zalem anymore. The Jazmardian blessing has no reason to exist now. We have Zavad with us—'

'I know you want to help, but I just don't think it's wise until we're sure you and Zavad are safe.'

I sighed, but it was a small expression of a deep frustration. Once again, I was forced to watch on.

Raggin rode out with the mounted archers. They shot the Zalems in their path with help from Alexia and the other archers on the rocks and drew close to the catapult. It fired another rock over their heads. The stone crashed in the field below Alexia and me, too close.

Raggin shouted, and his horsemen reached for the oil. The archers released a volley of arrows and cleared some of the men near the catapult. Raggin yelled again, and the black bags of oil flung into the sky like small, plump birds rushing to their prey. Some landed on the wood and broke, causing the oil to drip down it. Others landed in the grass.

The archers' fire arrows were alight. It was just as well, for the torchbearer who had ridden with them was already dead, just as it had been in Chettona.

'Shoot!'

The arrows shot through the air. The catapult caught fire, and we breathed a sigh of relief. But a few more Zalem soldiers ran to it and released the loaded arm again, sending another stone hurtling through the air.

Some of the patches of fire on the wood were burning out. Raggin yelled again, and even though I couldn't understand what he was saying, I could hear the panic in his voice. More bags flew through the air, bursting against the wood a second time. I held my breath and muttered a quick prayer. Without a torchbearer, we had to rely on it catching fire from the existing flames.

A Zalem pulled Raggin from his horse. The other Targian horsemen went to help him. As they fought off the Zalems, a breeze picked up, and the oil on the catapult set ablaze. Flames began to roar. The increasing heat caused the metal in the joints to expand. The wood started to crack. Then, it snapped altogether and exploded out over the men.

A large piece of it flipped towards Raggin. It hit him over the back of the head, and another piece landed on his legs.

'Look,' Alexia said, 'it's Bylon.'

He was riding onto the battlefield with the Dark Orb in hand. Nearby, Elhian was fighting with a Zalem. Darj impaled one he'd flung to the ground but hesitated before he went after another. Elhian leant on his knees and tried to catch his breath, when another Zalem attacked him. They were all exhausted.

'Come on,' Alexia said. She helped me down the rocks, and we hurried towards them both.

'Get Ren,' she said to Darj, 'and someone find me a white flag.'

A few minutes later, Ren came running towards us. Elhian helped me up onto Bagred. The five of us rode out to Sirvan, Elhian carrying a stick with a white piece of material tied to the top.

Sirvan waited until we were close and then charged at the queen with a bloodied sword. She didn't flinch but simply rode around him, and we followed. 'I have not come to fight you,' she said, 'but to offer you a truce.'

'You give me no reason to cooperate.'

'Six turns of the sand,' Alexia said, 'and the opportunity to collect our wounded and dead without fighting. Even you could see the sense in that.' She leant forward in her saddle. 'Or shall we see whether the Zalems respond better to their High Zalem than they do their captain?'

'They do not respond to a title but the power that goes with it. Thanks to her,' he pointed to me, 'you have forfeited your position, and we are leaderless. But don't worry. I'm sure I can manage in the meantime, and we have suffered loss before.' He gave Elhian a dirty look.

'Do you accept my truce or not?' Alexia asked.

Sirvan kept his sword up and his eyes on the queen. 'Four turns.'

'Five,' Alexia said, 'or nothing.' Elhian and Ren drew their swords.

'All right,' Sirvan said. He moved closer to Darj and thrust a long, bony finger towards him. 'But as soon as the time is up, you and I will meet.'

The others rode back to Tarcraig, but I saw Xander looking for Raggin amongst the fallen and went to help.

'I haven't seen him since this was destroyed,' Xander said, scanning the bodies near the catapult's wreckage.

'Perhaps someone already rescued him,' I said. 'We can look in the caverns if we don't find him. He might have been taken there for help.' I certainly hoped so. I'd seen the blow he'd taken. If he wasn't already getting treatment, there would be serious concerns for him.

'Raggin!' Xander called. 'Where are you, you stupid . . .' His words faded when he saw his friend lying under a block of wood. Part of it was still smoldering, and we coughed on the smoke. 'Had to be the hero, didn't ya?'

The field around us was eerie with soldiers searching the bodies for survivors. Some of the Zalems were finishing off their own men, and many screamed as they died.

Raggin tried to speak, but it came out as a mumble. Blood dribbled down his chin.

'Calm yourself,' Xander said. 'Let's get this off you.' With a great heave, he pushed the log off Raggin's legs. Underneath, Raggin's pants were stained with blood.

'I . . . I can't feel them,' Raggin said.

'It's all right,' I said, putting a hand on his shoulder. 'We'll sort you out. We need some help over here!' I called to a pair of Delyans. They made their way over, stepping between dead bodies.

I wiped the blood away from Raggin's head wound. The Delyans and Xander forged a stretcher from the scraps of the catapult and lifted Raggin onto it. By then, his face was a shade of grey and his legs limp.

'At least now I know it is possible to shut you up,' Xander said with a forced smile.

Raggin tried to respond, but the words caught in his throat again.

'Alexia, there's something I need to ask you.' Darj was talking to her in the caves when we arrived with Raggin. Alexia gave Darj a worried look as I settled Raggin on a bed a few steps away.

'If it's about me leaving with the Zalems . . . '

'It's not. It's about the High Zalem. Did he . . . ' He wrung his hands together and glanced at me. 'I really don't know how to ask this . . . '

'Did he what?'

'Did he . . . ' Darj leant closer to her ear and whispered the question.

Alexia stepped back, unmistakably repulsed. But she didn't respond straightaway. She stared at him with an open mouth. 'The truth is, so much of what happened while I was with him is a blur. I do remember feeling his lips on mine . . . '

'He kissed you?' Darj asked, snarling slightly.

'But I don't think he . . . ' She put a hand on her stomach, looking pale. 'Why do you ask?'

'I was hoping you could put me out of my misery. Adaliah is no longer ordained. I can't think of any other reason as to why.'

Alexia flashed me a confused look. Darj and I told her what had happened in Liane, surprising her with the information about the Targian Orb and the second butterfly.

'Darj . . . Adaliah, I am late . . . I thought it was just stress. But a child? His child? I cannot bear the thought!'

Darj reached for her hand. 'Don't trouble yourself until we know more. There may yet be a more satisfying answer.'

'The Ghosts are here,' I said to Prince Ren later. We stood side by side just beyond the rocks, having done everything we could for Raggin. I pointed at the soldiers who had been affected by the Zalems' Bane. They were appearing on the horizon.

I wondered what their lives would have been like before. Most would have been ordinary citizens caught up in the wrong place at the wrong time and made subservient to the High Zalem. Or perhaps they had dabbled in the black arts of the evil spirit Anash, like the original Zalems had in Delya. Or maybe they'd just been bakers, farmers, and other quiet folk.

Now they were marching towards us with no sense of purpose at all. '"Dead will the Ghosts be if the general does not recall",' I said. 'So many mysteries, and yet they must all be discovered soon, or we will be defeated. You would think we'd want them dead.'

'No,' Ren said. 'They're just like us. They only need the cure as Alexia did.'

'But we used it all on her. Even if we hadn't, there wouldn't have been enough for all of them.'

'I know. But there must be another way.'

The allies brought the last remaining bodies in off the field. They were piling them up in the largest clearing within Tarcraig. When the time came, a mass burial would be their final farewell. Other men were collecting arrows from the bodies and off the field. They would be used to restock the archers when the battle resumed.

'My ancestor, Dan,' Ren said, 'the one who defeated his brother Mors but let him live, wrote that facing the Zalems was like facing your innermost fear.'

'What is your fear?'

Ren thought about this. 'I am afraid that when the time comes, I will value my life more than the task set before me and that I will shame my kingdom and Ru'ach because of it. I don't want to be remembered because of something I didn't do, and a second son must work doubly hard to leave a mark on his kingdom.'

I wondered if my father had felt the same way. If he had, he'd never spoken of it to me, but then he'd had a special purpose in looking after Kest.

I looked at Prince Ren, taking in his youthful face, thoughtful eyes, and square shoulders. He had a small, round scar under his left ear that he kept running his finger over as he spoke. His eyes were a lovely hazel colour that reminded me of gold lying in a river.

'It's not wrong to want to live,' I said. 'You are more use to your kingdom and to Ru'ach with a beating heart. Ru'ach is the king of the living.'

'But what if that heart lacks the courage to do what is right?'

I sighed. 'You remind me of Alexia. She has been so determined to put duty before her heart that until now, she had forgotten how to feel. There are ones who could die if I fail to complete the task set before me, even though I'm no longer sure what that is and Erran is no longer here to tell me. Still, I will do my job, but not out of duty. I do it for the ones I love. Isn't that a worthy cause, too?'

Ren smiled at me. 'Duty is just love for a kingdom, for the people of that kingdom. Your cousin takes this seriously. I see this as very self-sacrificing, not unworthy.'

'As do I, but I still think it is an empty life that acts on duty alone.'

'Perhaps emptiness is your innermost fear.'

I raised an eyebrow. 'No . . . I think my greatest fear is despair, of suffering so much that I become as Alexia was—broken, a shell, alone. Empty, as you say. But the funny thing about life is that to risk love is to risk hurt. Still, I will never regret loving my family first, no matter what might happen in the future.'

He touched my upper arm. 'Nor will I.'

I woke later to find Kadram watching sand fall through an hourglass as Elhian, Darj, and Alexia entered their third hour of sleep. I'd slept two, but it was all I could manage. Darj was turning every few minutes despite his exhaustion. Alexia was breathing softly nearby, a reassuring sound.

'What are we going to do?' I heard Kadram whisper to himself. He poked a stick at the small campfire. 'With the Ghosts preparing to fight against us, we are too few, and our men are tired.' He looked at Darj again. '"Dead will the Ghosts be if the general does not recall." Oh, Lezan, dear brother . . . ' He turned his face upwards. 'What does it mean? What has Darj forgotten?'

He walked outside, and I lay staring at the cavern's ceiling, his questions echoing in my mind.

What does it all mean?

I thought about Erran and the power he had given me. I wondered what he would have wanted me to do in this situation, how he would have expected me to use the power.

Why had he called me?

I tried to think back to my first conversation with him. What had he said?

I can give you a blessing to help you overcome his power with the sword.

The High Zalem was dead, and I had assumed that meant his power was dead. So what had Erran meant about his power? Was it just a phrase, or had it meant something else?

But it must be done with the Kestian sword, the Life Sword.

'Can't sleep?'

I turned and saw Elhian with his eyes half-open, gazing at me.

I shook my head. 'I didn't mean to wake you.'

'You didn't. You're worried about how you're going to fight, aren't you?'

'Well, that . . . and . . .' I shared my thoughts with him.

'So, you think you have to destroy his power?' Elhian asked.

'I don't know what I think.'

Elhian kneaded my hand in his as he contemplated everything I'd said. 'Well, what gave him power? His men? No, you weren't supposed to spill any human blood but his . . .'

We sat up and leant against the cavern wall. My head felt so tired, like it was full of the sand from Kadram's hourglass. I leant into Elhian. I wanted to sleep, to escape, not to think about what it meant to destroy the power of the High Zalem.

Alexia rolled onto her side, still asleep.

'The balm healed Alexia,' I said, hoping a new train of thought might help. 'They gave her the Bane because they wanted to affect her physically and emotionally, and control her, and make her lose her sense of self. Her identity.'

'Right . . .' Elhian rolled his hand in the air as an encouragement to keep going.

Perhaps I was onto something. 'Was I supposed to put some of the balm on him?'

Elhian considered this. 'I don't think so. That's to heal people of the virus. He created the virus. Well, as far as we know . . .'

He used the virus as a weapon . . .

'What?' I asked when Elhian turned to me with a look of realisation.

'It's the Zalems' Bane, the Dark Orb.'

'What do you mean?' I asked.

'His power is in the Dark Orb, in the Bane,' Elhian said. 'The Jazmardian blessing must strengthen your immunity against it. It makes sense. In fact, maybe it wasn't just about killing the High Zalem, or Alexia. I think it's much more than that. You have to destroy his pestilence! Apart from Odavan, you are the only one with the blessing. And you have something Odavan doesn't—the Life Sword. That's why Erran wanted you to get it; it was cleansed for this purpose! Adaliah, you are the only one who can do it.'

I stared at him, amazed.

The last grains of sand fell through Kadram's hourglass, and the Zalem horn sounded out on the field.

33
ODAVAN RETURNS

Not long later, we reached the frontline of the battlefield, and Alexia turned to address the thousands of men.

'Today, we define our kingdoms' futures,' she said, raising her voice so she could be heard even from the top of the rocks. 'We will define it as good. I am so proud of your resolve and courage in my absence. Now that I am back, I will fight by your side until we eradicate our kingdoms of this disease. They have reinforcements'—she gestured towards the Ghosts, who now stood at the front of the Zalem army—'but we have Ru'ach on our side! We have a cause, and that is to fight as one against the darkness until the light prevails!' She raised her bow, and the Targians and Delyans cheered.

'We have already sacrificed too many men for Targe,' a Casmodian said. 'This is not our fight!'

'If we don't defeat the Zalems here, they will come to Casmodia,' Elhian said.

'You only fight because of her,' another said, thrusting a dirty finger towards me. 'Because she is one of them.'

'*She* is the queen consort!' Elhian said. 'But yes, our union does mean that Casmodia and Targe are also united. We will not let them die because we lack the courage to stand by them!'

'How many more men will be sacrificed for your cause? The Casmodian council would not approve of this.'

Elhian took a deep breath. 'Thousands of men died for Cades' cause—'

'Because you fought against him!'

Stop!' Elhian yelled. 'I fought against him because I would not see my kingdom defiled with sinful, power-hungering deeds in the name of a king who cared for nothing but his own selfish pursuits!'

For the first time, the Casmodians stopped bickering and listened.

'I fought against him because I believed that the men of that kingdom were not the same as him, that deep down I am from a holy kingdom, a kingdom of honour and integrity! Like Delya, we fight for Targe—not just for their sakes but for ours—but is it such a grief to you that they should also benefit from our help and support, that you might one day tell your children how you stood against evil for your allies, and in so doing also saved Casmodia?'

His men were silent. I could see a new emotion in their faces. It was shame at first—Elhian had reached their consciences at last—but then it was something different. Pride. Elhian had given them something to believe in, something bigger than themselves.

'To battle!' he called, raising his sword.

And the men from all kingdoms finally called back as one.

They began to move into position—archers to the top, infantry and cavalry to the front. I found Darj looking out at the enemy with more concern than usual. 'What is it?' I asked.

'I'm . . . I'm not sure we can win.'

I scoffed. 'When have we ever been sure?'

'General!' a man called before Darj could answer my question. I recognised the man as one of the scouts.

'Yes?'

'There are men coming!'

'What? More Zalems?' Darj asked.

'Not Zalems, sire!' The scout was grinning.

'Who?' I asked.

The scout pointed to the horizon. A battalion of men was approaching from the west. They held banners that were flying in the wind—green flags, edged with gold and embroidered with twelve stars. Others were yellow.

Darj squinted, trying to identify the man leading them. 'It's Lord Fenton with the militia!'

Alexia and Ren hurried to us. 'It's more Delyan men as well,' Ren said. 'My brother must have sent them to help us!'

The Zalems would soon begin their attack, but we didn't have to wait long for the new battalion to reach us. Lord Fenton came ahead of them, accompanied by a certain Delyan.

'Alel,' Darj said with amazement.

'General,' he said with a slight bow of his head. He acknowledged Alexia in the same way. The rest of the men arrived and stopped behind them.

'What are you doing here?' Prince Ren asked.

'We heard you had come to fight alongside the Targians,' Alel said. 'And as this is the first time Casmodia, Delya, and Targe have stood as one, we didn't want to miss it. Our people realise now that Queen Alexia was not responsible for the deaths of our loved ones.' He gave her an apologetic nod. 'And as the whole thing was a ruse by the Zalems to ensure our kingdoms would not stand together, we came with King Thane's blessing to make sure they would not succeed.'

'You are very welcome,' Darj said, patting him on the back. 'And, Lord Fenton, I am glad to see you rallying the councilors at last. Every man will help.'

'It is the least we could do. What I failed to tell Adaliah was that I'd already written to the men of the queen's council in Liane long before she arrived in Egra.'

I gasped at him. 'Why didn't you tell me? Why did you let me think they'd fail us?'

'Because I was afraid they would, that they would find an excuse not to come or come too late.' He stroked his moustache. 'Egra's militia alone would be nothing of the help you needed, nor would I grant them permission to die without at least some hope of success—unless I was overruled by General Darj or Queen Alexia, of course. The letter I sent while you were there was to instruct them where to meet, but it was only after you left that I received word that they had indeed mobilised. I've organised for supplies to come, and they should be here soon, too. We left Egra and came across these Delyans. We are not trained soldiers, you understand, but we will do our best.'

'I am most grateful, Lord Fenton,' Alexia said.

Darj began to call out instructions to the new men—'Form lines, get behind the cavalry'—until they were carefully arranged into the most advantageous positions.

The Zalem horn sounded again. They were beginning their attack.

'I don't suppose you could do what you're told for once and stay out of harm's way?' Darj asked Alexia.

'What do you think?' She gave him a bored look, but one corner of her mouth curved upwards a little.

Darj shook his head. 'To the top then, archer?'

She nodded. 'To the top.'

'Bylon will have the Dark Orb,' Elhian said to me as we rode behind Darj to the front of the army. 'Circle the battle and find him. I think this whole thing has been orchestrated to bring Sirvan to power, so be careful with them. Remember, Zavad is still at risk, and we don't know if you can spill blood yet without risking his life.'

'I won't be able to spill blood until the orb is destroyed. I've already thought of that.'

The Zalems were running towards us. 'Then you know what to do.' Elhian unsheathed his sword. 'Go!'

I turned Bagred and rode out of the way. The two armies clashed behind me.

A wave of Zalems climbed up the back of Tarcraig and attacked the archers from behind. Alexia spun her bow and knocked several of them down, then released a dual shot to kill two more. I hoped she could hold them back.

I need to find Bylon. I need to get to the Dark Orb.

'Where are you going?'

Before I could answer or turn, someone pushed me off Bagred. I rolled on the grounds a few times, and when I stopped, I felt cut all over. I struggled to my feet and found a Jazmardian standing before me. He tapped the point of his blade against his calf.

'Odavan,' I said, reaching for my sword, the Life Sword. 'What are you doing?'

'What is the power of the White Orb?'

'Where is Bylon?' I raised my sword.

'Are you sure you want to risk wounding me? Do not forget the boy—'

'Leave the boy out of this.'

As I fought him, I saw Bylon nearby, trying to open the Dark Orb. He had something in his hand.

'What are you doing?' I asked, thrusting my sword at Odavan for a second time. He deflected it, and I stumbled forward.

'Bylon is about to add an ingredient that will turn the Zalems' Bane into a gas. In a few minutes, everyone here will be infected.'

'What?' I looked about frantically, imagining all of us succumbing to the virus and becoming slaves to the Zalems.

I'd rather die.

'And to think I believed you were on our side that night.'

'You never believed that,' Odavan said. 'Not in your heart. Luckily for us, you did not trust your heart.'

There was some truth in that. I'd sensed something was wrong when I found out he'd left Alexia in the forest alone. 'I will not succumb to your pestilence.' I tried to sound calm, but I think I sounded more like a small child refusing to be told what to do.

'Do you really think you have a choice?' Bylon asked.

I had no answer. I hesitated, and Odavan took advantage of that and pushed me down.

As I lay winded on the grass looking up at the black sky, I saw a flash of purple. The second Armoured Butterfly floated above me as if beckoning me to get up. I wasn't sure if it was really there or if it were an illusion, but drawn to it, I sat up.

I was just in time. Odavan had been about to knock me out with a blow to the head.

I kicked him away and stood. I saw two things—Elhian riding towards me, and Bylon adding the new ingredient to the orb. A black cloud immediately began to form above it. I saw the Armoured Butterfly fluttering down towards Bylon, towards the Dark Orb. I knew then it was not an illusion.

Destroy his power with the sword.

The cloud grew bigger. It reached Elhian, and he fell from his horse as if the substance had knocked him down.

Only I have the blessing needed to get close to it without being infected.

I raised the Life Sword. I pushed Odavan away again when he tried to grab my arm and ran towards Bylon.

'No!' Odavan yelled, regaining his step and running after me.

I ran through the cloud and kicked Bylon so hard he sprawled backwards.

The orb was at my feet.

A sharp pain filled my mind. It felt like a hand had wrapped around my brain and was squeezing. I fell to my knees, my thoughts and focus all fading as I groaned.

'Do it, Adaliah!' The voice was Elhian's, but it was faint and pained as well. 'Do it!'

I opened my eyes. Bylon was trying to reach for the orb again.

I pushed him away for a second time, the action taking every scrap of my vanishing willpower. The noise of the battle—sounds of agony, desperation, and death—began to fade.

A thousand images flitted past my eyes.

My father: his love, his death.

Alexia and I playing as children.

Meeting Jeri for the first time.

Loving Elhian.

Defeating Jag.

Remembering who I was.

The word 'Life' lit up, and the sword's stone began to glow.

Elhian called to me from the ground. 'Do it, Adaliah!'

I stood and raised my sword. Bylon screamed. The wound Alexia had given him on his cheek stretched into a grotesque curve as his mouth widened.

I thrust my sword upon the Dark Orb as if slicing a melon. It split open, and then there was a light so blinding, I had to shield my eyes. The rest of the men on the battlefield did the same, and the fighting stopped.

A sound like thunder surrounded us, but much louder and longer. It felt like the sky would collapse and shatter to the ground. The earth began to move beneath me. Letting out a wild cry, I struck at the orb again, and this time, it fell in two. Lying inside was the Zalems' Bane. I raised the Life Sword one more time and brought it down on the glass vial.

It smashed, and the dark cloud vanished.

The Armoured Butterfly flew upwards. I followed it with my eyes and realised the vile storm that had filled the sky was receding just as fast as it had arrived. For the first time in weeks, a patch of blue was visible. It grew until it stretched from horizon to horizon. The world filled with the bright rays of the noon sun all at once. It was so warm, so golden, that the sensation was almost overpowering. The Armoured Butterfly began to shine. It landed briefly on my shoulder, then flew towards Elhian and did the same to him. It found Alexia and Darj amongst the soldiers and touched their shoulders, too. Then, it disappeared into the distance, leaving behind a world once more filled with light.

34
ZAVAD

Elhian staggered over to Bylon and raised his sword against him. Bylon attempted to fight back, but Elhian quickly cut him across the chest and Bylon fell to his knees. 'Guess whose turn it is to pay now?' Elhian asked.

'No, I didn't mean to!'

'Didn't mean to what?' Elhian shouted. 'Torture me in Sharlard? Attack Tiathi? Torment me about my father? Threaten my wife? I could let you live with your guilt.' Elhian impaled him with his sword. 'But I could not live with myself if I did.' He withdrew the sword, and Bylon fell down dead.

'No!' Odavan ran up behind me.

I turned and plunged my sword into his stomach, too, almost to the hilt. I held it there, so he could register his defeat. 'Look, Odavan,' I said. 'The A'zyon Warrior is back.'

I closed my eyes and soaked up the rays of sunshine while Elhian stumbled towards me. 'You ended it,' he said. He cupped my face. 'You brought light into a world of darkness.'

Some of the Zalems fell on their swords, forfeiting their lives. Some threw themselves at our remaining soldiers, inviting death with the hope of destroying just a few more enemies on the way.

The Ghosts had stopped moving altogether, now that the Bane was destroyed. Many were vomiting, the virus still at work in their systems.

Now, without the power of the Dark Orb sustaining them, they all needed a cure, and that was something we didn't have.

'Adaliah!'

Alexia had descended the crag, found a horse, and was riding at full speed towards me. I didn't think she was going to be able to stop in time.

'What's wrong?' I asked.

'Darj!' She pointed.

Darj was on his knees before Sirvan. Sirvan backhanded him across the face. Blood sprayed everywhere; Darj was nearly senseless.

'We have to do something,' Alexia said.

The three of us rode towards him, but Ren arrived from the other side first and pushed Sirvan away. 'Leave him be,' he said. 'It's over.'

'It will never truly be over,' Sirvan said. 'Your own ancestor Mors put everything in place to prevent our extinction. You think you have defeated us, but it is not over!'

Ren struck at Sirvan, while Darj spat blood onto the grass. Alexia knelt beside him. She put a hand on his shoulder; he shook it off. 'I have to finish this. My father . . . ' He saw Ren fighting with Sirvan and dragged himself to his feet.

'Darj . . . ' Alexia said, but when it came to stubbornness, we both knew she had met her match.

Sirvan kicked Ren out of the way. He had a dagger in his hand. He pitched it at Darj.

The moment that followed seemed to stop.

First, there was screaming, yelling—we all knew that Darj was going to die. Sirvan would only succumb to death if he could take Naythan Ryder's son with him in some reckless attempt to demonstrate his power, to finish what he'd started in that small house in Levanna.

Then, there was a boy. He was running across the field. It was the boy I had collected off the Path of the Dead, who, through Cades' campaign, had been separated from his family and almost died himself. It was the boy Darj had trained in the years that followed, personally dedicating hours to him and becoming the father he'd lost. It was the boy who had helped Alexia cope with the loss of her son, who had brought us both hope and purpose when there was only grief. It was the boy who had helped Elhian escape the Zalems, who had saved his life, and mine.

I didn't know he could run so fast. His dark hair flew out behind him, and his blue eyes, round and wild, remained imprinted in my memory for years to come.

The dagger flew through the air.

Zavad stepped in front of Darj, and the dagger landed in his back. He fell forward.

'No!' Darj said. He looked at Alexia and me, but we were both staring at the dagger in Zavad's back, incapable of speech.

Elhian was the only one of us able to function in any meaningful way. He carefully pulled the dagger out and helped him lie flat on his back while Darj, Alexia, and I knelt beside him.

'Darj . . . ' Zavad said, his breathing turning sharp and shallow. 'I wanted to help.'

'No . . . ' Darj swiped at his tears like they were insects. 'This is not how life is supposed to work. I'm supposed to protect you!'

'We protect each other.'

'You're too young,' Darj said.

'Being a soldier is about risking your life for a cause.' Zavad closed his eyes. 'And I get . . . to see . . . my father.'

Alexia reached for his hand. 'My boy, my boy . . . ' She sobbed and stroked back his hair. 'You have lived amongst kings and queens on earth; so shall it be in Ru'ach's presence.'

Zavad blinked a couple of times, and then his grip on Alexia's hand slackened.

'He's dead,' Alexia said to Sirvan with gritted teeth. Her eyes, like mine, were red with tears.

I did this. I must have spilt blood too early. Now Zavad is dead!

Or maybe it was much simpler than that. Maybe Zavad had run to protect someone he loved and died for it. Perhaps that was the pure, hateful entirety of it.

Darj put his hand over Zavad's motionless heart, his hand shaking and bloody. He took the dagger.

'He was a fool,' Sirvan said.

Darj collapsed backwards onto the grass and breathed heavily. Elhian and I stood over him with our swords raised. Alexia's bow was readied with an arrow.

'I'm disappointed in you,' Sirvan said, 'just as I was disappointed by your father's choice to stand against us. He failed to protect the ones he loved, just like you, and now you are alone.'

'Darj is neither alone nor a failure,' Alexia said, pulling back her arrow. 'And you have killed a child.'

A precious child. Our most precious Zavad.

'My father,' Darj said, struggling with the words, 'was a good man.'

With the dagger still in his hand, Darj suddenly pushed himself up and used his remaining strength to raise the weapon in one last act of survival. With an almighty grunt, he threw it as hard as he could. It cut through the air and sliced into Sirvan's chest.

Sirvan stiffened with the shock.

'No . . . ' He looked down at the dagger. 'Not like this.'

He swayed on his feet and collapsed to his knees. His body folded to the ground, and soon he was as spiritless as the grass he lay on.

Darj fell back near Zavad's body, exhausted and bleeding. Alexia pressed down on a wound on his stomach. He grabbed for my hand. '"Dead will the Ghost be if the general does not recall",' he said. 'I can see him now, Adaliah—my father, back in the house with the White Orb. "Sweet, holy wisdom", he said. I remember now. He was talking about the ingredients for the cure. Sweet, holy wisdom. He was talking about . . . about sweet myrrh, and holy oil, and wise sage.'

'What?' *Naythan had the orb?*

I thought fast. Yes, Naythan and Lord Benne had been involved in creating the cure with Erran—King Amaz had mentioned that in his letter. Sirvan must have realised they were up to something. That's why he went there, to try to get them on his side or to defeat them. In seeing that the cure was under threat, Naythan died to protect it and his family. He coded the information and gave it to the only person he could trust—his son.

'We have oil in the caves,' Alexia said. 'But as for myrrh and sage . . . '

'Samela gave me myrrh. If you find Guntar, it's in my saddlebag.'

'What about sage?' I asked. 'It doesn't grow around here.'

'Kadram will have some,' Elhian said. 'Jazmardian healers always do. It is one of the ingredients in the green paste they use to stay infections.'

'Do you know how many parts we need of each?' Alexia asked.

Darj grimaced. 'No. I don't.'

Darj convinced us to leave him and gather the ingredients. Elhian found Guntar and the myrrh. Alel, Ren, and some Delyan soldiers had even more. Alexia ran to the caves in search of olive oil. I went to talk to Kadram about the sage.

'Sage? What for?' he asked as he cleansed a soldier's arm wound.

'Darj said we need it for the cure,' I said. Elhian and Alexia joined us with the myrrh and oil.

'He didn't know how many parts of each were needed, though,' Elhian said.

'Did he have a name for this cure?' Kadram asked.

'He said his father called it "sweet, holy wisdom",' I said.

'In Jazmardian, that is "nanan halaza saag".'

'What?' I asked.

Kadram put the soldier's arm down and smiled. 'Erran was involved in the balm's creation, and Jazmardians always use the rhythm of the words to hide information. "Na-nan"—two part Delyan myrrh. "Ha-la-za"—three parts Targian oil. "Saag"—one part Jazmardian sage.'

We found and emptied a goatskin bottle. I poured a cap full of oil inside with some of the dried sage leaves Kadram had given me. I carefully added the myrrh, sealed the bottle, and shook the ingredients together. Opening it again, I poured the liquid into my palm.

'It doesn't look right,' I said. 'There were no visible leaves in the cure I gave Alexia.'

Kadram chewed on his lip. 'It must mean sage oil, not sage leaves. Sage oil comes from putting the leaves with the oil and leaving it for a day or two. That way, the oil absorbs the properties of the sage, and you strain the leaves out.'

'A day or two?' I asked. 'We don't have that much time.'

'Well, then,' Kadram said with a sparkle in his eye, 'it is lucky for you I already have some amongst my things.'

We soon made up a large batch of balm. Elhian collected a few more goatskin bottles. We filled them with the mixture and sent the walking wounded out to tend to the Ghosts. Following them with the last bottle, Alexia, Elhian, and I applied the cure to as many wounds as possible.

It wasn't long before they were healed of the virus just as Alexia had been, but quicker and easier as they hadn't been infected to the same degree. The redness came out of their skin. The infection faded, and their heads cleared. Life returned to their eyes. They looked at their hands, at each other, at the last few Zalems, trying to piece everything together—but the confusion seemed to pass quickly, too. They pulled themselves to their feet. Some picked up weapons and turned on what was left of the Zalem soldiers.

And in the midst of it, Darj raised himself up and walked away, leaving behind a red patch where he had bled for Targe, for victory.

35
LIFE FOR A LIFE

Zavad's brother Landor looked up when we walked across the cavern floor. He saw what Elhian was carrying, but I don't think he understood at first. The little body in Elhian's arms did not look like the exuberant and ever-passionate Zavad. Only a shell was left.

Zavad was gone.

It was only as we paused and met Landor's eyes, offering his brother to him as some sort of sacrifice, that he began to realise who we carried and why.

'Landor . . .' I began, but I didn't know what to say. We stood there stupidly, knowing all words were inadequate.

In the end, it was Alexia who spoke. 'He was so brave.'

Landor nodded, trying to be accepting as he peered down at Zavad's peaceful face. 'I saw him leave and did nothing. I thought he was just getting water.'

'This isn't your fault,' Elhian said. 'The only person at fault here is Sirvan. The Zalems—they did this to Targe and your brother. There is no point in tormenting ourselves over what could have been.'

I knew he was struggling to believe his own words, but I also knew if we didn't believe them, we would be haunted for life. Having seen the path Alexia had taken with Ethaniel and Jeri, I did not want to travel it now and knew it was better to blame the real enemy than to wonder what might have been.

Besides, Elhian was right. The Zalems had done this. Sirvan had thrown the dagger. It was his choice that decided the boy's fate. Nothing else mattered.

But it didn't make it any less devastating.

'What should I do with him?' Landor asked. 'Bury him here? Let him be buried with the soldiers?'

'No,' Alexia said, putting a hand on the young man's forearm. New tears were running down her cheeks. 'Cover him, but take him back to his mother. Adaliah left a cart just beyond Tarcraig. Leave now and take him home in that. Let your mother have a chance to say goodbye in her own way, to bury his body and understand what has happened in her heart. It will be easier for her in the end, I promise you. When we return to Liane, we will mourn with her.'

'You are the queen,' Landor said, embarrassed.

Alexia smiled through her tears. 'I am also a woman who knows what it is to lose a son.'

Landor took his brother into his arms. He cradled him, and the three of us watched as he took Zavad out of the caverns and away from us forever.

Alexia left me with a hug and said something about finding Darj. I hardly heard her as Elhian and I walked outside the cavern.

Elhian reached for my hand. 'Is it over yet? Have we paid the price yet?'

I tried to gain control over my voice. 'I hope so.'

He drew me into an embrace, and we held each other for several minutes. With everything else, there was almost no room to feel relief that the battle was done, but I knew it would come later. There had been death, but at least now death would stop.

'I'm so proud of you,' Elhian said. 'Because of you, we are free of them forever.'

'I hope so,' I said again. If I'd felt overwrought on the way to Egra, there was no word to describe how I felt now.

'Adaliah! Elhian! Your Majesties!' We turned and saw Kadram running towards us. 'You have to come.' He tried to catch his breath. 'Quickly!'

'Raggin, old friend,' Elhian said, gripping the hand of the man he had come to know well in the Northern Invasion. Kadram had led us to the cavern without telling us anything more about what was so urgent. When I saw Raggin, I decided it was because he had taken a turn for the worse, but something didn't feel right. The cavern was full of groaning and pain. The atmosphere was tense, and Kadram, normally so in control, seemed to be struggling to keep his emotions in check.

'How are you feeling?' Elhian asked Raggin.

'He is making claims that could rock Targe's very soul, including its queen's,' Kadram said. 'Especially the queen's!'

'What?' I gave the Jazmardian a confused look.

'I keep telling him, it's him!' Raggin pointed at Dayle, Zavad's poor friend who was once again alone and underground. He was tidying up some bandages and crying at the same time. 'It's the prince!'

'What?' I asked again, puzzled. 'The prince of the Zalems? Raggin, that's just a boy, and you're frightening him.'

'No . . . ' He groaned. 'Where's Xander?'

'His head wound is getting worse,' Kadram said to us. 'I have given him something for the pain and can only imagine that is the cause of this.'

'The cause of what?' I asked, now with frustration.

'I'll show you!' Raggin tried to get up but couldn't move the way he wanted to. 'What's . . . what's wrong with my legs?' he asked. Kadram looked away. 'Tell me the truth.'

Kadram pulled a blanket up to his neck; Raggin was shivering in the warm cave. 'They were crushed by part of the catapult.'

'Will I . . . will I walk again? The truth!'

Kadram forced a smile. 'Only time will tell.'

'The boy . . . ' Raggin said again, pointing at Dayle. 'You all tried to make me forget what I was saying, but it is him!'

The poor boy was now hugging his knees. 'Come here,' I said to him.

'I thought I was dead,' Raggin said. He flopped back onto the bed, sweat dripping down his face. 'For how is it that he is standing here before me? He is dead. I must be, too.'

Everyone was looking on now.

'You must try and rest, Raggin,' Elhian said uneasily.

'No, no. I know that boy.' He raised a weak finger at Dayle. 'He is our prince! He is the Targian prince!'

I began to feel angry. How dare he suggest such a thing? Jeri was dead and his memory sacred. Dear Zavad had just joined him, and I could not bear any more traumas.

But then I looked at Dayle with new eyes. For the first time, I studied the boy's face in detail. To begin with, he looked nothing more than a dirty orphan in need of a good wash and a warm meal. But as he unfolded himself and looked at me, I reached forward and brushed back his wild black hair from his face.

'Jeri!'

My legs felt so weak, I wondered how they were still holding me up. Kadram covered his mouth with disbelief. I melted to my knees.

'You're alive?'

'Adaliah?' he whispered.

I nodded, tears streaming down my face. I cupped his face with my hands, struggling to believe what I was seeing. 'But I buried you . . . in Hunt . . . I buried your body!' I searched his blue eyes and could see his mother staring out of them.

Jeri frowned and tried to remember. 'They pushed me into the burning house . . . '

'Yes, you tried to escape; Alexia—your mother—told me. And then they strung your little body to a post. I found you with Lezan later. You were burnt!'

'No . . . it wasn't me,' he said, looking up. 'I remember now. There was another one in the house. They took me out the other side before it fell down. The next thing I remember is Sharlard.'

'The body you buried was someone else, another poor boy used to deceive us,' Raggin said from his bed. 'The prince was alive, stolen for the Zalems' purpose, stolen as security should the queen not follow through with their plans. But they never bet on Zavad helping him escape. Imagine that, a young boy like Zavad rescuing the King of Casmodia and the Crown Prince of Targe!'

I wrapped my arms around Dayle—Jeri—and held him to me. 'I can't believe it. I can't believe it!'

Dead will the boy be if the lady does not abstain.

I knew then it hadn't meant Zavad at all. I hadn't failed him by spilling blood. The poem had meant Alexia's son. That was why I was becoming unordained—Alexia did have two living children! The only reason I hadn't died after touching the new butterfly was because Eva was underage; the position was still in transition, just as Darj had said.

It also meant Alexia wasn't pregnant with the High Zalem's child and that Jeri was the one the High Zalem had been referring to when he'd said they could wait for her child to grow up if need be.

It wasn't Eva I was thinking of, he'd said.

Tears spilt down both Elhian's and Kadram's faces as they watched on. 'I didn't recognise him in Sharlard,' Elhian whispered. 'I didn't know!'

I took a deep breath, trying to gain control of my emotions again. 'Your mother,' I said. 'We have to tell your mother!'

36
RECOMPENSE

Not a single Zalem was left alive on the battlefield. The Ghosts had finished them all, claiming revenge for centuries of hard labour, sickness, and stolen minds. Some of them were sitting on the field amongst the carnage, trying to understand what had happened. Others spoke together in groups. Some I could hear celebrating their freedom. Others were crying. The allied soldiers had already started the work of clearing the dead. They were piling up the bodies.

Alexia was walking through the field, and I ran towards her. 'Where is the general?' she called to Xander, who was a few steps away.

'We can't find him, Your Majesty.'

'What?' She gave him a panicked look. 'Darj is missing,' she said to me as I arrived by her side. 'I thought he went to rest or to be alone but now I don't know . . . '

'Alexia . . . ' My voice was fraught with emotion.

She turned and saw how my face was covered in tears and my eyes red. 'Oh, Adaliah,' she said tenderly. She hugged me. 'It's all right. It's over. We will both grieve Zavad, I know, but we won, and much thanks is owed to you and Darj.'

I pulled back. 'No . . . I have news for you.'

Alexia paled. 'Darj?' She held a hand over her stomach.

'No, no, I don't know where Darj is. But I have something important to tell you.'

Alexia continued to stare at me, not understanding.

'You must prepare yourself, cousin, for I fear this will shock and maybe even overwhelm you, as it almost did me.'

Alexia clutched my arm. 'Adaliah, for goodness' sake, what is it?'

'Just come! Quickly!'

Alexia followed me through the rocks and into the caverns full of wounded men. 'Adaliah, I don't understand. If it's not Darj, what else is there to tell me that requires all this? Is Elhian hurt?'

I didn't answer but took her hand and guided her between the injured soldiers. We found Elhian standing by a bed; he was wiping away tears, as was Kadram next to him. 'What's happened?' Alexia asked. 'Tell me, for nothing could be worse than my imagination.'

I stopped and turned to her. 'Do you remember what happened to Jeri?' I asked, searching her face.

Alexia frowned at me. 'Do you think I could forget?' I could see the mixed emotions rising in her face: anger, fear.

'You said he was pushed into a burning house—'

'He tried to escape, and they caught and burnt him—you know this!'

I shook my head, more tears spilling down my cheeks. 'No, they didn't burn him.'

Incredulity filled her face. 'What are you saying?' She shook me by my shoulders when I didn't answer. 'Adaliah, please don't do this to me, not now, not after Zavad . . . What are you saying?'

I turned and pointed to Elhian. He stepped to the side, revealing the boy hiding shyly behind him. They had washed his face, and now it was irrefutable: it was His Royal Highness the Crown Prince of Targe. It was Jeri Ethaniel Elryane, Alexia's beloved son.

Alexia's hands flew to her mouth, and she started to shake. Like me, she slipped to her knees. I knelt beside her and put an arm around her shoulders. 'He escaped the burning house, Alexia. The Zalems took him to use against us. If they didn't succeed with you, they were going to raise him to be the High Zalem. But none of that matters now . . . The Zalems have lost, and your son is alive!'

Alexia couldn't reply.

'Mother?' Jeri called, and she managed a small nod.

He ran towards her.

Alexia only just opened her arms in time. Then, the tears ran fast and freely as she wrapped her arms around her son and held him to her as if in a dream. 'I can't believe . . . I . . . You were dead!' She spoke in between sobs. 'I thought you were dead these near three years!'

I stood with Elhian as mother and son clung to each other in the midst of the hospice. Not one had a dry eye.

Alexia kissed her son's cheek, and it was some time before she could speak again. 'How . . . how did you survive?'

'They took me out of the house. They took me to Sharlard to work.'

'I am so . . . sorry . . . I am so sorry this happened to you. If I had known you were alive . . . '

Jeri leant into her again. 'I think it has been worse for you, Mother.'

Alexia sobbed once more. 'I thought you were dead,' she said again. 'You were dead, and yet you are here with me now. My prince has returned.' She smiled and laughed through her tears. 'My son is alive!'

37
THE PRICE OF BATTLE

'Where is he?' Xander asked when he arrived at the cavern a bit later. I took him to his friend's bed, leaving Jeri and his mother to continue their reunion in privacy.

'What's this stir you're causing now?' Xander asked when we reached Raggin. Elhian was sitting with him.

'You survived, then?' Raggin asked.

'Did you ever doubt me?'

'Of course not. Pity, though. I would have been happy to look after Jacinth if you were gone.'

Xander rolled his eyes at him while Raggin laughed at his own joke. But the laugh soon turned to a choke.

'Steady, old friend,' Elhian said. 'You've had a big day, discovering the prince. You should get some rest.'

'I do amazing things every day; no one usually notices, that's all.'

'Yes, they do,' Xander said.

Raggin grinned, revealing the gap where he was missing a tooth. 'I was joking.'

'I know, but I will still tell your children of the day you rode out against the Zalems' catapult.'

Raggin's smile faded. 'I think we all know I'm not going to have children, Xander, not now. You'll have to tell yours. I can just imagine

Serene asking to hear about good, ol' Uncle Raggin every night before bedtime. You'll grow tired of it.'

'As her guardian, it would be expected.' Xander smiled, but it was tinged with sadness. The colour in Raggin's face was fading.

'You are one of the bravest men I know,' Elhian said. He gripped the captain's hand.

'You were the one . . . who saved me at Chettona. One man riding out . . . against an army.'

Elhian smiled down on him while Xander took Raggin's other hand.

'Travelling with you both . . . to Jazmarda . . . was one of the best times in . . . my life.' He looked at Xander. 'And I will never . . . never forget your friendship.'

'Nor I yours,' Xander whispered.

'Today . . .' Raggin said, 'if they ask where I am . . . tell them I never left . . . never will.'

'Look after Zavad for us,' I said, 'and Ru'ach be with you both.'

He nodded. His breathing became shallow and strained. This lasted for a minute or two. Then, with the three of us watching over him, he quietly passed away.

It wasn't long after that a caravan of wagons arrived at Tarcraig. At first, I couldn't figure out what they were, but I followed Lord Fenton over to them and realised it was the supplies I had asked for.

There were barrels of fresh water, some wine, rolled oats, salted beef and fish, nuts, dried bread, bags of apples and potatoes, more chickens (our last wagon had been lost when we had to retreat to Tarcraig) and, most importantly, healing products: bandages, needles, and pain-relieving tonics.

'I will have men set it out in rows so the soldiers can pass through and pick up rations of each,' Fenton said.

'Good. Could you see that anything used for healing is taken to the hospice caverns?'

'Of course, Your Majesty.'

'Father died, didn't he?' Jeri was asking his mother when I returned to them. They were sitting just outside the cave, and Kadram was with them, making us something to eat over a small campfire. The stars were beginning to dawn over us. I gazed up at them in wonder; I'd forgotten how splendid they looked hanging in the night sky.

Alexia nodded in answer to Jeri's question, tearing up again. 'Do you remember?'

'Yes, I think so.'

'He was a brave man,' I said.

'He was,' Alexia said. 'And he gave me one last gift before he died. You have a sister, my darling. Little Eva.'

Jeri brightened. 'The princess! I met her while I was staying with Zavad in Liane.'

'You did?' Alexia asked. 'Was she all right?'

'Yes, she was fine. She was well-looked after by lots of guards and maids. That's how we knew she'd be safe.'

Relief filled Alexia's face at this. I gave her a fond smile as Kadram dished up some fish stew for us all.

'I can't wait to see my little princess again and watch the two of you getting to know each other.'

Jeri took in her beautiful face and loving eyes. He couldn't stop staring at her. 'We have been very lucky,' he said.

She kissed his temple again. 'No, we have been very blessed. Ru'ach has dealt with me much more kindly than I deserve.' She looked up at me, noting my silence. 'What is it?'

Alexia, Jeri, and I walked back inside the cavern to Raggin's bedside. Kadram was cleaning Raggin's face. His hands had been placed over his sword, which lay on his torso. Xander sat beside his friend with his head bowed.

'We have lost two special people today,' Alexia said, resting her hand on Raggin's. 'First Zavad, and now this.'

Elhian put a hand on her shoulder. 'Alexia, I'm hoping it won't be three.'

'Darj . . . Has he still not been found?' she asked.

Elhian shook his head. 'And if he is wounded, every minute matters.'

Alexia clutched her son's hand.

'Are they talking about the general, Mother?' Jeri asked.

'Yes.'

'I saw him in Liane with Zavad. Zavad said he was kind to him.'

'Yes, and he would like nothing better than to see you again. Elhian, I want every man available to search for him. We cannot rest until I know he is all right. As for Raggin . . . ' She met Xander's eyes. 'We will honour him with a Targian warrior's funeral.'

Elhian and I turned over bodies on the field as we searched for Darj. A hundred or more men from all three kingdoms did the same. Every now and then, a wounded soldier was found alive and a stretcher brought to him. We hoped it was Darj every time. But another hour passed, and still he was missing. I returned to report this to Alexia. Jeri had fallen asleep. She kissed his temple and stood.

'Stay here, if you wish,' I said. 'No one would blame you if you didn't let Jeri out of your sight for months.'

'I'll be here when he wakes. Darj is my friend, too.'

'He is a strong man,' Alel said as we joined him and the others on the field.

'He is a legendary one,' Lord Fenton said. 'Targe will feel it if he dies.'

'He is not going to die,' Alexia said as if Fenton had blotched ink on a scroll. A Delyan called out for another stretcher, but we were soon informed it was for a Casmodian soldier named Jon.

Alel studied her face while she wasn't looking, a mischievous gleam in his eyes. 'Well, he has something to live for,' he said. 'He is in love with you, Your Majesty.'

Alexia opened her mouth with astonishment. 'That is impertinent, Alel. I am sure he said no such thing.'

'No, a man does not need as many words as a woman,' Lord Fenton said. He shared a smile with Alel. 'But even I knew this about the general. If you had not been so blinded by grief these past years, you would have seen it, too.'

I held my breath, certain that would be going too far for Alexia. She scoffed. 'I suppose next you will be telling me how imperative it is I marry, like Archbishop Dennear has for so long. Lord Fenton, as you have done Targe a great service today by bringing us reinforcements, I will not chide you for your words. But I warn you, be careful not to tread where you are not wanted.'

Alel and Fenton watched as she walked off into the field ahead of us.

Fenton turned to me with a grin. 'I imagined myself as a potential suitor, but I soon saw the truth. Darj is the best man for her.'

I hurried after Alexia, feeling more exhausted than I could ever remember. The emotional turmoil of the last few days was weighing on me, and the fear of not finding Darj was making my very body hurt. Alexia had to be feeling the same, if not more so, but she scoured the field with keen, alert eyes. Across the field, Elhian lifted another wounded Casmodian onto a stretcher. 'Darj, where are you?' I whispered to myself.

'Is there any way we might recognise him?' a nearby Delyan soldier asked.

'He wears a band here.' Alexia indicated her upper arm. 'Ethaniel gave it to him in honour . . . '

As she spoke, we saw the very band she was referring to. It was on a bloodied arm that was sticking out from underneath another body. I hurried forward and began to push the body off. It was a Zalem soldier. I saw pain stiffened in his dead face, but my main concern was the man underneath.

He was so covered in blood, I wouldn't have recognised him had it not been for the band on his arm.

'Oh, Darj,' Alexia said, grasping his hand. 'Don't leave me, not now.' She placed two fingers on his wrist, and I did the same on his neck. His skin was cold. I couldn't feel anything, and judging by the way Alexia was pressing harder and harder, she couldn't either. She took off her cloak and draped it over his torso. She tried his wrist again. 'Adaliah, please tell the others to come.' She was doing her best to sound calm, but I still heard the edge in her voice.

I stood and yelled across the field several times until Elhian and a few others started running towards us.

'Come on, Darj.' Alexia rubbed his hand, trying to coax life back into it. 'We did not survive all this just to lose you now.' She stroked the hair back from his forehead and found the head wound responsible for the blood. It was deep.

'Is he alive?' Elhian asked, appearing behind me.

'I . . . I don't know.' Alexia grasped his wrist again, still trying to find a pulse. 'I keep thinking I can feel something, but I don't know if I'm just imagining it.'

'We need to get him to Kadram,' Elhian said, putting a hand on her arm. 'He's going to need a lot of help.'

I reached for her hand. 'I cannot lose him now, Adaliah,' she whispered.

'I know.'

'Gently now,' Elhian said to Fenton and Alel as they lifted Darj onto a stretcher. 'We don't yet know the extent of his wounds and must be very careful. We'll take him into the cave and examine him more there.'

'He is breathing,' Kadram said, holding up a small, now foggy mirror.

Alexia rolled up her sleeves and began to peel back Darj's bloodied shirt.

'You do not have to do this, Your Majesty,' Kadram said. 'You have had an exhausting night already. You all have.'

'He is my friend,' Alexia said, looking up. 'I will not leave him now.'

Kadram and Elhian began to clean Darj's arms and legs while Alexia tended his head. The three of them rinsed the cloths in buckets of water, turning it red. Alel and I continually refreshed their supply from the small spring that flourished in Tarcraig.

Elhian stitched Darj's worst wound back together. It was across his abdomen; Elhian said it might have injured his inner organs.

'What does that mean?' Alel asked.

'It means the damage may be beyond my skill to heal.' Elhian was pale. Blood still had this affect on him from time to time.

Kadram dressed Darj's smaller wounds with his greenish-brown cream and then wrapped them in bandages. By the time we'd finished, Darj was recognisable again but still as unresponsive as he had been when we'd first found him.

'I think all we can do now is get some rest,' Elhian said. 'But he will need more care, Alexia. It will not be easy, but we need to take him home.'

'Fine,' Alexia said. 'We will leave in the morning.'

38
DAWN RISING

Alexia didn't sleep that night. She alternated between holding Darj's hand as he lay unconscious and studying her son's face while he slept. I knew she was still trying to comprehend all that had happened, still trying to reverse the truth she'd believed for the past few years. We all were.

I woke just before dawn. A horn had sounded outside, and I knew what it meant. There was to be a memorial service for Captain Raggin, Zavad, and the rest of the fallen. I could already hear the men singing outside as they had done to honour Alexia's loss in the Northern Invasion and my father's death before that.

I blinked and tried to focus. I saw Alexia leaning over Darj across the room. She planted a tender kiss on his forehead. I raised my eyebrows when she lingered a second more and left another on his lips.

I didn't get a chance to talk to her about it. I walked with my husband and the others outside, joining the thousands of men who stood ready to welcome the sunrise, ready to say farewell to those who had died on the path to victory.

A pile of stones had been constructed as a memorial. In front of that, a hole had been dug for the grave of the man who would be honoured most.

The men stopped singing. Xander walked up to the rudimentary coffin he'd built. 'You were my best friend,' he said. 'Now you join the ranks of many other war heroes before you.'

It was the first sunrise any of us had seen since the dark storm had receded. It was beautiful with flecks of orange and pink. I could feel it was going to be a warm day, and I relished the light. It encouraged me to see how big and lovely the sky was, how majestic the sun looked as it climbed up above the horizon. I thought of poor Jeri, who had barely seen it for years, and dear Zavad, who would now only see it from above.

Xander lit the bowl of oil on top of the stones. Then, he and another lowered the coffin into the ground. As the oil burned, the men began to sing again. The Casmodians and Delyans didn't know the words, but they listened with quiet respect.

The men then turned to Alexia, who was standing at the back of them with Jeri. She was watching the flames and remembering the stone monuments the men had made for her near the Tiathi Basin, I think. There'd been so much grief in saying goodbye to the two she loved most, and yet, one had been restored to her.

She walked between the soldiers to the front. 'We have lost many good men in this battle,' she said, 'but we have also been victorious in our cause. The last battle was won by life!'

The men cheered at this.

'My son, Prince Jeri, has been returned to me.' She held up his arm, and the soldiers cheered loud and long. 'We will never forget those who died so valiantly in battle. It is time for us to go home, but we will take them with us in our hearts forever.'

'Goodbye, Your Majesty,' Prince Ren said, bowing low. 'Should you ever come to Delya again, I promise you our people will welcome you most warmly.'

'Thank you, Your Highness,' Alexia said.

'Please let me know how Darj recovers,' Alel said. 'I hope very much to hear some exciting news in the near future.'

Alexia narrowed her eyes but didn't say anything. I was glad. There wasn't a lot she could say after the affection she'd shown the unconscious general that morning. I wondered if it meant she loved him, but in a way, I was scared that she did.

What if he doesn't survive?

'Please tell your brother I am indebted to him for his people's sacrifice,' Alexia said, handing Ren a note addressed to King Thane. 'I hope you can both take pride in the part Delya played in defeating the Zalems.'

'Indeed, we do,' Ren said.

Ren said farewell to Elhian and me, and then he and the Delyans turned south to take the news of our victory back to their people.

Kadram was leaving us as well. He was due back in Jazmarda, and there was little he could do to help us now.

'Well done,' he said to me as Alexia and Elhian stood nearby. 'You stopped the dark prophecy from coming true and showed true heroism once again.'

'The prophecy?' I asked. 'Do you mean the poem the Zalems left for us?'

'Yes. It was written in Dragon's Breath ink, you know.'

'I remember that you said that—and I know that Dragon's Breath is a poison—but I don't know what the ink is.'

'It is a rare, enchanted ink, used for deadly purposes,' Kadram said. 'Whatever is written in it must come true. The Zalems wrote the first part of each sentence centuries ago. Mors had a gift of prophecy, but it came from Anash, not Ru'ach, and was impure. He condemned you and the Ghosts to death by determining your futures with Dragon's Breath ink.'

'Why would he want the Ghosts dead?' I asked. *Especially when he wanted to turn us all into them?*

'He only wanted the Ghosts to help conquer the world. After that, he planned to obliterate them and live with the Zalems, those who had chosen him.'

'How was it stopped?' Elhian asked.

'Queen Cazine learned of his plot. She could not take back what he had written, but she could alter it. She added clauses based on what she could see of the future. To "dead will the boy be", she added, "if the lady does not abstain", and so on. She had a pure gift of prophesy from Ru'ach, Adaliah, and she knew you would take the Jazmardian blessing.'

'Why would she want Elhian to pay, though?' I asked.

He squeezed my shoulder with a sad smile. 'She didn't. There is only one way to counter the curses written in Dragon's Breath ink, and that is with the selfless sacrifices of the innocent. All four of you made the sacrifices necessary to right the wrongs.'

'She gave us ways out,' Alexia said, 'even if they were painful ones.'

'She did the best she could,' Kadram said. 'You see, there are always people looking out for you, even if they lived centuries before.' Kadram gave me a final hug. 'Dragon's Breath, the poison, was a diluted ingredient in the Zalems' Bane.'

'The rash on your back did look a bit like what Dragon's Breath can do,' I said to Alexia.

'Yes . . . ' she said thoughtfully.

'Alexia,' Kadram said. 'I will be praying for Darj. The four of you are the guardians of all that is good. There are many people to be proud of, people who will always be remembered. People like Zavad.'

I blinked back tears. 'Especially Zavad.'

Elhian took charge of organising the men to travel home. With poor hygiene and Fenton's medicine supplies quickly depleting, we were already losing many to infection. Too often, those who escaped the sword succumbed to disease instead.

Those who didn't carved the names of the lost in the stones of Tarcraig. Xander did this for Raggin and cut a large circle around his name, so it stood out from amongst the others. I did the same for young Zavad, marking his age.

The trees that still grew in the tough crevices of the rocks were rustling in the light wind. They seemed lusher and greener now that the sky was blue and the sun was shining again. I walked amongst the men and quiet stones with my cousin. The soldiers bowed to us as we passed. We reached a tall, gnarled tree and stood under it while the men continued about us.

'I'm not quite sure how to do it, you know,' Alexia said, 'how to understand all that has happened . . . How can people traumatise another person's life for nothing but their own gain? I thought Jeri was dead. I grieved for him. And now I have lost Zavad. That's all life is, isn't it? We trade lives like merchandise. One is returned; another is lost. And all because of those who believe their way is supreme and worth the life of others. They took my son from me, stole three years from his life and mine. I want to hate them for it. But I won't.'

I looked up at the leaves above, glistening in the sun. 'I guess the Zalems never knew the love we did, never knew how to value the lives of others.'

'Yes, and I'm so proud of the boy my son has become, despite everything. He is kind and compassionate, like his father—'

'And his mother,' I said.

'I just wish I could have spared him from all he went through. I wish we could have saved Zavad.'

'I know, truly. But there's nothing we can do now except rejoice that Jeri is back with us.'

Alexia turned to me and linked her arm through mine. Without her bow and arrows, she was more feminine in her appearance and less burdened. Her eyes disclosed her tiredness but also her hope. 'You are right, of course, and I will never cease to be grateful for it. I will forgive them as I forgave the others, for his sake and mine.'

We continued walking, and I thought of Darj, whom Elhian was now preparing for travel. 'Alexia,' I said, 'Elhian is not sure Darj will survive the move to Liane.'

She didn't answer straightaway, but I felt her arm stiffen. 'We can't leave him in a damp cave, and the rest of these men need to see their home and families. We also have evacuees in Liane desperate to return to Chettona and Hunt.' Alexia swallowed hard. 'Darj will be fine. He must be.'

'You don't always have to be so brave, you know.'

A tear escaped onto her cheek. 'That's what he said once. But I am not trying to be brave, Adaliah. I am just trying to cope.'

39
RETURN TO LIANE

We travelled slowly for almost ten days across a distance that could be covered in seven, but many of the returning soldiers were wounded. Some, like Darj, had to be carried.

The men took turns in holding his stretcher, all of them conscious of trying to make his journey as smooth as possible. Alexia gave permission for Elhian and me to ride ahead to Liane, but while this had appealed to part of me, I couldn't bring myself to leave Alexia alone. In finding her son, there had been much joy, but if Darj were to die . . . Besides that, he was my friend. I couldn't abandon him for his sake, let alone Alexia's.

Elhian had refused, anyway. Throughout the journey, he checked on Darj's condition and redressed his wounds every morning and night and sponged his mouth with water. He occasionally became semi-conscious. When he did, we helped him to take some broth.

Liane finally appeared like a bride in the distance, and it was with great relief that I rode through the eastern gate with Alexia.

The streets were lined with people who cheered when they saw us. The hour it took to get to the palace was a blur. There were speeches and praises in the town square; Alexia announced our victory from her horse and reintroduced Jeri to the people. Some of them cried to see him, and I think the poor boy was overwhelmed by it all. It was a big transition from a slave in Sharlard to the crown prince of a kingdom.

She told them what I had done, and another round of cheers followed. But while I appreciated their support and acknowledgement, it did little to relieve my current level of confused emotions.

'I urge you all to pray for the general's quick recovery,' Alexia said to the people as Darj was carried between them, 'for without him, Targe would not have been victorious.'

The Targian soldiers began to reunite with their families. I saw Captain Xander hurry to his wife and kiss her. She was holding their child in her arms; the small girl was engulfed in a desperate embrace between her parents. I knew Xander would tell Jacinth of Raggin's heroics and that she would comfort him, but I also knew there would remain a sense of loss always.

There were cries of pain as people heard about their loved one's death. Captain Raggin and Zavad were just two who had given their lives to stop the Zalems. I thought of the many other families who would now have to decide how they would live without the men who had supported them or brought them so much happiness. I thought about what Alexia had said—how could those who had caused all this, who had fought for the Zalem cause, justify so much death? I realised then she hadn't just been talking about her own suffering. There were many more across Targe, Casmodia, and Delya who would now be asking the same question.

Alexia, Jeri, and I entered the palace, and a maid came to us with the princess.

'Eva! Come here, darling.' Alexia leant down and opened her arms to her, but Eva hid her face in the maid's skirt.

There was no mistaking the hurt on Alexia's face, even for someone accustomed to hiding her emotions. I put a hand on her shoulder. 'It's all right. She just needs time to remember.'

'I've let her down,' Alexia whispered as Jeri ran to Eva and took her hand. 'She no longer trusts me.'

'She's still just a babe,' I said. 'All such things can be repaired with love.'

Jeri chatted to Eva and made her laugh. Then, he brought her over to us.

'Come, my darling,' Alexia said to her daughter. 'Can I hold you?' She reached her arms out again.

Eva studied her face a bit longer and then gave a little nod. She wrapped her arms around Alexia's neck. 'Mother back now?' she asked into Alexia's shoulder. 'Mother better now?'

Alexia held back tears. 'Yes, darling, I'm better now.'

Later, several maids helped the queen clean and change back into one of her gowns, as I already had. The one she chose was a beautiful summer dress that fell to the ground. It wrapped around her figure perfectly, draping down like a blue waterfall. The scar where the arrow had hit her in the Northern Invasion was just peeking above the bodice.

'Alexia, there's something you need to read.' I'd already fetched the letter her father had written to her, the one we had opened in her absence. I explained why, but she didn't reproach me or the others for breaking the seal.

She dismissed the maids, and I sat with her as she read and began to understand more and more about herself, her heritage, and her father. 'I miss him so much,' she said as she finished. 'And my mother. I have longed for them both so much these past few years.' She blinked away tears.

I thought of my parents. The grief of losing them so early was also never far from my mind. Life would have been so different had even just one of our parents survived. 'Me, too,' I said. 'It's a comfort to know how much they loved each other, though.'

'Indeed. Poor Darj, even he was caught up in our mess as a child and suffered loss for it. His father helped create the cure, and with it, he saved my father's life. And mine.'

I reached for her hand. 'I'm sure Amaz and Ethaniel are proud of you, just as Naythan must take pride in Darj.'

She put the letter down. 'Thank you for all you've done for us, Adaliah. For all you did for me. Please don't ever think I take that for granted. Targe owes you a great deal. I don't even know how to honour you for that.'

'That's simple: with your love and your friendship.' I hugged her, and we held each other tight for some time.

'I'm going to see Darj,' she said.

'Do you love him?' I asked, studying her closely.

'You know I do.'

'I know you love him as your general and as your friend, but do you love him?'

'Adaliah . . . '

'He's a good man.'

'I don't doubt that for a second.'

I glanced over my shoulder, leant towards her, and spoke quietly. 'I saw you kiss him, you know.'

Her cheeks flushed a little, like she'd been caught stealing from the kitchen. I think she was inclined to admonish me for spying on her at first, but she just laughed and stepped around me, artfully avoiding my questions. 'I just want to check that Jeri and Eva have had enough to eat,' she said, 'and then I will join you in Darj's room.'

Elhian was waiting for me at the general's door. 'Is he all right?' I asked.

'No, I can't say he is.' I knew he was preparing to be strong, not only for me but for Alexia, who would need us both should the worst happen. I ran my fingers through his thick crop of brown hair, knowing he had many troubles of his own that we had yet to speak about.

'We shouldn't have let him go,' I said. 'After he killed Sirvan . . . We should have made sure he got help, but we were too shocked about Zavad.'

'Do you think he would have listened?' Elhian asked. 'He was angry about his father's death and Zavad's. I think we all become foolish when our loved ones are hurt, even if we only find out about it years later. Darj wouldn't have let you stop him, even if you'd tried. I don't think he even would have listened to Alexia.'

I nodded. 'I suppose they are even then. She doesn't listen to him either.'

'And yet the two work harder to earn each other's approval more than anyone else's.'

I raised my eyebrows. 'That's very insightful.'

He nodded sagely. 'We men often are.'

I smiled and turned towards Darj's room.

'Adaliah,' Elhian said, putting a hand on my arm. 'Prepare yourself.'

I didn't know what he meant. I'd travelled with Darj all the way from Tarcraig and seen him at his worst. Three of his ribs had been broken, as well as his collarbone. Several days after the battle, the bruising had come up. He'd become red and swollen, like a butchered deer. Nothing could surprise me now.

But when I saw him, I understood. He was deathly pale; the laceration across his abdomen was purulent. When I reached over to his hand, it felt heavy and dead.

Alexia arrived a few minutes later. I don't know what I expected from her at the sight of him: not panic perhaps, but fear at least, or distress, or even anger. But none of those were visible in her eyes. There was sadness there, of course—she had not wished this on her most trusted friend—but most of all, there was calmness and acceptance.

She took a cloth and began to clean his infected wound, despite the fact she was dressed no longer as a commoner but as a queen.

The physician pulled off Darj's socks. The feet beneath were dirty and swollen again. I dipped another cloth in a cool bowl of water and started to wash them.

Alexia finished cleaning his laceration, and the physician helped her bandage it back up again. It was as she began pulling the bandage tight that Darj stirred and groaned. The sound turned into more of a whimper. I knew what it meant: *I've had enough. I'm done.*

Alexia cupped his face with her hand and stroked back his hair.

'A . . . Alexia?'

'Shhh . . . ' she said. 'It's all right. I'm going to take care of you. All you need to do is rest.' She kissed his forehead.

The pain left his face, and it was then that I knew two things: Alexia had transferred her peace to him in a beautiful exchange, and she loved him, more than she loved anyone.

It wasn't until the next morning that he took a bit of water and gruel on his own. I fell asleep that night in a chair near his bedside, the fatigue of the last few months catching up with me. I had no idea what was sustaining Alexia, especially as I suspected she was the most tired of us all. I heard her voice, and it drew me back into the conscious world.

'I know you and I have fought,' she was saying to the sleeping Darj. 'We've driven each other mad at times, and I'm sure I've taken you for granted.' I opened my eyes and saw her clasping his hand. 'But I do care for you. Jeri's alive, Darj. I want so much for you to see him again. I want so much for you to enjoy the life you fought so hard to make worth living. Please, come back to me.'

There was quiet for a bit, and I was tempted to go back to sleep, but then I saw him moving, waking. 'You're here,' he said. His voice was frail. It was the first time I'd heard it properly in weeks.

Alexia's eyes filled with tears, and she looked down, trying to conceal her emotion. It seemed the more she tried to hold it back, the more the tears came.

Darj brought her hand to his lips and kissed it.

I didn't know whether to pretend to be asleep or leave them alone. I worried that alerting them to my presence in their conversation would embarrass them and stop whatever they might otherwise say. And to leave, I would have to walk past them. So I stayed.

'Don't you ever do that to me again,' Alexia said.

'While ever I live,' Darj whispered, 'I will always put myself between danger and the things I love—whether that be my kingdom, my comrades . . . or you.'

'But I can't bear it,' she said with a sob. 'I have seen too much death, endured too much grief to even risk losing you as well.'

Darj wiped away some of her tears. 'And what am I but a common man?'

'You are not common to me.'

A shadow appeared at the doorway. Alexia and Darj didn't notice, but I saw Elhian peek around the door and step back again. His shadow remained, and I knew he was eavesdropping, too.

'After all you have done, no one could say you are common,' Alexia said. 'And they certainly couldn't if you were the prince consort.'

Darj stared at her.

I held my breath. *What?!*

'Prince . . . consort?' he asked at length.

Alexia gave a small laugh. 'Marry me,' she said. 'If you can bear to be royalty, to be the father of princes and princesses, to become my closest companion, advisor, friend, and lover, then marry me, please.'

I clasped both hands over my mouth as I contrived to keep my joy to myself.

Darj struggled for words. 'I . . . I didn't know you even cared for me in that way.'

'Nor did I, but over the past few months, I realised you were the only other man I could love after Ethaniel. And I do love you, Darj.' She blushed in a rare show of vulnerability.

It was now Darj's eyes that glistened with tears. He pulled himself up into a sitting position, groaning at the pain that filled him. But he didn't seem to care. He caressed Alexia's cheek and drew her closer to him. Then, he pressed his lips against hers, and they kissed slowly, lovingly.

Now I really should go.

I tried to see an escape while they were distracted, but there was none. I comforted myself with the thought that Alexia knew I was in the room. Elhian's shadow was still by the door, so I knew he had no intentions of leaving either.

'I never once dreamed I would be able to do that,' Darj said as they drew apart.

Alexia smiled while he lay back down again. 'I can't promise you it'll be easy. It will mean so much more than just marrying me. Even Ethaniel sometimes struggled with having a wife who was also a ruler, and you . . . I never want you to betray who you are. But as my husband, you will no longer be just "the general" but a prince, and you must be willing to grow into that role. It will also mean you will be father to the children of another man—'

'What do you mean "children"?' Darj asked with alarm. 'Are you pregnant to him after all?'

Alexia laughed. 'No, I'm not. The reason Adaliah was not ordained to touch the orb was because Jeri never died!' She explained what happened, retelling her joy at finding her son alive. 'He will come and see you as soon as he knows you're awake.'

'Two shocks in as many minutes,' Darj said, bewildered. 'I can't remember the last time I felt so happy!'

'Yes. We have been unhappy for a long time, you and I.'

'That's true,' I said before I could stop myself.

Alexia swung round to look at me. Her cheeks flushed again, but then she just laughed, as did Darj. Elhian realised the pretense was over and came into the room, too, smiling at them both. 'It is about time,' he said, putting an arm around me and pulling me in against him.

'Yes,' Alexia said with another laugh as she turned back to Darj. 'My father once said that the deepest wounds are caused by people but that it is also from people that we find the deepest healing. I'm sorry I pushed you all away when in reality, I needed you so much.'

Darj took her hand in his again. 'None of that matters now. I . . . I have loved you forever.' He weaved his fingers through hers. 'But they would never accept me. You should marry a lord, or a prince, or a king. You're born to it, and it's what you deserve. I am a commoner, and any association you have with me will only lead to comment and criticism.'

Elhian and I opened our mouths to voice our disagreement, but Alexia stopped us with a raised hand and a smile.

'Are you saying you don't think the archbishop will be pleased?'

'Yes, that's exactly what I'm saying.'

Alexia met his lips with another affectionate kiss. 'Good.'

40
RAISING HOPE

When Alexia wasn't with Darj or the children, she was with her council, making plans to strengthen the Targian army, to travel to Sharlard and make sure it was destroyed, and to improve relations with Delya. Elhian and I sat in on some of the meetings to discuss Casmodia's place in the post-war world. Elhian offered to send men to help rebuild Chettona and Hunt, while Alexia proposed to send us all the resources we would need to rebuild Tiathi.

'Without cost?' Elhian asked as the three of us discussed it around Darj's bed. 'Are you sure?'

'Of course,' Alexia said. 'I haven't forgotten you are the reason my Eva didn't die at Cades' hand. Now you've helped bring my son back and fought for Targe again. Moreover, I'm sure your careful and ongoing attention to Darj is the reason he pulled through.'

'You saved my life,' Darj said, putting a hand on Elhian's shoulder. 'I couldn't ask for a better friend.'

Elhian smiled. 'Soon to be family.'

'Yes, and any men brave enough to marry Elryane women must stick together.'

Alexia rolled her eyes at him. 'We'll ignore that. But in terms of the resources we can gift you, Elhian, it's my pleasure to give it. Truly, it's the least we can do.'

On the sixth day of our return, Alexia invited Zavad's family to the palace chapel, where a service was held for the young boy. It was the first time a civilian family had ever entered the private worship room of monarchs past. Zavad's mother kept thanking us for the gesture. I was relieved she didn't hate us for what had happened.

She had remarried since the Northern Invasion and added another child to her brood, another son named after her first husband. Including Zavad, that was nine children, and nine it would always remain in her heart.

The queen embraced her at the end of the service, the boundaries of class fading away as two women acquainted with grief comforted each other.

'Goodbye, Zavad,' I whispered upwards. 'You were loved by the best of people.'

'The Casmodian Council will try to overturn our decision to help Targe,' Elhian said to me later as we walked through the palace gardens. 'But Casmodia must realise that if it wasn't for Targe standing strong, the Zalems would have invaded us. What happened to Tiathi would have been just the beginning.'

I saw the earnestness in his dark brown eyes. We were still so young in the view of our home council, but they could not ask for a more passionate or caring king. 'Casmodia will grow to be great again,' I said, 'this time for the right reasons.'

'Yes, I hope we can build something worthwhile for our children,' he said.

I rested my hand on my stomach. I still wasn't sure what kind of mother I would make. Perhaps it was because I had never known my mother and didn't know how to be one. I knew I wasn't yet pregnant. I wasn't sure how to feel about that. On the one hand, I feared parenthood. I was a warrior after all, independent for the most part, despite my love for Elhian, and the thought of having a little one relying on me was frightening. I knew Elhian wanted a child not only to love but also to help secure his throne, but I didn't want to bring one into the world for that alone. Besides, we'd been married for months and had conceived nothing. What if something was wrong?

'If we ever do have a son, do you think we could call him Karlen?' I asked, thinking of the guard who had died protecting me.

'Yes, I'd like that,' Elhian said. 'And it will happen when we're both ready,' he added as if he'd been reading my mind, 'and when there is less stress in our lives, I think.'

'I worry about you, you know,' I said.

'Why?'

'Because ever since killing Cades, you have been uneasy.'

'I know,' he said and paused. 'For so long, I feared becoming like my father, but I think now it is actions, not heritage, that defines a person. Look at Alexia. She is said to have the Zalem blood in her, and yet aside from you, I don't know a better person. If I hadn't killed Cades, he would have killed Eva and continued a war that would have brought both our kingdoms to their knees. We are already struggling to stand as it is.' He paused again. 'I have little to offer you.'

'No,' I said and gave him a kiss. 'You have offered me everything.'

FOUR MONTHS LATER

The white stateroom in Liane Palace was full of people. Women wore beautiful gowns and fluttered about like swans. Men also looked important in their stunning outfits. Many flocked around Elhian, making quips that were intended to be intelligent but which I could see were straining him. I stood talking to the Lady of Rorinhall for a while, a short woman who had a nice smile but not much conversation.

'The queen will be here soon, but do not be anxious,' I heard a gentleman say to a lady a few steps away. 'Her Majesty is most adept at putting people at ease in her presence.'

When she wants to, I thought with a smile.

I could hear the crowd cheering and singing outside, and earlier, I'd seen the streets of the city covered in white rose petals. Everyone was celebrating the marriage of their queen.

The room fell silent when Darj, now surnamed Ryder-Elryane, entered from the left door of the ballroom. He stood tall with long, black pants and a royal green sash about his waist. His white coat was covered in gold braiding. For the first time in I don't know how long, his hair wasn't hanging over his forehead in that rugged but messy way but was combed back. He walked to the middle of the floor. I marveled at how handsome and regal he looked: no longer a soldier, but a prince.

He caught my eye and winked.

Judging by his frown, Archbishop Dennear was not as pleased to see him. He was permitted to join us for the reception but had not been invited to perform the wedding. When I took a step towards him, prepared to settle our differences after what happened outside the Jewel Room, he flustered and moved away but came near Darj instead.

The archbishop's expression darkened. 'Her Majesty should have taken my advice,' he muttered.

'And what advice was that?' a new voice asked.

Her Majesty stood in the doorway on the right. Everyone in the room bowed and curtsied low, including me.

She was stunning. Her hair was up with several tresses curled and pinned in place under a glistening tiara. She wore diamond earrings and an exquisite satin gown embroidered with swirls. She met her husband in the middle of the room and linked her arm through his.

'Nothing, of course, Your Majesty,' Dennear said, though his expression did not match the humility of his words. He turned to Darj and bowed. 'Your Highness.'

There was a moment of uncertainty amongst the nobles as Dennear scuttled away. But then the music started, and the room filled with the warmth of it. Darj took Alexia's hand. They began to dance, and all else was forgotten.

When we rode through the Targian countryside on our way back to Casmodia several days later, I convinced Elhian to travel past Kest River. There, the water flowed ever peaceful and undisturbed, as if all that had passed since I met Odavan there had been a dream.

I ran my hand across the tree where I'd found my father's blade. 'I hope we have made you and your brother proud, Father.'

Something caught my eye. There was a flag caught in the tree—a crescent moon overlaid with an eye was on one half, a butterfly with a broken wing on the other. I hadn't seen that particular symbol before.

A broken butterfly?

Something about it seemed strange. I closed my eyes and breathed in the crisp, autumn air. When I looked back, the flag was gone. I turned my face back to the sky.

'Watch over us always, Father.'

Enjoy this sneak peek of

THE CROWNED GUARDIANS

BY TRUDY ADAMS

THE ARMOURED BUTTERFLY
BOOK THREE

PROLOGUE

I couldn't remember the name of the cave. Someone had told me about it only a day earlier, but a day earlier we'd been with Elhian and Darj. A day earlier we'd still had our belongings, including our clothes and weapons and horses. We'd been warm and uninjured and not caught in a snowstorm.

I didn't need to know the name of the cave, of course. I just wanted something to take my mind off the cold. Icicles hung from the ceiling. The air was still, but there was an unnerving whistling in the distance. The ground was a surly mixture of gravel, dirt and snow. My feet were cut and blue. I wondered how long it would take for my toes to die. Would I have the courage to cut one off, if I needed to? Would I still be able to run? My back was sore from huddling against the stonewall. I wanted to sleep, but I had to remain alert. Even in the stormy weather, we could still be attacked.

But I had no sword. I wasn't wearing any armour, and I had no strength to put up a bare-fisted fight.

I'd forgotten all that.

My cousin's lips were already blue. Her clothes were tattered, too. She'd dug me out of the snow and dragged me for several minutes before we reached the cave. She only managed to get us a few steps inside, just out of the wind. We'd been able to talk at first—she tried to keep us awake by talking of our childhood memories through chattering teeth, but then she drifted off. She was stroking my arm in a distracted attempt to keep my blood moving, but I knew it wouldn't be long before we both fainted away. I imagined someone finding us generations later—two frozen women in a forgotten and nameless cave, only identifiable by the signet ring Alexia had hidden in her bodice.

She held me closer, joints stiffening. 'Keep breathing . . . dear cousin.'

A moment later, there was the blackness I longed for.

For more information about
Trudy Adams
&
The Zalem Crisis
please visit:

www.trudyadams.squarespace.com
www.facebook.com/trudyadamsauthor

For more information about
AMBASSADOR INTERNATIONAL
please visit:

www.ambassador-international.com
@AmbassadorIntl
www.facebook.com/AmbassadorIntl

If you enjoyed this book, please consider leaving us a review on
Amazon, Goodreads, or our website.

More from Ambassador International

Darcentaria has been invaded by the Outside. El of the Outside has been captured, and Torsten Eiselher, the once-formidable warrior-has been injured and is lost in the woods. Will he ever be able to find his way back to El and discover the true Way? Or will the darkness and his thirst for revenge swallow him whole? El has her own choices to make between the man she loved from the Outside and the man she loves now. Will her heart make the right choice?

Determined to survive, an orphaned Esther must fight a rising new order in a broken America. This new order, the Federation of Acceptance, enforces directives that jeopardize human rights and beliefs. Esther must decide where she stands as she faces disappearing teachers, murdered classmates, and a traitorous ex-flame. Haunted by the mistakes of her parents' past, Esther is forced to make decisions that will affect the lives of everyone around her.

Polar opposites, pretty girl Willow Rysen and humble nerd Christian Blythe, find themselves forced to work together on a project for their science class at Bethel Private School. As the two work together, Miss Popular finds her world turned upside down after a night of partying, made even worse when Christian is the only one around to rescue her. Will she find that the grace of God can overcome her past failures or will she allow the lure of the world's ideologies to keep her tight in its grasp?

www.ingramcontent.com/pod-product-compliance
Lightning Source LLC
Chambersburg PA
CBHW070047030726
47506CB00002B/388